# PAYBACK TIME

As soon as the outlaws were out of sight, Smoke and his men came down off the hillock overlooking the railroad tracks and approached the wreckage site.

"Jesus!" Louis whispered at the number of bodies lying scattered on the ground.

Their horses snorted and shied at the smell of so much blood and at the sight of so many horses and men torn apart by the explosions.

When the group would find men still alive, the boys would try to make them comfortable, covering them with blankets against the cold and telling them help was on the way.

Louis glanced back over his shoulder at the bodies lying dead all around them. "I've seen a lot of bad men in my time out West, Smoke, but I don't know as I've ever seen anyone who could do this and just ride away as if nothing had happened," he said, a look of deep disgust on his face.

"I know what you mean, Louis," Smoke said. He took a deep breath, trying to get the stench of burnt flesh out of his throat, and turned to look at the dead bodies. "I want you all to remember this sight when we finally catch up with the men that did this, 'cause I do not intend to give them any quarter or mercy." He turned his eyes to Louis. "and if any of you have any reservations about what I'm going to do, you'd better head on back to the rail yard with Van Horne and the wounded men when he gets here."

Louis shook his head. "Don't worry about me, Smoke. Whatever you've got planned for the bastards that did this is too good for them." Louis's cultured face had turned grim and his eyes looked like those of a hawk, black and ferocious and unforgiving.

Smoke's lips curled in a s

"Just remember you said that,

flow and the outlaws' bodies st

# BOOK YOUR PLACE ON OUR WEBSITE AND MAKE THE READING CONNECTION!

We've created a customized website just for our very special readers, where you can get the inside scoop on everything that's going on with Zebra, Pinnacle and Kensington books.

When you come online, you'll have the exciting opportunity to:

- View covers of upcoming books
- Read sample chapters
- Learn about our future publishing schedule (listed by publication month *and author*)
- Find out when your favorite authors will be visiting a city near you
- Search for and order backlist books from our online catalog
- Check out author bios and background information
- Send e-mail to your favorite authors
- Meet the Kensington staff online
- Join us in weekly chats with authors, readers and other guests
- Get writing guidelines
- AND MUCH MORE!

**Visit our website at
http://www.kensingtonbooks.com**

# QUEST OF THE MOUNTAIN MAN

## William W. Johnstone

**PINNACLE BOOKS**
Kensington Publishing Corp.
http://www.kensingtonbooks.com

PINNACLE BOOKS are published by

Kensington Publishing Corp.
850 Third Avenue
New York, NY 10022

All Kensington Titles, Imprints, and Distributed Lines are available at special quantity discounts for bulk purchases for sales promotions, premiums, fund-raising, and educational or institutional use. Special book excerpts or customized printings can also be created to fit specific needs. For details, write or phone the office of the Kensington special sales manager: Kensington Publishing Corp., 850 Third Avenue, New York, NY 10022, attn: Special Sales Department, Phone: 1-800-221-2647.

Pinnacle and the P logo Reg. U.S. pat. & TM Off.

First Pinnacle Books Printing: July 2003

10  9  8  7  6  5  4  3

Printed in the United States of America

# Chapter 1

Spring had come early to the Sugarloaf this year, and Smoke Jensen's hired hands were well on their way to getting the spring branding and separating of the winter calves from their mothers done a month earlier than usual. It had been a mild winter, and the snow accumulation on the lower slopes of the Rocky Mountains was already beginning to melt and disappear under the rays of the spring sun.

Smoke sat on the top rail of the corral, a half-smoked cigar in his mouth, and watched as Pearlie, his ranch foreman, cussed and hollered at the hired hands to get the last of the calves in the corral branded so they could stop for lunch. The wiry young man was working like a dervish, moving from place to place within the corral, kicking and shoving the branded calves into the chute that would lead them out to pasture even before the smoke was cleared from their fresh brands.

Smoke smiled around his cheroot as he glanced upward at the morning sun as it shone through mild cloud cover. He figured it was only about ten-thirty in the morning, and Pearlie was already yelling about lunch. That figured, since Pearlie rarely let more than a few hours pass without putting something or other in his mouth. He was, as Cal, his young protégé, called him, a real food hog, with Cal usually putting heavy emphasis on the word "hog."

Hearing light footsteps behind him, Smoke turned and saw his beautiful wife, Sally, approaching the corral with a metal pot of fresh coffee in one hand and a platter of her well-appreciated doughnuts, called bear sign, in the other. Her long, dark hair was hanging down to caress her shoulders, just the way he liked it, and her hazel eyes were bright and clear and full of life, as usual.

"Hi, darlin'," Smoke drawled, jumping down off the rail. "What's this?" he asked as he took the platter of bear sign from her hands.

She smiled, and it was if the clouds parted and the sun shone brighter to Smoke. "I could hear Pearlie shouting about lunch all the way in the cabin, so I thought a short break for some coffee and doughnuts might help him make it until noon when I'll serve the boys lunch."

Pearlie, who was busy lying across a calf's neck so Cal could apply the branding iron, hadn't seen Sally's approach.

Smoke whistled through his lips and held up the platter for the men in the corral to see. "Hey, we got coffee and bear sign, boys," he shouted.

Pearlie's head whipped around at the words "bear sign," and he jumped up off the calf and literally ran toward the corral gate. As soon as he was up and off the calf, it kicked out with both hind legs and scrambled to its feet, knocking Cal on his ass and sending the branding iron flying.

Pearlie didn't take time to undo the latch on the gate, but just jumped up on top and leapt on over. He didn't intend for anyone else to get first pick of the doughnuts. When Pearlie arrived next to Smoke and Sally, skidding to a stop in the mud that was a result of the spring rains earlier in the week, he ignored the coffee and grabbed a double handful of the bear sign, while simultaneously tipping his hat at Sally.

"Mornin,' Miss Sally," he said just before he popped an entire doughnut in his mouth and began to chew.

"Good morning, Pearlie," she said with a laugh, shaking her head at the way he was making the food disappear.

Cal and three other hands walked up at a much slower pace, showing a good deal more restraint than Pearlie had. When Cal got close enough, he reared back and kicked Pearlie in the seat of his pants with the side of his boot.

"Gosh darn it, Pearlie," he groused, "that calf dang near took my leg off!"

Pearlie juggled the bear sign in his hands to keep from spilling them onto the ground when Cal's kick made him jump. "Dagnabbit, Cal, you almost made me drop these here bear sign!" he shouted, holding the doughnuts in one hand while he rubbed his posterior with his free hand.

Cal pointed at the platter heaped full of doughnuts. "Well, what was your hurry, Pearlie? Miss Sally made plenty enough bear sign for all of us."

Pearlie shrugged. "I just wanted to git'em whilst they was hot, Cal. You know they taste better that way," he answered, looking not at all ashamed of his actions.

"Horsesh—uh, stuff!" Cal rejoined, glancing at Sally as he reached over and took a couple of the bear sign for himself. "You just wanted to make sure you got more'n everybody else, that's why you was in such a hurry."

"There's plenty for everyone," Sally said, stepping between the men. "And I made a fresh pot of coffee to go along with the bear sign."

When Pearlie opened his mouth to ask a question, Sally interrupted him. She pulled out a small brown sack containing sugar and held it up. "And yes, I did bring you some sugar for your coffee, Pearlie."

Cal shook his head as he poured himself a cup of the steaming brew. "I swear, Miss Sally," he said, smiling slightly, "you done spoiled that man rotten."

"What?" Pearlie asked as he dumped the entire packet of sugar in his coffee without asking anyone else if they wanted any. "Just 'cause I like a little sugar in my coffee, you think I'm spoiled?"

Cal smirked. "You mean a little coffee in your sugar, don't you?" he asked. "And what's next, Pearlie? Pretty soon you're gonna be putting cow's milk in it like the ladies in town all do."

Smoke laughed and put his arm around Sally. "You boys finish up your coffee and get back to work. I'm not paying you to sit around on your backsides jawing at each other all day," he said as he walked Sally back toward their cabin.

"Thank you kindly for the food and coffee, Miss Sally," called Pete, one of the hands.

"Yes, ma'am," Pearlie mumbled through a mouthful of doughnut, "thanks."

Cal took off his hat and slapped Pearlie in the back of his head with it. "Don't talk with your mouth full, Pearlie. Didn't your momma never teach you no manners?"

"Hell," Pete said laughing, "if'n Pearlie didn't talk with his mouth full, he'd dang near never get to say nothin'."

Smoke liked the way his men had an easy camaraderie on the job. Out in the High Lonesome, he knew that on any given day their lives might depend on their coworkers, and he reasoned the better friends they were, the less chance there was of anyone getting hurt or killed in the dangerous business of ranching out on the frontier.

He was especially fond of Pearlie and his young sidekick, Cal. They'd been with him for several years now, and after standing next to them in some pretty hairy situations, he knew he couldn't ask for any better men to be by his side or to guard his back. In the parlance of the West, they would both do to ride the river with.

Pearlie had come to work for Smoke over five years before, after he'd found he couldn't stomach a man he'd hired his guns to in a range war against Smoke Jensen. Pearlie had gone to the man, named Tilden Franklin, after Franklin had raped a young woman, and told him he was through. Franklin was enraged, and he had his other gunnies beat Pearlie almost to death, finally shooting him and leaving him for dead. Wounded and near death, Pearlie had made his way to the Sugarloaf to warn Smoke about Franklin, and he'd been a fixture on the ranch ever since.

Calvin Woods, a year or two later, was just fourteen years old when he found himself in Colorado, broke and starving after leaving his parents' hardscrabble farm to try and make a living on his own. Sally had been on her way back to the Sugarloaf with a buckboard full of supplies during the spring branding, and Cal, railthin from not eating anything but wild berries for the past week, had stepped from the bushes at the corner of the trail with a pistol in his hand.

"Hold it right there, miss," he'd called.

Sally could see right away the boy was half-starved and could hardly hold the old pistol up, he was so weak.

She slipped her hand under a pile of gingham cloth on the seat, grasping the handle of her short-barreled Colt .44, and eared back the hammer, just in case.

"What can I do for you, young man?" she asked, no fear in her voice.

"Well, uh, you can throw some of those beans and a cut of that fatback over here, and maybe a portion of that Arbuckle's coffee too."

"Don't you want my money?"

The boy frowned and shook his head. "Why, no, ma'am. I ain't no thief. I'm just hungry."

"And if I don't give you my food, are you going to shoot me with that big Navy Colt?" Sally asked, trying hard not to smile.

Cal hesitated for a moment, and then he grinned ruefully. "No, ma'am, I guess not." He twirled the pistol around his finger and he slipped it into his belt, and then he turned and began to walk down the road toward Big Rock.

Sally, feeling sorry for the boy instead of angry, called out to him and offered him a job on the Sugarloaf, which he eagerly accepted. When they got back to the ranch, Pearlie took the boy under his wing, even though he was just a couple of years older than Cal. They'd been best friends ever since.

Both Smoke and Sally thought of Pearlie and Cal as more members of their family than hired workers, and the boys, who would gladly lay down their lives for either of them, reciprocated the feelings.

As Smoke and Sally approached their house, Smoke heard the sounds of hoofbeats in the distance, and they were coming closer at a rapid rate, as if the rider was in a hell of a hurry.

Smoke's hand went to the Colt in his holster. Visitors in the High Lonesome weren't always friendly, and Smoke had more than his fair share of enemies still walking around.

"Step into the cabin, Sally," he said as he turned and looked down the road leading to their house, "until I see who this is."

Sally, who'd learned never to question Smoke's instincts, ducked into the cabin and took a Henry repeating rifle off the rack next to the door.

She held the gun expertly and waited to see if she would need to use it to back Smoke's play.

After a minute or two, she saw Smoke's hand come away from his pistol and a smile break out on his face as he called out, "Hey, Monte, come on in and have some coffee."

She hung the rifle back up on the rack and went into the kitchen to get Monte Carson, sheriff of Big Rock, a cup of coffee and some bear sign.

By the time Sally came out onto the porch, Monte and Smoke were sitting on chairs and Monte was tamping tobacco in the pipe, which was rarely out of his mouth.

Monte jumped to his feet and tipped his hat. "Howdy, Miss Sally."

"Hello, Monte," she responded, smiling and waving him back to his seat as she handed him a mug of coffee and put the plate of bear sign down on a table between him and Smoke.

Smoke took the other mug, and watched as Monte grabbed a doughnut and swallowed it in two bites. Cowboys throughout the valley around Big Rock prized Sally's bear sign.

"How is Mary?" Sally asked, speaking of Monte's wife. "We've been so busy with the spring branding, I haven't had a chance to visit her in a while."

"She'd doin' just fine, Sally," Monte said. "Her rheumatiz is botherin' her a bit, but now that warm weather's on the way, it'll soon get better."

"Winter up here does have a way of getting into our bones, especially as we all get older," Sally said, dusting her hands off on the apron tied around her waist.

Monte's face sobered and he pulled an envelope out of his vest pocket. "Well, I guess I might as well get to the reason I came out here. Jackson over at the telegraph office gave me this telegram for you and said I needed to get it out here right away."

"Bad news?" Smoke asked.

Monte gave a half smile. "You know ol' Jack, Smoke. He wouldn't say, but I 'spect it is or he wouldn't have been in such an all-fired hurry for me to bring it to you."

Sally took the envelope and opened it. As she read it, Smoke saw her face pale and her eyes fill with tears.

He got immediately to his feet and stood by her side, putting his arm around her waist, waiting for her to tell him what it said.

After a moment, she folded the letter and placed it in her apron pocket. She looked up at him, her face sad. "It's my father," she said quietly. "My mother says he's real sick. The doctor in Boston thinks it might be his heart."

Smoke hugged her. He knew how close Sally was to her parents, and it'd been over two years since she'd been back to see them. He looked over her shoulder at Monte. "Would you make arrangements for us to take the next train out heading east, Monte? We'll get packed and be in town first thing in the morning."

"Sure, Smoke," he answered, and he looked at Sally, "I'm real sorry to hear about your paw, Sally."

"Just a minute, Monte," Sally said. She turned to Smoke. "You don't have to come with me, Smoke."

When he started to protest, she held up her hand. "No, I know how much you hate to go back East, especially when there's still a lot of work to do around the ranch. I'll just go out there by myself and see what the situation is. By the time you're through with the branding and such, I'll know how my father is and I'll let you know then if you need to come."

Smoke hated to think of Sally making such a long trip by herself, but she was right. He hated the big cities of the East, and could hardly stand to visit for very long. The crowded streets and the dudes with their fine clothes and insincere manners grated on his nerves worse than a burr in his boots.

When Sally saw the indecision on his face, she smiled gently. "I'll be all right, dear. After all, I've made the trip many times before."

Finally Smoke nodded, though it was clear he wasn't happy with the idea of her traveling alone. "All right, if you say so."

Sally prepared a large lunch of fried chicken, mashed potatoes, and several loaves of fresh bread. She had a lot of hungry cowboys to feed before she could start her packing, and she cooked extra portions at lunch so she wouldn't have to cook later for supper.

Even though Smoke was among the richest ranchers in the area and they could easily afford a full-time cook, Sally enjoyed cooking for the men. She'd been a teacher in the local school, and she wouldn't have known what to do with her time if she couldn't make herself useful in this way. At times, even though Smoke hired a cook for trail drives, Sally would ride along and help him prepare the meals from the chuck wagon. When Smoke asked her why, she said it helped keep her cooking skills sharp—and the men all agreed she was right, for she was widely known as the best cook in the county.

After lunch, she went into the bedroom to get her things together, while Smoke went out to the corral to help with the branding.

Some six hours later, Smoke entered the cabin and found their wooden bathtub set up in the spare bedroom, and it was full of steaming hot water.

"What's this?" he said with a grin. "I'm a mountain man—you know it's not time for my annual bath yet."

Sally appeared from their bedroom, wearing a frilly pink nightgown, a half smile on her face. "Smoke Jensen, I'm leaving in the morning and I won't see you for I don't know how long. If you think I'm going to spend my last night with you with you all covered with dirt and sweat, well, then, you've got another think coming!"

Smoke laughed and began to quickly shed his buckskins. "Well, dear, when you put it that way . . . "

# Chapter 2

Two weeks later, on the day Sally was supposed to wire him and let him know what was going on with her father, Smoke called Cal and Pearlie to the cabin just after breakfast. They'd been riding fence all week, fixing up the areas where the winter storms had torn them down. The branding and separating of the calves from their mothers had been done, and there was nothing much else to do around the ranch. They were all just about bored to death.

When they entered the cabin, Smoke looked up from his coffee. "I've got to go into Big Rock this morning to pick up Sally's telegraph, and I thought you boys might like to go along."

"Boy, Smoke," Pearlie said with feeling, "you got that right! I'm so tired of Buttermilk's cookin', I'm 'bout ready to go on a diet."

Buttermilk Wheeler was a local cook that Sally had insisted Smoke hire to cook for them while she was away. "Otherwise," she'd said with a twinkle in her eyes, "I'll come back to find you all dead of food poisoning."

Cal laughed at Pearlie's claim. "That'll be the day when you pass up food of any kind, Pearlie."

"Well, it's true," Pearlie argued, looking at Smoke with a pained expression on his face. "Now I know why they call his biscuits 'sinkers,' and the coffee . . . well, let's just say it tastes like ol' Buttermilk flavors it with axle grease."

Buttermilk, who was standing over at the stove kneading biscuit dough, turned his head, looking hurt. "I'll remember that, friend, next time you hold out your cup for your third helping."

Pearlie ignored him. "You think we could have lunch over at Longmont's, Smoke? I got me a real hankerin' for some of that there French cuisine," he said, pronouncing it *queeseen.*

Smoke laughed. He knew a day in town with the boys was just the thing to get him over his boredom. "I don't see why not."

"Maybe we can get Andre to fix up some of those frog legs in butter sauce he's always trying to get Pearlie to taste," Cal teased, knowing Pearlie got sick at the very thought of eating any part of a slimy frog.

"And maybe he can wash it down with some coffee that ain't flavored with axle grease!" Buttermilk added from the other side of the room.

Pearlie held up his hands, his nose wrinkled. "Thank you, but I think I'll just stick with a steak about two inches thick, some of those fried taters, and maybe some of that peach cobbler Andre makes so good."

"It's a mite early for the peach cobbler, Pearlie, but I think we can manage the rest of it," Smoke said, standing up and getting his hat.

"I don't know, Smoke," Pearlie said, walking out of the door behind him. "You know, Andre has that greenhouse of his and he's just about always got some fresh vegetables, even in the dead of winter."

"Peaches ain't no vegetable, you idiot," Cal said. "They're fruit."

"Oh, so now you're a gardenin' expert along with everthing else you think you know, huh?" Pearlie said, swinging at Cal's butt with his boot but missing.

"If you'd ever try and read some of those books Miss Sally gave me, you'd know a little something too," Cal said, a superior air about him.

Smoke stopped walking and turned as if to go back in the cabin.

"What'd you forget, Smoke?" Pearlie asked.

"Some cotton. If you boys are gonna go on like this all the way to town, I'm gonna stuff my ears full so I don't have to listen to it."

Once they got to town, Smoke sent the boys on ahead to Longmont's Saloon while he stopped off at the telegraph office. He picked up a long telegraph that had just arrived from Boston and took it outside to read.

Sally wrote that her father had indeed had a heart stroke and, though he'd survived it, he was extremely weak and the doctors didn't know how long it was going to take for him to recover. Sally said she thought she'd better plan on staying for an extended visit to help her mother cope with her father's illness.

Smoke grimaced, and carefully folded the telegram, stuck it in the pocket of his buckskin jacket, and headed for Longmont's. It was bad enough to be sitting around on his duff bored to death, but to do it without the steadying influence of Sally was going to be almost intolerable. And to make matters worse, he was having trouble sleeping without Sally's warm body next to him in their bed.

He chuckled to himself. It was funny, but when he

was camped out on a trail drive or on a hunting or fishing trip to the High Lonesome, he slept like a baby even on the hardest ground. Guess he was getting spoiled, and he missed the feeling of being spoiled by Sally.

He stepped through the batwings of the saloon, and out of long habit learned from years of watching his back, stepped to the side with his back to the wall until his eyes adjusted to the darkness of the room.

Longmont's was a combination restaurant, bar, and poker parlor, with tables for eating situated off to the left, a long mahogany bar against the far wall on the right, and a few felt-covered tables in front of it for the poker players to sit at while they drank and gambled. Louis Longmont, the owner, had no fancy-dressed women or piano players or faro tables, and offered only the simple pleasures of excellent food prepared by his French chef and longtime friend, Andre, honest liquor, and an honest game of straight poker in a dignified, quiet atmosphere.

Smoke saw Louis himself seated at a table off to the left with Cal and Pearlie, his usual spot until the nighttime poker games heated up. He and Smoke had been close friends for longer than Smoke liked to remember.

Louis was a lean, hawk-faced man, with strong, slender hands and long fingers, the nails carefully manicured, the hands clean. He had jet-black hair, turning slightly gray over the ears, and a pencil-thin mustache. He was dressed as always in a black suit, with white shirt and dark ascot—the ascot something he'd picked up on a trip to England a few years back. He wore low-heeled boots, and had a pistol on his right hip in tied-down leather; it was not just for show, for Louis was snake-quick with a short gun and was a feared, deadly gunhand when pushed. He was just past forty years old, had come to the West as a young boy, and had made a fortune due to his sharp intellect and fearless nature.

When he saw Smoke enter the door, Louis waved him over and poured another cup of coffee out of the silver pot on the table. Smoke took a seat and looked at the coffee. "I may need something stronger than that, Louis."

Louis's eyes grew concerned. "Bad news from Sally, Smoke?"

"Yes and no. Her father is doing all right, but he had a heart stroke and the doctors say there's no telling how long he might be laid up. The bad news is that Sally plans on staying up there with him until he's better, and that could be months according to her telegram."

Pearlie's face fell at the news. "You mean we're gonna have to keep on eatin' Buttermilk's food for months?"

Cal nodded in sympathy with Pearlie. "I'm sure gonna miss Miss Sally's cooking," he said morosely.

"Yeah," Smoke agreed. "The place just won't be the same without her around, that's for sure." Though his mind was more on the coldness in their feather bed than on the quality of her cooking.

Louis's eyes narrowed. "You say Sally is going to be gone for some months, and you are finished with most of the immediate work that needs to be done on the Sugarloaf?"

Smoke nodded. "That's just about it, Louis, and I'm going to get real tired of sitting around watching the grass grow."

"Have you thought about the possibility of taking a trip, maybe going off somewhere on an adventure?" Louis asked, a speculative glint in his eyes.

"Why, what do you mean?" Smoke asked. "What kind of adventure are you talking about?"

"Let's order lunch first, and then there is someone I want you to meet," Louis said, a secretive smile on his face as he held his cards close to his vest.

"I thought you'd never offer," Pearlie said. "My

mouth's been waterin' ever since we came in here and I smelled Andre's cooking."

While they were eating, Louis went over to the young black boy who served as his waiter, handed him a note, and then returned to the table.

"What was that all about?" Smoke asked around a mouthful of steak, cooked just the way he liked it, red and bloody inside and charred on the outside.

"I sent Lincoln over to the hotel with a note for a man I want you to meet," Louis answered.

"Oh?"

"His name is William Cornelius Van Horne," Louis said. "He was one of the builders of the Illinois Central Railroad, and he's out here to do a little antelope hunting before heading on up into Canada to build another railroad."

"And he's here to hunt antelope?" Smoke asked. "Why? You can't eat the damned things. They taste like leather."

Louis shrugged. "He says he wants a head to put on his wall, seems it's about the only big-game trophy he doesn't already have."

Smoke put his fork down, a look on his face like his steak had suddenly gone bad. "Louis, you know how I feel about that. I don't believe in killing anything you're not going to eat. I hope you don't think I'm gonna take this idiot out hunting for a trophy to put on his wall."

Louis held up his hand and shook his head. "No, Smoke, it's nothing like that, but I think you'll like this man. And what with Sally going to be gone for so long, I think you might want to hear what he has to say."

*    *    *

The lunch dishes had been cleared away, and Smoke and Louis and the boys were on their third cup of coffee, when the batwings swung open and the sunlight from outside was blocked by a massive figure.

The man who entered was of average height and had the approximate size and shape of a whiskey barrel, with broad shoulders, a thick paunch, and hands as large as hams that looked tough enough to drive railway spikes with. He looked to Smoke to be in his mid-to-late thirties, and had a full but neatly trimmed beard and mustache.

He was dressed in a suit and vest, and when he waved and walked over toward Louis's table, he had that graceful, light-footed gait common to many big men.

When he got to the table and spoke, his voice was deep and gravelly—a whiskey-and-cigar type of voice, Smoke thought. As he appraised the man, he was impressed. The man had an air of authority about him, and of strength. He was used to leading men and to having his orders carried out without hesitation or question, Smoke surmised, and he didn't appear to be the kind of man who has to prove his manhood by killing animals and hanging them on a wall.

"Good afternoon, Louis," the man said, inclining his head, but his eyes were on Smoke. Evidently he too was appraising Smoke even as he was being appraised.

"Hello, Bill," Louis said, getting to his feet. "Mr. William Cornelius Van Horne, I'd like you to meet Smoke Jensen," Louis continued. "He's the man I was telling you about yesterday."

"Ah," Van Horne said, "the famous mountain man." He stuck out his hand to Smoke.

When Smoke stood up and took the hand, he was surprised to find it hard and rough, with calluses on it. This was not a man who rode a desk all day, he thought, smiling as Van Horne squeezed his hand hard enough to make a lesser man wince.

"Hello, Mr. Van Horne," Smoke said. "I don't know about the 'famous' part, but I was a mountain man for a while in my younger days."

"Call me Bill, Smoke. I'm not much one for formalities."

"This is Cal and Pearlie," Smoke said, "my friends."

"Howdy, Cal, Pearlie," Bill said, smiling and nodding as he took a seat on the other side of Louis.

"Would you care for some lunch?" Louis asked the newcomer.

Bill smiled. "I will never pass up a chance to partake of Andre's excellent cooking, Louis. A steak and some of those wonderful fried potatoes would go nicely, I think."

While Louis gave the order, Bill spoke to Smoke. "Has Louis told you why I was asking about you?"

Smoke glanced at Louis and shook his head. "No, but he did say something about you wanting to hunt antelope."

"Pshaw," Bill said, waving a dismissive hand. "That was just something to pass the time while I waited to get in touch with you."

"Oh?"

"Yes. I've heard about you and your . . . rather special relationship with those men who live up in the Rockies who call themselves mountain men."

Smoke smiled. "I've ridden with a few of them over the years, though their numbers aren't what they used to be, what with the coming of civilization to the mountains."

"Smoke, I have been commissioned to undertake a great task. The government of Canada has asked me to build a railroad from Winnipeg all the way to the western coast, near Vancouver Island."

Smoke pursed his lips, visualizing what he knew about Canada. "That's some pretty rough country, Bill.

You'll be crossing at least three mountain ranges that I can think of, not to mention forests so thick you can barely ride a horse through them, and that's not even taking into account the various Indian tribes who won't take kindly to your trespassing on their lands."

Bill laughed, a great booming sound that came from his gut. "You do have a way of putting it into perspective, Smoke. Yes, you're right, but the Canadian government didn't say it was going to be easy."

"Easy is the last word I would use, Bill. Danged near impossible is probably more accurate."

Bill's brow knitted. "You don't think it can be done?"

Smoke shrugged. "I don't know. For one thing, I don't know a whole heck of a lot about what it takes to build a railroad, and I don't even know if there are any passes over the mountains you'll have to traverse. I've never been that far north."

"You're right about the mountain passes, and I don't know either. There have been several expeditions through the area, but the men on them haven't finished their journeys yet, so there is no word on where the passes might be, if there are any."

He leaned back in his chair so the waiter could place his plate of food in front of him on the table.

As he cut up his steak, he added, "That's why I needed someone who might be able to persuade some of these mountain men down here in Colorado Territory to come up there and act as advance scouts for my expedition."

He took a bite of steak and rolled his eyes. "This is delicious, as always, Louis. Are you sure I can't hire Andre away from you?"

Louis grinned and shrugged. "Andre is a free man, Bill, so you can try."

Bill shook his head. "No, that would be worse than trying to steal another man's wife, but tell him if he ever has a hankering to travel up north to give me a shout."

He took another bite and said, "The pay would be excellent, Smoke, probably more money than any of your friends could earn in ten years of trapping."

"Money is not important to mountain men, Bill," Smoke said, a half smile on his face. "Their lives center around being on their own and away from civilization, not on earning a living."

"Well, what better challenge than going where few have gone before," Bill said, pointing his fork at Smoke as he spoke. "I hear there are fewer than twenty-five hundred white men in an area of several hundred thousand square miles in Canada. You can't get much further from civilization than that."

Smoke thought about it for a few minutes while he got a cigar going and drank some more coffee. He knew several of his old friends up in the High Lonesome who thought Colorado was getting too crowded and who might be willing to try a new place, just for the adventure of it.

"I might know some men who might be willing to take you up on such an offer, now that you mention it," Smoke said.

Bill smiled and finished off his steak. He pushed the plate to the side, took a leather case out of his breast pocket, and extracted a long, thick cigar. He struck a lucifer on his pants leg and puffed the cigar alive. He eyed Smoke through billowing clouds of blue smoke. "Louis tells me you have a wife and a ranch to run and that you would likely be unavailable to leave the country for an extended period of time."

Smoke started to nod, and then he thought. *Wait a minute. Why not? Sally's going to be gone for many months, and I'm bored with ranch life. Why not go off on an adven-*

*ture? It might be the last chance I get to traverse uncharted, uninhabited land in the company of my mountain-man friends.*

"Ordinarily, that would be true, Bill, but as it so happens, my wife is away on an extended trip just now. Let me think it over for a day or so and I'll get back to you."

"Excellent," Bill said. "Let's have a drink to your making the right decision."

# Chapter 3

Van Horne pulled a gold watch from his vest pocket and glanced at the time. "It's still a little early for hard liquor, but it's never too early for beer."

He glanced around, but the waiter was nowhere to be seen. He got to his feet. "I'll just go to the bar and get us a pitcher of Louis's finest beer."

He walked over to the bar and squeezed in between several men who were standing at the bar.

"My good man," he said to the bartender, "would you be so kind as to bring a pitcher of beer and five mugs to my table?"

One of the cowboys at the bar stepped back and looked at Van Horne, his eyes going up and down. "Well, just listen to Mr. High-and-Mighty here," he said in a loud voice, slurred by too much whiskey too early in the day. He was tall and slim, with a wide leather belt inlaid with silver conchos, and his boots had silver toes. He was wearing twin Peacemaker Colts with pearl handles tied down low on his hips.

To Van Horne, he seemed to be trying to look like the desperados in the penny dreadfuls.

"Pardon me?" Bill asked, turning to look at the man.

"Pardon you?" the man responded sarcastically. "Pardon you for what? For being so fat you can't hardly get through the door?"

"Oh-oh," Smoke said in a low voice to Louis. "Looks like trouble at the bar."

Louis started to get up, but Smoke put a hand on his arm. "Wait a minute, Louis, let's see how Bill handles this," Smoke said, wanting to see how the big man handled himself. If he was going to be out in the wilderness with Van Horne, he wanted to see what he was made of. Smoke didn't think Van Horne was heeled, so he loosened the rawhide hammer thong on his own Colt just in case the confrontation turned deadly.

Bill snorted and turned back to the bar, trying to ignore the drunk, but the man grabbed him by the shoulder and whirled him around. "Don't turn your back on me while I'm talking to you, fatty."

Bill's hand moved so quick that Smoke could hardly see it as he reached up, grabbed the lout by the throat, and lifted him up until his feet dangled a foot off the floor. As the man's face turned purple and he grabbed Bill's hand, trying to pry it loose, Bill said calmly, "You, sir, are rude and obnoxious, and I cannot abide rudeness." He cocked his head to the side and stared into the man's bulging eyes. "Often rudeness is prevalent in men whose intelligence is akin to a dog's," he added contemptuously.

He gave a final squeeze and without apparent effort threw the man across the room, where he landed flat on his back, still gasping for breath.

One of the man's friends stepped away from the bar and dropped his hand to his pistol butt. Smoke was just about to draw, for he would never allow an unarmed man to be gunned down, when Bill drew back his right arm and punched the man in the face so hard he splattered his nose flat and knocked the man to his knees.

A third man, his eyes wide, let his hand drop toward his gun and Smoke called out, "I wouldn't do that, partner."

The man glanced at Smoke and saw the barrel of his .44 pointed right at his head. "This ain't no fight of yours, mister," the man said uncertainly, but his hand stopped moving and hung there in the air, shaking slightly.

"It is when you're drawing on a man who isn't heeled," Smoke said. "You want to say something to Mr. Van Horne, say it with your fists, not that hogleg on your hip."

Bill squared off with the man, his fists at his side. "Well, sir, do you have something you wish to add?"

The man looked around at his friends, one still blue and gasping and the other with his nose spread all over his face. "Uh, no . . . I guess not."

"Then I suggest that the next time you want to drink your lunch, you do it someplace else," Bill said, picking up the tray with the pitcher of beer and mugs on it. He turned his back on the man and walked back to the table, as if nothing had happened.

Smoke smiled at him. Van Horne hadn't even broken a sweat. "You pack a mean punch, Bill," he said as Bill poured them all beer.

Bill looked at him out of the corner of his eye, a slight grin on his face. "When you supervise thousands of men building a railroad, Smoke, you either learn to be good with your fists or you stay behind a desk." He upended his beer and drained it in one long swallow. As he sleeved suds off his mustache, he grinned. "And I never was one for staying behind a desk."

"How come you don't carry a gun, Mr. Van Horne?" Cal asked.

Bill poured himself another beer. "Oh, I do when I'm

out in the field working, Cal, but when I'm in town, I don't usually see the need." He took a swallow, smaller this time, and added, "Of course, I may have to change my mind about that in the future."

"Are you any good with a short gun?" Pearlie asked, impressed by Bill's coolness under fire.

Bill shrugged. "I'm not the fastest gun around, Pearlie, but I hit what I aim at, and I'm told that's more important than being fast."

Smoke held up his mug. "I'll drink to that," he said, laughing.


After they'd said their good-byes to Bill and Louis, Smoke and the boys stepped out of the saloon and walked toward their horses.

The three cowboys from the bar were waiting out in the street, one of them with his nose still dripping blood onto his shirt.

"Hey, you!" one of the other two called.

Smoke stopped and looked over at him. "Are you talking to me?" he asked calmly.

"Yeah. You're gonna learn not to stick your nose in other people's business."

When they heard the commotion outside, Louis and Bill stepped to the window to see what was happening.

Bill started to move toward the batwings, but Louis stopped him. "But I can't let Smoke fight my battles for me," Bill said.

"Just watch, Bill. I want you to see Smoke in action."

"Oh," Smoke said to the gunny. "And I suppose you're going to teach me?"

"That's right, asshole," the man said, crouching with his hand held over the butt of his pistol. "Me and my friends."

"You want some help, Smoke?" Pearlie said, covering

a yawn with the back of his hand, seemingly unconcerned about the men standing before them.

"No, I don't think so, Pearlie," Smoke said. "After all, there's only three of them."

"All right," Pearlie said, and he and Cal moved to the side. Pearlie leaned back against a post with his arms crossed.

"By the way, gentlemen," he said conversationally, "what are your names?"

The man with the bloody nose looked over at him. "Why do you want to know?" he asked angrily.

Pearlie shrugged. "Most people like to have their names on their tombstones, so I thought I'd ask."

Sweat began to appear on the man's forehead, and he turned back to face Smoke.

Smoke looked at him, his eyes as mean and black as a snake's. "Either draw or go back to the hole you crawled out of," Smoke said, his voice hard. "I got things to do."

"You son of a . . ." the man snarled as he went for his gun.

Quicker than it takes to tell it, Smoke drew and fired three times. The man with the bloody nose was hit high in the left shoulder, the slug spinning him around to fall facedown, screaming in pain. The second and third men were both hit in the middle of their chests and blown onto their backs, dead before they hit the ground. Not one of them had cleared leather.

Bill and Louis came out of the saloon, Bill shaking his head. "I'd heard you were fast, Smoke, but I never believed just how fast."

Smoke punched out his empty brass and reloaded his pistol. "Like you say, Bill, it's more important to be accurate than fast."

Bill laughed. "But it's even better to be both, Smoke."

Smoke walked over to stand over the injured man,

who was moaning and crying and holding his shoulder, blood dripping between his fingers.

Smoke dropped two twenty-dollar gold pieces on his chest. "Here you go, mister. Use this to bury your friends and to get your arm taken care of."

He started to walk away, and then stopped and looked back over his shoulder. "And do it by sundown and then get out of town, 'cause if I ever see your face again, ever, I'll kill you."

# Chapter 4

Smoke spent the next two days working around the ranch, overseeing his men as they tended fences, worked cattle, and made sure the new calves they'd separated from their mothers were all doing all right. As he worked, he found himself increasingly looking at the snow-covered peaks of the Rockies in the distance, a longing in his heart he'd ignored for far too long.

Finally, he'd had enough. He was bored silly, and Sally's absence just made matters worse. Smoke decided to take Van Horne up on his offer to help with finding a suitable route for the Canadian railroad. After all, he'd been wanting to get back up into the mountains and see his old mountain-man friends for some time, and this would be a perfect opportunity, what with Sally gone for who knows how long.

He rode over to the ranch nearest the Sugarloaf, and asked his old friend Johnny North if he'd keep a watch on the place for him while he was gone. North agreed to ride over every week or so and make sure the hands Smoke had working for him didn't need anything, and to keep a close eye on his livestock in his absence.

Smoke decided to take Cal and Pearlie along for company, and to teach them a thing or two about mountain living. Both men had long been fascinated with the High Lonesome and had met some of Smoke's mountain-man friends on previous occasions, and were overjoyed at the chance to ride with them once again.

So, when the packhorses were loaded with the supplies Smoke thought they would need, he and the boys rode into Big Rock, ready to travel. Smoke sent a telegram to Sally in Boston telling her of his plans and promising to keep in touch whenever they were near a telegraph, and then they met up with Van Horne in front of Louis Longmont's saloon.

This time, instead of his three-piece suit, Van Horne was dressed for the trail in trousers, riding boots, and a flannel shirt that looked large enough to use as a sleeping blanket. He had a Smith and Wesson nickel-plated pistol in a holster on his belt and a brand-new Winchester rifle in his saddle boot.

His packhorse was loaded down with enough food for a year, and Smoke grinned and shook his head. It was clear Van Horne did not intend to go hungry on this trip up into the mountains to find some mountain men to ride with them.

"Hello, Smoke, boys," Bill called as they approached.

"I can see you've got plenty of provisions for the trip," Smoke said, smiling.

Bill looked over his shoulder at the boxes piled high on the back of the packhorse and nodded. "Yes, of course, I'm packed for two people."

"Two?" Smoke asked.

The batwings of the saloon swung open and Louis Longmont stepped out. "Yes, Smoke. I decided that it was not fair for you to have all the fun this time, so I have elected to join you on your little jaunt."

Longmont had also given up his trademark black

suit for trail clothes, though his still looked as if they'd
been made by a French tailor. His black pants were
freshly ironed and his dark leather coat was as shiny as
his knee-high black boots. He wore a brace of Colts on
his belt, and had a Henry repeating rifle slung over his
shoulder as he walked toward his horse.

"Is Andre gonna come too, Mr. Longmont?" Pearlie
asked, licking his lips in anticipation of fine meals being
cooked every night.

Longmont shook his head. "Not on your life, Pearlie.
Andre's place is in the kitchen, not on the back of a
horse."

"Oh," Pearlie said, disappointed.

Louis and Van Horne swung up into their saddles
and looked at Smoke. "Ready?" Louis asked.

"As I'll ever be," Smoke answered, and spurred his
horse into a slow canter down the main street of Big
Rock, heading north toward snow-covered mountain
peaks in the distance.

As they swung into line behind him, Pearlie leaned
over in his saddle and said to Cal, "I sure hope they
ain't expectin' you to do the cookin' on this here trip."

"Why not?" Cal asked, raising his eyebrows.

"'Cause I plumb forgot to bring any stomach salts to
ease the bellyache your food causes."

Two days later, as their horses moved slowly up the
side of a mountain slope that was still covered with
snowdrifts two feet deep, Smoke held up his hand and
the procession slowed to a halt.

Bill Van Horne pulled his horse up next to Smoke's
and said, "What is it? Why are we stopping?"

Smoke raised his nose in the air and sniffed. "I smell
smoke—campfire smoke."

Van Horne sniffed. "I don't smell anything?"

Before Smoke could answer, a loud booming gun-shot echoed through the tall ponderosa pines that surrounded them on all sides, followed quickly by several higher-pitched cracks of rifle fire in the distance.

"What the hell?" Van Horne said as his horse stamped and jumped to the side.

Smoke's forehead wrinkled as he stared in the direction of the sounds. "That first shot was from a Sharps, and the ones that followed were from a Winchester."

"Don't most of the mountain men use Sharps?" Cal asked, standing tall in his stirrups to try and see through the forest.

"Yeah, and it sounds like someone's in trouble," Smoke said, spurring his horse forward as he leaned over its head.

As the men road up the side of the mountain, pistols out and ready, they heard more gunshots from up ahead, the sharper cracks of the Winchesters being answered by the deeper booming of a Sharps Big Fifty.

After riding as fast as the horses could run through the deep snow for twenty minutes, Smoke reined his horse in and was out of the saddle before it came to a complete stop.

He jerked his Winchester out of his saddle boot, and crouched down as he jogged up to the crest of a small hillock and peered over the edge.

The others joined him, all holding rifles cradled in their arms. Below, they could see a small campfire with four paint ponies tied to a tree nearby and a makeshift shelter made out of pine limbs piled at an angle against a large boulder, forming a lean-to.

There was blood in the snow around the fire and tracks where a body had been dragged into the lean-to. A long, black barrel was sticking out of the pine limbs and firing at several men who were lying behind logs and rocks in a semicircle around the camp, firing back into the lean-to.

"What's going on?" Van Horne whispered to Smoke as he peered down at the scene below.

"Looks like some mountain men are being fired on by those fellows over there," Smoke answered, nodding toward the men on the ground below.

"How do you know they're mountain men in the camp?" Van Horne asked.

"They're riding Indian ponies, and they're using a Sharps Big Fifty." He pointed his finger down at the camp. "And see, there's a pile of beaver and fox pelts over next to the horses. That's probably what the men are after."

Van Horne nodded. "I see."

Smoke laid his rifle barrel on a rock in front of him, took careful aim, and fired.

One of the men below screamed in pain, grabbed his leg, and rolled over onto his back, shouting, "I'm hit!"

Smoke levered another round into his Winchester and stood up. "Drop your weapons, or I'll put the next one in your head!" he shouted, pointing the barrel of his rifle at the men below.

One of the men made the mistake of turning his rifle toward Smoke, who quickly fired, hitting the man square in the forehead. As his blood and brains sprayed all over the snow around him, the other men slowly put their rifles down and stood up, their hands in the air.

"Now, come on out from behind those rocks so I can see you," Smoke yelled.

Three men walked out into the open, one stopping to help the wounded man get to his feet and limp out with them.

"Bring the horses," Smoke said over his shoulder as he stepped over the ridge and walked down toward the men, the barrel of his rifle still pointing at them and his finger on the trigger.

"Yo, the camp," he called, not wanting to be shot by whoever was in the lean-to.

"Who be you?" a gravelly voice called from behind the barrel of the Sharps as it swiveled to point toward Smoke.

"Bear Tooth, is that you?" Smoke called, a grin on his face.

"Smoke? Smoke Jensen?" the voice answered as a huge man, well over six and a half feet in height, appeared in the opening of the lean-to, a Sharps cradled in his arms.

While Smoke's eyes were on Bear Tooth, one of the men in the clearing dropped his hand and went for a pistol on his belt.

Smoke jumped as a rifle went off behind him and a hole you could put a fist through appeared on the man's chest. He dropped like a stone.

"Thanks," Smoke said to Van Horne, who was still aiming his smoking Winchester at the men below.

"Don't mention it," Bill replied, impressing Smoke with his coolness under fire.

Soon, the three attackers still remaining alive were trussed up and tied with their backs to trees.

Bear Tooth disappeared inside the lean-to, and reappeared moments later with his arm around a man with flaming red hair and beard and a bloody left shoulder.

"Red Bingham, you old beaver," Smoke said, grinning. "I heard you were dead."

"Naw, he ain't dead," Bear Tooth said as he helped Red to sit down next to the fire. "He just smells that way."

Red turned his bright blue eyes to Bear Tooth. "You can talk. At least I took'n me a bath last spring, which is more'n I can say fer some."

Smoke laughed. Bear Tooth was famous among the

mountain men for never going near water. He was known to say if God had intended men to bathe, he would've given them fins like fish.

Smoke glanced at the men tied to the trees nearby. "Poachers?" he asked.

Bear Tooth glared at the men. "Yeah, seems they wanted some skins to sell and were too lazy or too dumb to trap their own."

Louis knelt next to Red and used his knife to cut away the buckskin over his wound. He looked up at Smoke. "Looks like the bullet went all the way through. Doesn't appear to have hit the bone and the blood's oozing and not spurting."

Smoke nodded. That was good news, for a broken bone was almost always fatal up here in the mountains, and the slow bleeding meant no artery had been hit.

Red gritted his teeth and pulled out a long, wide-bladed knife from a scabbard on his belt. He leaned over and stuck the blade in the coals of the fire. After a moment, when the blade was glowing red, he looked at Louis. "You want to do the honors, mister?"

"Do you want me to pour some whiskey on it first?" Louis asked as he reached for the knife.

"Waste good whiskey on a little scratch like this?" Red asked. "No, sir, but if'n you have some, a little nip'd do me nicely."

Smoke laughed and nodded at Pearlie, who pulled a small bottle of red-eye from his saddlebags and handed it to Red.

Red looked at the bottle and shook his head. "When I said a little nip, son, I was speaking figuratively, not meaning to be taken so seriously." Without another word, he upended the pint bottle and drained it as Louis picked up the knife from the fire.

When Louis put the red-hot blade to each of the bullet holes, Red's face paled and his jaw muscles bulged, but he didn't make a sound as his flesh sizzled and smoked under the knife.

After Louis was finished, Red took a deep breath and said, "Now, if you happen to have another bottle of that there firewater, stranger, I'd be much obliged for another taste."

Bear Tooth snorted. "A taste, he says. That means he'll drink the whole danged thing if'n you're not careful."

He hesitated, and then he added, "Now me, on the other hand, I'm a gentleman. I'd only take a small dollop of a man's whiskey, just to be sociable-like."

# Chapter 5

While Red Bingham was drinking his whiskey, Bear Tooth dumped a couple of handfuls of coffee into a blackened pot that sat next to the fire, and added some water from his canteen before pushing the pot onto the coals.

Smoke looked over at Bill Van Horne. "Bill, you're in for a real treat now. You're gonna get to sample some mountain-man coffee."

Bill glanced at the pot. "I noticed he put quite a bit of coffee into the pot."

Bear Tooth nodded. "As they say, the thing 'bout makin' good coffee is it don't take near as much water as you think it do."

"Yeah," Pearlie said, grinning. "Like Puma Buck used to say, if it won't float a horseshoe, it ain't near strong enough."

At the mention of Puma Buck, Bear Tooth looked over at Pearlie. "So, you knew Puma?" he asked.

"Yes, sir," Pearlie answered, his face sober at the thought of the old mountain man who'd given his life to save Smoke and Cal and Pearlie in a fracas a few years back.

Bear Tooth looked down at the fire, his eyes suspiciously wet and shining. "I miss that ol' beaver something fierce," he said in a low voice.

Smoke nodded. "Like a lot of our old friends, he's gone on to better things," he said.

While the coffee was cooking, Red Bingham struggled to his feet, his left arm held close against his side. He bent over and picked his knife up off the ground, and walked slowly toward the men tied to trees off to the side of the camp.

The men, sullen-faced and angry, suddenly looked apprehensive when they saw the way Red was holding the knife. One of them, in a strong French accent, asked, "Hey, what the hell are you planning on doing with that knife?"

Bill looked at Smoke, his eyebrows raised in question, but Smoke just winked and stood watching Red with folded arms.

Red knelt next to the dead man with a hole in his chest and grabbed a handful of his hair. He lifted the head up and quick as a wink sliced the scalp off, and held the bloody mop of hair up in the air, crimson strings of blood running down his hand and onto his arm.

He glanced over his shoulder at Bill, who had a sick expression on his face. "This one's your'n, mister. You want it?"

As Bill quickly shook his head, one of the French poachers leaned over and vomited in the snow, while the other two just watched with horrified expressions on their faces.

Red carried the bloody scalp over to the body of the other dead man, the one Smoke had shot in the forehead. He poked at the head with the toe of his boot and looked over at Smoke. "I think you just about ruined this one, Smoke. The back of it's all blowed away where the bullet came out."

Smoke gave a tight smile. "Sorry about that, Red. I was aiming for his chest, but he must've ducked."

"Well, no matter," Red said as he sliced the torn scalp from the head and held it up with the other one. "It'll still do to hang from my lodge pole."

He stood up and moved toward the men where they sat tied to trees, grinning as they cringed back as far as they could.

One of the men hollered at the men around the fire, "You ain't gonna let this crazy old bastard scalp us, are you?"

"He's not really going to do it, is he, Smoke?" Bill asked in a low voice, his face pale.

Smoke again shrugged. "According to mountain-man ways, Bill, it's his right. These men tried to kill him and his partner, and they would've taken everything they worked all winter for in the process. If he wants to take their hair, I'm sure as hell not going to try and tell him not to." He glanced at Van Horne. "This is part of the ways out here in the High Lonesome, Bill. There aren't any sheriffs or marshals to call when someone does you wrong, so you take care of it yourself, or you don't live to see too many winters."

Bear Tooth, who was in the process of pouring mugs of coffee for everyone, looked over at Red. "Hey, Red, we done got enough scalps already. You're gonna plumb stink up the place if you take three more."

Red stood over the men, blood from the scalps dripping off his knife and hand. "I guess you're right, Bear Tooth. Maybe I'll just take their balls. We ain't eaten no mountain oysters fer months now."

As the French men's faces blanched, Bill hiccupped

and put his hand over his mouth to keep from throwing up.

"I've got a better idea, Red," Smoke said, moving over to stand next to the mountain man.

"What's that, Smoke?" he asked, smiling grimly though his eyes, which had a characteristic twinkle in them.

"Let's take their guns and boots and set them loose on the mountain without any horses. It'll be interesting to see how long they can go before they end up eating each other to stay alive."

Red pursed his lips and nodded. "That's a good idee, Smoke. After a day or two, if they live that long, they'll be sleepin' with one eye open watchin' each other to see who's gonna be the next meal."

Bill looked at Louis, who was watching the proceedings with wry amusement. "Louis, you can't let them do that. It's barbaric."

"Bill, like Smoke said, this isn't a town where you can turn men like that over to the law," Louis explained as he pulled a long, black cigar from his coat pocket and lit it with a twig from the fire. "Justice out here in the mountains is not always pretty, but it is fast and efficient. If these men are allowed to live, sooner or later they'll try to kill some other trapper and steal his skins." He smiled grimly. "At least this way, they have a chance to live, if they're willing to live the rest of their lives knowing they turned to cannibalism to survive."

"That's right, Mr. Van Horne," Pearlie said as he sipped his coffee. "The Indians would've just hung 'em upside down over a bed of coals and cooked their brains whilst makin' bets on who'd die first."

"Of course, they would sing songs in tribute to the man who died showing the most courage," Bear Tooth added.

"That's an honor I think I can live without achieving," Van Horne said, still looking sick.

As Red cut the ropes holding the men against the trees, he asked Smoke, "Should I let 'em keep their knives and flints?"

"Sure," Smoke answered, his eyes flat and hard. "We want them to be able to make a fire and not freeze to death. That would be too easy on them."

"Yeah," Bear Tooth added, again smiling wickedly. "And human flesh tastes better if'n it's been cooked a little." He hesitated, and then he added with a wink at Bill, "At least, that's what I've been told, never having partaken of it myself of course."

Red stepped back and pointed at the men's feet. "Throw them boots over here and get the hell outta my camp, you bastards, 'fore I change my mind 'bout your scalps."

"You can't let him do this to us, mister," one of the men said to Smoke as he took off his boots. "It ain't right."

Smoke shrugged and turned away, saying, "Well, I suppose you got a choice, just like you had when you decided to kill him. You can take your chances on foot, or you can let him gut you and scalp you and end it all right now."

While the men were taking their boots off, Red went over to their horses, took their flints and striking stones out of their saddlebags, and threw them on the ground in front of them.

"You boys better get a move on. You only got 'bout five more hours of daylight an' then it's gonna get really cold."

"I figger it'll take you 'bout four days to walk down the mountain to where it's warmer," Bear Tooth called to the Frenchmen. "After two days, if'n you live that long, your stomachs will be growlin' enough to keep you awake, which is good, 'cause long about then your partners are gonna be lookin' at you like steak on the hoof."

After the Frenchmen slunk off down the mountain, Bear Tooth pulled a slab of elk meat out of their lean-to and sliced some thick steaks off it with his skinning knife. He threw them into a cast-iron skillet, added some wild onions for flavor and a piece of fatback for grease, and put the skillet on the coals. While the steaks were cooking, he put some water in a kettle hanging from a trestle over the fire and poured in several handfuls of pinto beans.

"Reckon it's 'bout time to eat," he said as he took a squat next to the fire and used his knife to cut a chunk off a large square of chewing tobacco.

As the men sat around the fire, drinking coffee and waiting for the meal to cook, Red glanced over at Smoke. "You gonna introduce us to your partners or not, Smoke?"

Smoke laughed and introduced everyone to the mountain men, who didn't offer to shake hands but merely nodded, as was the mountain-man way.

"Been a long time since we seen you up here in the High Lonesome, Smoke," Bear Tooth observed, speaking around a large wad of tobacco in his cheek. "You up here to do some trappin' or huntin'?"

Smoke shook his head. "No, Bear Tooth, as a matter of fact, we came up here looking for you."

"Me?" Bear Tooth asked, surprised at the answer.

"You and some of the other old beavers that are still up here trapping," Smoke said.

"Not too many of us old-timers left anymore, Smoke," Red said, his eyes sad as he stared into the fire. "It's just not the same anymore. Time was, you could go all winter an' not see nary another white man, 'ceptin' your partner." He glanced off in the direction the French poachers had taken. "Now, you got pond scum like those men crawlin' all over the place." He looked at Smoke. "Hell, it's getting plumb crowded up here now."

Bear Tooth nodded. "He's right, Smoke. A lot of the men been here for years have headed up north, 'cross the border into Canada, where civilization ain't ruined everthing yet."

Smoke looked over at Bill. "That's the reason we're up here, Bear Tooth. Mr. Van Horne, Bill, is planning on building a railroad across Canada, from Winnipeg to the West Coast over near Vancouver Island, and he needs some experienced mountain men to help with the surveying of the route across the Canadian mountains."

Bear Tooth leaned to the side and spat a stream of brown tobacco juice into the fire, making it hiss and sizzle. "That so?" he asked, his eyes moving to fix on Bill.

Bill nodded, leaning forward. "That's right, Bear Tooth. We're going to cross twenty-five thousand square miles of the most desolate and wildest country in the world, making trails through land that hasn't seen more than a handful of white men in the last hundred years. I'm going to need men like Smoke and you and Red to find us a way through mountains that may not even have any passes in them. It's going to be a big job, one of the biggest ever undertaken."

"When you plannin' on doing all this, Bill?" Red asked as he stroked his beard.

"As soon as we can get up there. I've got several thousand men waiting in Winnipeg for us right now to get the surveying done so they can start to lay tracks."

"T'aint possible," Bear Tooth said as he got to his feet and flipped the elk steaks over to brown.

"Why not?" Bill asked.

"'Cause even if we left now, it'd be the middle of next winter 'fore we could get up there on horseback, an' winter in the mountains is no time to be doin' no surveyin'."

"That's right, Bill," Red added. "You'd have snow up over the horses' heads." He shook his head. "Can't be done 'fore next spring at the earliest."

"Yes, it can, gentlemen," Bill said. "I've got a train waiting for us down in Pueblo, just a few days ride from here. I figure the trip from Pueblo to Winnipeg will take only about a week, give or take a couple of days depending on how deep the snow is in the passes."

Bear Tooth and Red both looked aghast at the suggestion. "You mean you want Red and me to ride on one of them iron-horse contraptions?" Bear Tooth asked incredulously.

"Why, yes," Bill answered. "I have my own special cars on the train for us to ride in. I promise you you'll be quite comfortable."

Red stared at Bill through narrowed eyes. "I hear them things go so fast that the wind'll flat tear the skin offen your face if you hang it out the window."

Bill had to bite his lips to keep from laughing. "No, I assure you, Red, riding on a train is quite safe. People do it all the time."

"What 'bout our hosses?" Bear Tooth asked. "I don't plan on ridin' through no mountains on a hoss I don't know."

"There are special cars on the train for your animals," Bill said. "You can take as many of them along as you wish."

Bear Tooth got to his feet and began to serve steaks and beans to everyone on tin plates. "How many of us old coots you plannin' on takin' up there?" he asked.

Bill looked at Smoke, who said, "I'd like at least two more in addition to you and Red."

Bear Tooth and Red were silent for a few moments as everyone got started eating, and then Bear Tooth looked over at Red. "I heard Rattlesnake Bob Guthrie an' his ridin' partner, Bobcat Bill Johnson, was a couple'a peaks over to the south, toward Pueblo, last month. Maybe they'd be willin' to go along."

"Maybe," Red said as he chewed his steak. "Last time I saw Bobcat, he was complainin' 'bout how crowded it was getting up here, so maybe he'd be ready to try some new stompin' grounds."

"You haven't asked me what the job pays," Bill said, smiling at the wonderful flavor of the elk steak.

Bear Tooth shrugged. "Don't matter much," he said. "We ain't exactly up here in the High Lonesome to get rich."

Red nodded his agreement. "That's right. It might be fun to go somewhere's where we ain't steppin' on other men's toes ever time we go for a ride."

"Do you think you can find Rattlesnake and Bobcat?" Smoke asked.

Red looked down his nose at Smoke as if he'd just been insulted. "If'n they're still alive, we can shore as hell find 'em."

Bear Tooth laughed. "That's right, Smoke. Red can track a snake across granite if'n he has a mind to. If they're up here an' still wearin' they scalps, we'll find 'em."

"Then, you're saying you'll go with us?" Bill asked, excitement in his voice.

"Shore," Bear Tooth said as he cut a chunk of elk steak and stuck it in his mouth. "If'n we don't, ol' Smoke there's liable to get you lost, since he's become so civilized lately."

"That'll be the day," Smoke said, laughing.

# Chapter 6

The next two days were an arduous mixture of slogging through deep snow on the sides of mountain peaks and then, when they proceeded lower on the mountainsides, wading through mud and melted snow in the valleys, where spring was already producing myriads of wildflowers and green grass for the horses to munch on.

Van Horne glanced around at the beautiful scenery and said to Smoke, "This country reminds me a lot of Canada."

Smoke nodded. "Sometimes, when I've been away too long down in the flatlands, I forget just how beautiful it is up here."

Bear Tooth harrumphed. "Beautiful? This ain't nothin', men. You should see it 'bout two or three weeks from now when spring is full on an' the snow is all gone. The colors will damn near take your breath away."

Red Bingham slapped at his neck and snorted. "Yeah, an' most of these damned black flies will be gone by then, thank God."

Smoke and Cal and Pearlie were riding the Palouse

horses from Smoke's remuda, while the mountain men road pinto ponies like the Indians used. Van Horne was on a Morgan, one of the few horses large enough to carry his 250 pounds up and down the mountainsides without tiring. The group used the horses left behind by the French poachers as additional pack animals, tying them with dally ropes to the packhorses they already had.

By the time the group reached the mountain area where Rattlesnake Bob Guthrie and Bobcat Bill Johnson had last been seen, they were tired, saddle-sore, and covered with bites from the thousands of black flies the spring had brought up into the mountains.

Just after noon on the third day of their search, they made camp in a valley with plenty of grass for the horses to eat. The sun was out and the day was clear, the temperature climbing into the mid-fifties.

Pearlie climbed stiffly down from his horse and rubbed his aching backside. "Damn, boys," he said grumpily, "I think my butt's done grown to this saddle."

The two mountain men, who were used to spending days at a time in the saddle, looked at him and grinned. "Pearlie, boy, I got just the thing for those blisters," Bear Tooth said, pulling a dark brown bottle from his saddlebags.

"What's that?" Pearlie asked.

"It's a liniment I make from pine sap, whiskey, an' bear fat," Bear Tooth said, tossing the bottle to Pearlie.

Pearlie pulled a cork from the bottle and sniffed it cautiously. "Whew," he exclaimed, making a face and holding the bottle out away from his face. "That smells strong enough to peel paint off'n a barn."

"Don't waste it," Red Bingham said, laughing. "Bear Tooth's been known to drink it when we run low on whiskey."

"Works pretty good to tan the hides of the skins we

trap too," Bear Tooth said. "It's guaranteed to either kill ya or cure ya."

While the rest of the men set up camp and started a fire to cook lunch on, Pearlie moved off into some brush nearby, dropped his trousers, undid the flap on his long underwear, and gingerly rubbed some of the liniment onto his sore buttocks.

Suddenly, his skin on fire, he came running out of the brush, his pants down around his knees, jumping and hollering and fanning his butt with his hands. "Good God Almighty!" he yelled. "Somebody help me!"

Bear Tooth laughed as he stirred a pot of beans warming on the fire and winked at Smoke. "Told ya it'd make him forget all about how sore his ass was."

After a few minutes, Pearlie quit shouting and stopped jumping around. He stood there, his eyes wide as a smile slowly appeared on his face. "By gum," he said, looking at the bottle he was still holding. "It does feel better now."

He pulled his pants up and walked over to the fire. "What's for dinner?" he asked as he poured himself a cup of coffee from the pot on the coals.

Red Bingham looked up at him from over the tin plate on his lap. "Fer the main course, we got beans an' fatback, an' fer dessert, we got more beans an' more fatback."

"Yeah," Cal said, scooping a spoonful of beans onto his plate, "you ate the last of the elk yesterday, Pearlie."

Smoke smiled at this, and then he froze, his hand going to the Colt on his hip as he raised his nose and sniffed the air. "Don't look now, boys, but we got company," he said in a low voice as he eased the Colt from his holster.

A gravelly voice came from a copse of trees fifty yards away. "You plannin' on shootin' somebody with that hogleg, Smoke?"

Smoke grinned and let the pistol fall back into its holster.

Bear Tooth made a face and stood with his hands on his hips facing the trees where the voice came from. "Well, I'll be damned. That sounds like a bobcat, boys."

Two scruffy, well-worn mountain men wearing buckskins so dirty they looked black eased their ponies out of the trees and walked them slowly towards the camp.

Smoke got to his feet and waved. "Howdy, Bobcat, Rattlesnake," he called.

The two men nodded without speaking and rode on into camp. As they dismounted, Bobcat Bill Johnson, a short, wiry man with dark skin and sun-streaked blond hair and beard, sniffed loudly. "That coffee and beans sure do smell good," he said.

Bear Tooth sniffed loudly, his face screwed into an expression of distaste. "At least somthin' smells good around here," he said, staring at the two men as they approached the fire. "What happened?" he asked. "You men forgot to take your annual bathing this year?"

Bobcat stared back at him. "Hell, Bear, it ain't hardly spring yet. We usually wait till the snow's all gone 'fore we take a bath."

"Set an' take a load off," Red said, smiling at the byplay. "You're welcome to dig in, we got plenty."

Rattlesnake Bob Guthrie moved to the packhorse he was leading and took a slab of meat wrapped in burlap and waxed paper off the back of the animal. "You boys want some venison to go with them beans?" he asked.

"Here, let me help you with that," Pearlie said, jumping to his feet and taking the meat from Rattlesnake's hands.

Rattlesnake looked at Pearlie, sniffed a couple of times, and grinned. "Don't tell me you let ol' Bear Tooth talk you into usin' that liniment he makes up."

Pearlie blushed as he cut steaks off the venison and

put them in an iron skillet to cook. "He said it'd take the soreness outta my butt," Pearlie said in a low voice.

Rattlesnake laughed. "I let him put some on a pony of mine once that had some saddle sores on its back. The animal took off up the mountain and we didn't find it for damn near a week. It'd run so long, it was two feet shorter an' fifty pounds lighter when we finally found it."

"But them sores were healed, weren't they?" Bear Tooth said haughtily.

Smoke smiled. It was a mountain-man tale in the best traditions of the High Lonesome—outrageous, with just a touch of humor and truth in it.

After introductions had been made all around, the men sat down to venison steaks, beans, and canned peaches that Van Horne had brought along on his pack-horse.

While they ate, Smoke outlined the job offer Van Horne was making to the mountain men, emphasizing the opportunity they would have to travel and explore land largely unseen by anyone before them.

Rattlesnake put the last of his venison in his mouth, added a generous spoonful of beans, and chewed slowly, his eyes on the fire as he thought over the proposition. After a few minutes, he looked up at Smoke. He pointed to the pile of beaver, fox, and bear skins they had piled on one of their packhorses. "You see them skins there, Smoke?" he asked, a look of disgust on his face.

Smoke glanced at the skins and nodded.

"That's 'bout half what we trapped last year by this time, an' last year's amount was less'n half what we got the year before."

Bobcat nodded, his eyes sad. "Yep, there's just too blamed many folks up here trappin' an' huntin' nowadays. Hell, it wasn't more'n a month ago we seen some other men up on that peak over there," he said, pointing off to the side at a mountainside ten miles away. "Used to be, we wouldn't hardly ever see another white man in these parts the whole winter.

"Damned place is getting so crowded a man might as well live in the city—can't hardly turn around without bumpin' into some other sumbitch trappin' in our streams."

Van Horne leaned forward, setting his plate down on the ground. "Well, boys, you won't see that where we're going. To my knowledge, there's only been a handful of men even try to cross the mountains we're going over, an' that was more than five years ago."

Rattlesnake dropped his plate next to the fire and picked up his tin coffee cup. After he took a big swallow, he said, "Well, me'n Bobcat ain't much fer joinin' up with other men when we go travelin', but"—he cut his eyes at Smoke—"we might just make an exception seein' as how we'd be explorin' with the famous Smoke Jensen."

Bobcat smiled. "Yep, ol' Preacher used to give us an earful 'bout how good a man you was to spend time with, Smoke, back when he was still around. Might be nice to give it a try an' see if'n he was right or just pullin' our legs."

"Preacher told me many times, men, that you were all good men to ride with, and even spend the winter with if it came to that," Smoke said, looking at each of the mountain men in turn. "I'd be honored if you'd care to join us on our expedition."

Rattlesnake looked up at the clear blue sky and down at the melting snow all around them. "Hell, trappin's 'bout over fer this year anyhow," he said. "It might be kind'a fun to go see what Canada's like, see how it compares to the High Lonesome of Colorado."

"One thing they didn't tell you, boys," Bear Tooth said, a malicious gleam in his eyes.

"What's that, Bear?" Bobcat asked as he cut a slice off his plug of tobacco and stuffed it in his cheek.

"We gonna have to ride the train to get to Canada 'fore next winter."

"A train?" Bobcat said, almost swallowing his chaw.

"That's right," Red said, smiling at Bobcat's discomfort.

Bobcat stroked his chin thoughtfully and shook his head. "Well, now, I don't know 'bout that, boys. I ain't never been on one of those contraptions before."

"Well, if'n you're too scared, Bobcat," Bear Tooth said with a grin, "we'll understand if you back out."

"Too scared?" Bobcat asked, his eyes wide. "Why, you young pup," he said, "I ain't scared of nothin' nor nobody. If'n you're willin' to risk your life on one of them things, why, then, so am I."

Once they'd decided to go along, the men didn't waste any time. They packed their horses, broke camp, and headed down the mountain in the direction of Pueblo, where Van Horne had a train waiting to take them north toward Canada.

# Chapter 7

The trip to Pueblo was uneventful, the mountain men keeping the group entertained with increasingly outrageous tales of life in the High Lonesome, and the group arrived just after noon on the third day of their journey. As they rode into town, Rattlesnake Bob pulled his pony up next to Smoke and glanced over his shoulder at Louis Longmont, who was riding in the rear.

"Smoke," he said, after leaning to the side and spitting a stream of brown tobacco juice at a mangy dog who was running alongside his pony, "I gotta ask ya' somethin'."

"What is it, Rattlesnake?" Smoke answered.

"What is the story on that Longmont feller? He looks awful soft to be comin' on a trip like this."

"Oh?"

"Yeah. I took notice of his hands. The feller don't look like he's ever done a lick of hard work in his life. His hands are soft an' don't hardly have no calluses on 'em at all." He squinted his eyes in an expression of distaste. "Hell, even his fingernails ain't go no dirt under 'em."

Smoke chuckled. He was used to men underestimating Louis's toughness. His fine clothes and refined manner often made men make the mistake of thinking he was soft. "Don't let his appearance fool you, Rattlesnake. Louis is tough as a boot under those fancy clothes, and in a pinch there is no man I'd rather have watching my back than him. He's saved my life on more occasions than I like to think about."

Rattlesnake chewed in silence for a moment, and then he nodded. "I'll have to take your word fer it, Smoke, 'cause I just don't see him as the kind who'll take to the High Lonesome well."

"Like I said, don't underestimate Louis, Rattlesnake. He came out West when he was knee-high to a horse, and he came with nothing but the clothes on his back. He's now one of the richest men I know, and he's earned every cent of his money the hard way. He doesn't have any back-down in him, and he'll put his life on the line for any man he considers a friend."

"If'n you say so," Rattlesnake said doubtfully, but it was clear he was reserving judgment on Louis until he proved himself to the mountain men in the only way that counted, by being as tough and as mean as they were.

From a few places back, Van Horne called, "Hey, Smoke. Why don't we grab some grub before we head over to the train station?"

"I'll second that," Pearlie said with conviction. "My stomach is pushing up against my backbone I'm so hungry."

"I agree," Louis said. "I find myself missing Andre more and more as time goes on."

Van Horne pulled the head of his Morgan toward a

dining place with a sign over the door that said simply THE FEEDBAG, and the others followed, tying their mounts and packhorses to a hitching rail in front of the building.

The Feedbag was set up similarly to Longmont's saloon back in Big Rock. It consisted of a large room with eating tables on one side and a bar and smaller tables for the men who just wanted to drink their meals on the other side. It was about three quarters full. Most of the men wore the canvas trousers of miners, but there was a smattering of men dressed in chaps, flannel shirts, and leather vests who were obviously cowboys from nearby ranches.

Van Horne pushed through the batwings and walked directly toward a large table in the front corner of the room, while Smoke, Pearlie, Cal, and Louis spread out just inside the door with their backs to the wall waiting for their eyes to adjust to the gloomy lighting. The mountain men stopped and eyed Smoke with raised eyebrows.

"You expectin' trouble, Smoke?" Rattlesnake Bob asked, his hand dropping to the old Walker Colt stuck in the waistband of his buckskins.

Smoke smiled as his eyes searched the room for anyone who might be paying him special attention. "No, Rattlesnake, but I've found the best way to avoid trouble is to be ready for it when it appears."

When he saw no one was looking their way, Smoke walked on over to the table where Van Horne was already sitting down talking to a waiter, and took his usual seat with his back to the wall and his face to the rest of the room.

As they all took their seats, Bill said, "I ordered us a couple of pitchers of beer to start with while we decide what food to order."

Bear Tooth smacked his lips. "That sounds mighty good, Bill. I ain't had me no beer since last spring."

Before Bill could answer, a loud voice came from a group of men standing at the bar across the room. "God Almighty! What the hell is that smell?" a man called loudly, looking over at their table. "Did somebody drag a passel of skunks in here?"

The young man, who appeared to be about twenty years old, was wearing a black shirt and vest with a silver lining, and had a brace of nickel-plated Colt Peacemakers tied down low on his hips. He had four other men standing next to him, all wearing their guns in a similar manner, and all were laughing like he'd just said something extremely funny.

Rattlesnake Bob glanced at Bear Tooth and grimaced. "I hate it when that happens," he said in a low, dangerous voice. "Now we're gonna have to kill somebody 'fore we've even had our beer."

"Take it easy, Rattlesnake," Smoke said. "He's just some young tough who's letting his whiskey do his thinking for him."

Rattlesnake eased back down in his chair. "You're right, Smoke," he said, smiling. "If'n ever man who was drunk-dumb got kilt, there wouldn't hardly be none of us left."

Smoke continued to keep an eye on the man across the room as the bartender tried to get him to be quiet, without much success.

When their waiter appeared with the beer and glasses, Smoke asked him, "Who's the man with the big mouth over there at the bar?"

The waiter glanced nervously over his shoulder, and then he whispered, "That's Johnny MacDougal. His father owns the biggest ranch in these parts."

"Well, I don't care if'n his daddy owns Colorado

Territory," Bear Tooth growled. "You go on over there an' tell the little snot if'n he wants to see his next birthday he'd better keep his pie-hole shut."

The waiter's face paled and he shook his head rapidly back and forth. "I couldn't do that, sir," he said.

"Why not?" Rattlesnake asked.

"Just last week Johnny shot a man for stepping on his boots." The waiter hesitated, and then he added, "And the man wasn't even armed at the time."

"How come he's not in jail then?" Louis asked.

"Uh, his father carries a lot of water in Pueblo," the waiter said. "The sheriff came in and said it was in self-defense, though it was plain to everyone in the place that the man wasn't wearing a gun."

"So that's the lay of the land," Van Horne said, pursing his lips.

"Yes, sir," the waiter said, and hurried off back to the kitchen before these tough-looking men could get him in trouble, or worse yet, get him shot.

A few minutes later, after he'd downed another glass of whiskey, the young tough and his friends began to swagger across the room toward Smoke and his friends.

Smoke and Louis both eased their chairs back, took the hammer thongs off their Colts, and waited expectantly for the trouble they knew was coming. Smoke eased his right leg out straight under the table so he'd have quicker access if he had to draw.

MacDougal stopped a few feet behind Rattlesnake's chair and made a show of holding his nose. "Whew, something's awfully ripe in here," he said loudly, looking around the room to make sure he had an appreciative audience. "I think something done crawled in here and died."

Rattlesnake eased his hand down to the butt of the big Walker Colt in his belt, and as quick as a snake striking, he whipped it out, stood up, and whirled around, slashing the young man viciously across the face with the barrel.

MacDougal screamed and grabbed his face as blood spurted onto his vest. Before the other men could react, Rattlesnake grabbed MacDougal by the hair, jerked his head back, and jammed the barrel of the gun in his mouth, knocking out his two front teeth.

As MacDougal's eyes opened wide and he moaned in pain, Rattlesnake eared back the hammer and grinned, his face inches from the young tough's. "Now, what was it you was sayin', mister?" he growled. "Somethin' 'bout somebody smelling overly ripe, I believe?"

As one of MacDougal's friends dropped his hand to his pistol, Bear Tooth stood up and had his skinning knife against the man's throat before he could draw. "Do you really want some of this?" he asked, smiling wickedly at the man. "'Cause if'n you do, you'll have a smile that stretches from ear to ear 'fore I'm done with you."

"Uh, no, sir!" the man said, moving his hands quickly away from his pistol butt.

MacDougal's eyes rolled back and he almost fainted from pain and embarrassment, and he sank to his knees on the floor of the restaurant.

Rattlesnake shook his head in disgust, pulled the Walker out of his bleeding mouth, and pushed him over with his boot until MacDougal was lying flat on his back, crying and moaning with his hands over his face.

Rattlesnake waved the Walker at MacDougal's friends, who cringed back, and said, "You boys better take this little baby off somewheres an' get him a sugar tit to suck on 'fore he pees his pants."

The men all bent down, picked MacDougal up, and helped him stagger out of the batwings, their eyes fixed on the barrel of the Walker as they left.

Rattlesnake stuck the gun back in his belt and turned back to the table. "Now, then, where's my beer?"

After they'd all eaten their fill of beefsteak, potatoes, corn, and apple pie for dessert, Van Horne threw some twenty-dollar gold pieces on the table and they walked toward the door.

Smoke hung back for a moment and whispered to Cal and Pearlie, who broke off from the group and exited through a side door.

Smoke glanced at Louis and nodded. Louis nodded back and kept his hand close to the butt of his pistol. Both of them knew the trouble wasn't over yet. Men like MacDougal didn't take treatment like he'd received without trying for revenge, especially when they'd been shamed in front of their friends and neighbors.

Just before Van Horne got to the batwings, Louis and Smoke stepped in front of him. "You'd better let us go out first, Bill," Smoke said, his eyes flat and dangerous.

Smoke and Louis went through the batwings fast, Smoke breaking to the right and Louis to the left, their eyes on the street out in front of The Feedbag.

Sure enough, MacDougal and his friends were lined up in the street, pistols in their hands, cocked and ready to fire.

As they raised their hands to aim and shoot, Smoke and Louis drew, firing without seeming to aim. An instant later, Cal and Pearlie joined in from the alley where they'd come out to the side of the men in the street.

Only MacDougal, out of all the men with him, got off a shot, and it went high, taking a small piece off Smoke's hat.

The entire group of men dropped in the hail of gunfire from Smoke and Louis and the boys, sprawling in the muddy street, making it run red with their blood.

"Damn!" Rattlesnake said in awe. He had started to draw his Walker at the first sign of trouble, but it was still in his waistband by the time it was all over. "I ain't never seen nobody draw an' fire that fast," he added, glancing at Smoke and Louis with new respect.

Smoke and Louis walked out into the street and bent down to check on the men. They were all dead, or so close to dying they were no longer any risk.

A few minutes later, a fat man with a tin star on his chest came running up the street. "Oh, shit!" he said when he saw who had been killed.

He looked over at Smoke and the group and moved his hand toward his pistol, until Smoke grinned and waggled his Colt's barrel at him. "I wouldn't do that, Sheriff," Smoke said, jerking his head at the group of people standing at the windows and door of The Feedbag. "There are plenty of people in there who will say we acted in self-defense, so there's no need for you to go for that hogleg on your hip."

"But . . . but that's Angus MacDougal's son," the sheriff stammered.

Van Horne moved forward. "I don't care if it's the President's son, Sheriff. These men drew on us first."

"And just who are you?" the sheriff asked.

"My name is William Cornelius Van Horne," Bill said, pulling a card from his vest pocket and handing it to the sheriff. "And if you'd like to send a wire to the United States marshal over in Denver, I'm sure he will vouch for me."

The sheriff eyed the men standing in front of him, and wisely decided not to make an issue of it. "All right, if it went down like you say, you're free to go." He took his hat off and wiped his forehead. "But I don't think Mr. MacDougal is gonna like this."

Rattlesnake bent over and spat a stream of tobacco juice onto Johnny MacDougal's dead face. "If'n the man has any sense, he'll be relieved that we took that sorry son of a bitch off his hands," he said. "If he'd had any sense at all, he would'a drowned him in a barrel a long time ago."

# Chapter 8

Van Horne left the sheriff standing open-mouthed in the middle of the street staring down at the dead bodies, and walked over and got on his horse. After the rest of the men were mounted up and ready to go, he led them down the streets of Pueblo toward the train station.

When they got there and Van Horne had identified himself to the stationmaster, he had them walk their horses to the rear of a train waiting on a siding. The last couple of cars were fitted out as transports for horses, with two feet of hay on the floor and several buckets of sweet-feed and water hanging from nails on the wooden rails of the car.

Men working under the direction of the stationmaster put a ramp in place, and the horses were unsaddled and the packhorses were unloaded and led up into the cars.

Van Horne stepped back and spread his arms. "There you go, boys. All the comforts of home for your mounts," he said, grinning at the mountain men, who were eyeing the car with some suspicion.

Bear Tooth stepped up into the car, stuck his hand down in one of the buckets, and pulled out a handful of the feed, bringing it close to his nose and smelling. He grinned and looked over at Van Horne. "What the hell is this?" he asked, taking a lick of it with his tongue.

"That's called sweet-feed," Van Horne answered. "It's grain mixed with molasses and corn and oats. It's used to put weight on horses after they've been out eating only grass."

"Damn, this stuff tastes good enough for *me* to eat," Bear Tooth said. He glanced over at his pony, which had its head already buried in one of the buckets. "I don't know if we gonna be able to git our hosses outta here after they've got a taste of sweet-feed."

Van Horne laughed and motioned for Bear Tooth to get down out of the car. "Now," he continued, waving them to follow him, "let me show you where we'll be riding."

He walked several cars forward and then climbed up a small set of steps into another car. This one was evidently fitted out for officials of the railroad, for it was very plush, with Oriental rugs over gleaming oaken floors, heavy brocaded drapes over the windows, and comfortable chairs and couches arranged around the car. A large bar stood in the corner with over twenty different kinds of whiskey and brandy and wine in circular racks behind it, and a plate of sandwiches and fried chicken lying on it. The car even had its own potbellied stove in one corner, in case the weather turned inclement.

"Now this is what I call travelin' in style," Pearlie said, moving around the car with wide eyes, pushing on the cushions of the couch to see how soft they were.

"The car just behind this one is fitted out with bunks and curtains in case we want to sleep along the way," Van Horne said proudly.

Rattlesnake Bob and Bobcat Bill stood in the door-way, along with Bear Tooth and Red Bingham, not ven-turing inside the beautiful car. Rattlesnake whispered something to Bobcat, and he nodded in agreement.

"If'n it's all the same to you, Mr. Van Horne," Rattlesnake said, "Bobcat an' me'll just mosey on back to the car with the hosses in it. This one's too nice fer the likes of us."

"But—" Van Horne started to object, until Bobcat cut him off.

"No, sir," Bobcat said, "we thank you kindly fer the offer, but we'd feel better 'bout it if we just stayed with our hosses."

"All right," Van Horne said finally, shrugging. "If that's the way you want it."

"Howsomeever," Rattlesnake added, moving over to the bar and picking up a bottle of Old Kentucky bour-bon and a handful of chicken and sandwiches and stuff-ing them in his pockets, "we will take a bottle of this tonsil paint an' a little of this here food to keep our-selves warm just in case it gets a mite chilly out."

Van Horne laughed as the two mountain men backed out of the car and moved off back down the line of cars toward the car holding the horses.

"How about you, Red and Bear Tooth?" he asked. "This car seem too fancy for you?"

Bear Tooth grinned, exposing yellow stubs of teeth. "Hell, no, Bill," he said as he stepped over to the couch and sat down, putting his feet on a coffee table that probably cost more than he made in two years of trap-ping. He leaned back with his hands behind his head and smiled at Van Horne. "I figure it's your money and your play. If'n you want to waste this good liquor and food and furnishin's on the likes of us, then it's all right by me."

"Course, if'n you're gonna let Bear ride in here with the rest of us," Red said as he entered the car and moved toward the bar, "you might want to open them windows a mite." He glanced over at Bear. "'Cause much as I hate to say it, that boy in the bar back there was right. Somethin' does smell kind'a ripe in here."

Smoke and Louis and Cal followed Bear Tooth into the car, and all took seats except Pearlie, who was already over at the bar next to Red Bingham, filling his face with chicken as fast as he could chew and swallow it.

Van Horne moved to a funnel-device on the wall and pulled it down and spoke into it, telling the engineer they were ready to proceed.

As the train pulled out of Pueblo, Sheriff Wally Tupper loaded the bodies of Johnny MacDougal and his friends onto a buckboard and prepared to make the long trip out to the MacDougal ranch.

He looked down at the dead men and shook his head. Angus MacDougal was gonna be plenty upset about the death of his son, and old Angus was not a man who would take such a thing lying down. Tupper sighed. He sure as hell wouldn't want to be in the shoes of the man who'd shot Angus's only son. There was going to be hell to pay, and that was a fact!

As he climbed up on the hurricane deck, Tupper took a deep breath. He just hoped Angus wouldn't shoot him for bringing him the bad news.

As the wagon pulled up to the ranch house, Angus MacDougal was waiting on the porch, already dressed in a black suit. Evidently, word had preceded Tupper's arrival with the bodies.

Tupper brought the wagon to a halt and Angus stepped down off the porch, followed by his wife and his twenty-two-year-old daughter, Sarah.

Sarah was a looker, all right, Tupper thought. It was too bad she was every bit as tough as her old man, and just as good with a gun if the stories about her could be believed. The last man who'd tried to court her had been run out of town with a load of buckshot in his ass for having the effrontery to think he was good enough for Angus's baby girl, or so the story went. Since then, suitors had been far and few between for the pretty woman, though, Tupper thought, if I were twenty years younger and fifty pounds lighter, I might give her a try myself, and Angus be hanged.

Angus walked up to the wagon and pulled back the sheet over his son's body. His wrinkled face showed little emotion, but his eyes blazed with a hatred so intense, it made the hair on the back of Tupper's neck stand up.

"Who did this to my boy, Wally?" he asked, his eyes still on his son.

"I don't know his full name, Angus," Tupper said deferentially as he took his hat off in respect. "There was a group of men involved in the fracas who worked for a fellow named William Cornelius Van Horne."

Now Angus's eyes shifted and bored into Tupper's. "Van Horne, huh? I've heard of him. A railroad man if memory serves."

"That's right, Angus," Tupper said, nodding his head vigorously. "I checked him out with the U.S. marshal over in Denver, an' he said the man's plenty powerful, all right. Word is he's goin' up to Canada to build a railroad up there."

"He the man fired the bullet that killed my boy, Wally?"

Tupper shook his head. "No, sir. The man who actually shot Johnny was named Smoke, but I didn't get his last name. He was a big man wearing buckskins, and there were a couple of old mountain men with him, but they didn't fire on Johnny and the others."

"Smoke, huh?" Angus said, his eyes narrow.

"That's what some of the boys in The Feedbag heard him called. Another fellow with him was named Louis, who also did some shooting."

"Well, I want you to go back to town and find out if anyone heard anything else, especially that bastard's last name."

"Uh, Angus," Tupper said, "it was a fair fight. Johnny and his friends drew down on Van Horne's men first. They didn't have no choice but to fire back."

Angus's face flamed red and he slammed his fist down on the side of the buckboard. "And I don't have any choice either, Wally! I'm going to make sure the son of a bitch who killed my boy is planted in the ground, and if you don't plan on helping me find out who it was, then I have a feeling we'll have a new sheriff in Pueblo before the snow melts."

"Now hold on, Angus," Tupper said. "I didn't say I wouldn't help. All I meant was Johnny was plenty liquored up and he forced the other men's hands, that's all."

Sarah walked up to stand next to her father and stare down at her dead brother. "I told you Johnny's drinking was going to get him killed someday, Father," she said.

He whirled on her and raised his right hand as if to strike her, but the look in her eyes stopped him. She showed not the slightest trace of fear.

"Go on, Father," she said through tight lips. "Hit me if it'll make you feel any better. But Johnny's the one you should've hit when he needed it, and maybe this would never have happened."

Angus whirled back around, his eyes flashing. "Tupper, what are you still doing here? Do like I said and find out what the man's name was who killed my son!"

# Chapter 9

John Hammerick sat drinking coffee laced with brandy at his favorite café in Grand Forks. Though it was spring in most parts of the country, winter still had a harsh grip on this northern corner of the state, and John felt the brandy would help keep the cold at bay.

Hammerick was what had been called a highwayman in the olden days—a rather romantic name for a thug and robber who had never, as far as anyone knew, done an honest day's work in his entire life. He was, for all of that, a man of many talents, and would prey on trains, stages, banks, and just about anyone or any place that had what he wanted and was too lazy to work for, namely money.

Known as Hammer by the men who followed him in his daily endeavors to extract as much money as he could from anyone who happened to have some, Hammerick had fallen on hard times lately. A two-year-long drought in the area had caused a dip in the economy, with farmers and the banks that supplied them all being extremely low on cash. Hammer was having a hard time finding anyone with enough money to make it worth his while to rob them, and his men were getting antsy, and some had even moved south looking for greener pastures.

Hammer would have done so himself, except for the fact he was too lazy to make the effort to relocate. Also, he rather enjoyed his local status as a man to be reckoned with and one that you shouldn't turn your back on.

He unfolded the *Grand Forks Gazette*, and read it as he drank his coffee, hoping to find some news that would help to enrich him and keep his men happily following his lead. Though he'd been kicked out of school long before he graduated, he had managed to master reading, after a fashion. Long words still gave him some trouble, but the writers of the *Grand Forks Gazette* weren't noted for using fancy language.

An article on the second page caught his eye, and he reread it a second time, his lips pursed in thought. After a while, he smiled and looked across the table at his second in command, Bull Bannion. Hammer didn't bother to show the article to Bull, who'd been kicked out of the only school he'd ever attended for being a bully, because Bull couldn't read. He could sign his name, but he did misspell it more often than not.

"Bull, I think I've found the answer to our prayers," Hammer said, draining his cup and signaling the waiter for a refill.

"Prayers?" Bull asked, his forehead wrinkled. "What are you talking about, Hammer. I ain't prayed since that time the bull gored me in my privates a few years back."

Hammer shook his head. Strength of intellect wasn't one of Bull's strong points. But since Bull was a little over six and a half feet in height and weighed in at almost three hundred pounds, Hammer didn't need him for his mind, but for his ability to beat the living shit out of anyone who happened to question any of Hammer's orders.

"No, Bull. I mean I've found something in the paper that's going to make us rich."

"Oh?" Bull said, putting his coffee cup down. Bull's coffee wasn't laced with brandy, but with the cheapest brand of rotgut whiskey he could find. He always said he didn't care what his liquor tasted like, as long as it got the job done.

"It says here," Hammer continued, "that they're starting to build the Canadian Pacific Railroad up in Canada in the next month or two." He glanced down at the paper. "In fact, they're going to begin the line in Winnipeg."

"How's that gonna put any money in our pockets?" Bull asked. "You ain't plannin' on going to work for the railroad, are you?" Bull grimaced. "You know I got a bad back and I can't do no heavy liftin', Hammer."

Hammer sighed. Trying to have a conversation with Bull was like trying to herd cats—damn near impossible. "No, Bull. But the article says they're going to be hiring over fifteen thousand Chinamen, and another five or six thousand whites to help build the railroad."

"So?" Bull asked, waving his empty coffee cup at the waiter to signal he too needed more. "I done told you I ain't gonna take no job laying track."

"Think about it, if it's not too much of a strain," Hammer said, beginning to get exasperated. "Twenty thousand men, more or less, each of them making about a dollar a day. I hear the railroad pays their men in gold once a month. That means the men that run the railroad are going to be transporting almost six hundred thousand dollars a month through some of the roughest country in the world."

Bull still didn't get it. "You mean they pay them

Chinamen a dollar a day?" he asked, shaking his head. "Hell, I never earned that much back when I worked cows, an' I'm a white man," Bull said, clearly feeling discriminated against.

Hammer bit his lip to keep from shouting, for shouting at Bull was a sure way to get your face smashed in. "I don't know, Bull, but even if it's only fifty cents a day, that's still almost three hundred thousand in gold coming through Winnipeg every month just waiting for someone to come and take it."

Suddenly, Bull got the idea. "Oh, I see what you mean." He hesitated. "But just how far is this Winnipeg from here?"

"A goodly ways," Hammer said. "But it's not too far from Noyes, up in the northern part of Minnesota. The sheriff in Noyes is an old friend of mine. I figure if we give him a split of our take, he won't mind if we take the men up there and set up our base there. Then, every month or so, we can ride on up into Canada, pick us up a little gold, and then hightail it back to Noyes and the Canadians won't be able to follow us."

"But Hammer," Bull argued, "that much money is bound to mean a lot of guards. That payroll is going to be a tough nut to crack."

Hammer shrugged. "Well, if it does turn out to be too tough, there's still going to be a lot of Chinamen and other workers who have their pockets full of gold. I imagine they'll be bringing it in by train, rather than stages or wagons, and you know how good I am at robbing trains."

"Still, there's bound to be plenty of men watching that much gold. It won't be as easy as it is down here, Hammer, where they only carry a few thousand dollars."

Hammer gritted his teeth to keep from telling Bull

he was full of shit. "Well, even if we can't get it off the train, then we'll just take it off the men after they're paid. Either way, it's still a lot of gold that's gonna be spread around up there, and I don't see how we can lose."

Bull glanced out the window at the gray snow still blowing in the streets of Grand Forks. "I hear it's even colder up there in Canada than it is down here," he said.

Hammer laughed. "Who said getting rich was going to be easy, Bull?"


When it came time for supper to be served on the train, Van Horne reached up and pulled on a cord hanging on the wall next to the large easy chair he was sitting in. A few minutes later, a young black man entered the car.

"Willard, would you please go back to the cattle car and ask the two gentlemen riding there with the horses to join us for dinner?" he asked.

Willard's eyes widened. "They's riding with the animals, sir?"

"Yes," Van Horne answered, smiling. "They thought they'd be more comfortable there." He hesitated, and then he added, "And Willard, once the men have joined us, would you ask one of the porters to gather up all the clothing from the packs in the car and give them a good cleaning while we eat?"

"Yes, sir," Willard said, and left the car.

Pearlie, who was sitting near a window on the other side of the car, looked up eagerly. "Did I hear you mention food?"

"Yes," Van Horne answered. "We'll have it served to us here in this car."

Bear Tooth looked over at Pearlie. "For once I agree with you, Pearlie boy. I'm so hungry I could eat a bear."

"That won't be necessary, Bear Tooth," Van Horne said. "I believe the menu tonight consists of beefsteak, potatoes, corn, and apple cobbler for dessert."

Red Bingham nudged Bear Tooth with his elbow. "That do sound better'n bear, son," he said grinning.

Once everyone was gathered in the car and dinner was served, Smoke turned to Van Horne. "Tell me a little about how we're going to get all the way up into Canada on the train. I wasn't aware the lines went that far."

As he ate his steak, Van Horne explained. "The man who hired me to build the railroad from Winnipeg west to the coast, James J. Hill, along with some partners, bought the old St. Paul & Pacific Railroad a couple of years back. He then laid some tracks and connected the St. Paul to a Canadian Pacific line from Fort Gary up in Winnipeg down to St. Vincent, Minnesota, and renamed his railroad the St. Paul, Minneapolis, and Manitoba route. The route has been so successful that two of his partners, Donald Smith and George Stephen, got a contact from the government of Canada to extend the Canadian Pacific Railroad west all the way to the Pacific Ocean, and that's just what he's hired me to do."

Van Horne paused and pushed his empty plate away from him on the table. He took a long, thick cigar out of his coat pocket and lit it. As clouds of aromatic blue smoke billowed out, he looked directly at Smoke. "Of course, there are those who think this route cannot be completed since the country we'll be going through is so rough. In fact, they've given our little project the name 'Hill's Folly.'"

Smoke jerked his thumb at a large map of Canada hanging on a wall across the room. "I was looking at that map earlier, and from what I can see you've got at least three mountain ranges to cross, with no guarantee there's any passes low enough for a train to go through." He reached into his pocket, brought out a cigar, and puffed it into life. "And what's more," Smoke added, "I've heard the Stony Indians up there in Canada aren't near as civilized as those here in Colorado Territory. They might have some objections to a railroad being built through land they consider their own."

Van Horne nodded through the smoke. "That's right, and that's exactly why I've hired you gentlemen. You and your friends are going to have to help us find a route through those mountains, and you might have to do a little convincing of the Indians along the way that we will not be denied our chance to bring progress to the area."

"Getting through them mountains ain't gonna be no problem fer us, Bill," Bobcat Bill Johnson said around a mouthful of steak, "but findin' a pass that ain't gonna be snowed in the entire winter is somethin' else again."

Smoke nodded. "Bobcat's right, Bill," he said. "There's almost always passes in the mountains that a man on horseback can get through, if he knows what he's doing. But even if we do manage to find them and you are able to get the tracks laid, they're probably going to have quite a bit of snow covering them for at least part of the year."

Van Horne waved his cigar in the air. "That's not a problem, gentlemen. We now have snow-trains that have huge plows on the front of them that can keep the tracks clear of snow."

Smoke smiled and went back to his meal. Evidently, Van Horne had never been in a High Lonesome blizzard that could easily drop several feet of snow in the course of a night or two. Of course, that wasn't Smoke's problem. His problem was going to be finding a way through the mountains while fighting off hostile Indians, trappers, and anyone else who didn't want the railroad coming through that part of the country. He smiled to himself, thinking they were surely going to earn the money Van Horne had promised them for the job.

After they'd finished their meal and all the men were sitting around drinking coffee with cigars and cigarettes, Willard came into the car with a large bundle of clean clothes in his arms.

"Here's them clothes you wanted washed, Mr. Van Horne," he said, placing the bundle on a table. "They's still a mite damp, but they's suitable to wear."

Bobcat and Rattlesnake glared at the pile of buckskins on the table. "Them looks suspiciously like our clothes, Bill," Bobcat said.

"Yes, they are, Bobcat. I . . . um . . . I thought that since we're going to be traveling in such close proximity to one another, clean clothes and baths might be in order for everyone."

"You what?" Rattlesnake asked. "Are you plannin' on stoppin' this here train and makin' us get into a river an' bathe?" He glanced out the window. "Hell, it's still snowin' out there."

Van Horne laughed and got to his feet. "Of course not, gentlemen. Follow me."

He went through the rear door, passed through the sleeping car, and emerged into a car with four large copper bathtubs bolted to the floor. In one corner of the room was a large copper barrel hooked up to a stove device that would heat the water.

Van Horne waved his hands. "There you go, men. Each tub is supplied with hot water, soap, and a brush to scrub the dirt and grime off with." He pointed to another wall on which were three basins with mirrors above them. "And there, should you care to shave, are all the necessary implements at your disposal."

The four mountain men walked over and looked at the tubs dubiously. "Well, I'll be hanged," Bear Tooth said. "I've heard of these things, but I've never seen one up close before."

"You mean, we just fill that thing with hot water and get right in?" Rattlesnake asked, running his hands over the copper tub.

"Yes, and while you're bathing, I'll have the porter wash the rest of your clothes," Van Horne said.

Bobcat raised his eyebrows. "You mean we have to take our clothes off 'fore we get in there?"

Van Horne had to bite his lip to keep from laughing, since he didn't want to hurt Bobcat's feelings. "Yes, that is the customary way to bathe," he said simply.

Red Bingham picked up a bucket, held it under a spigot on the copper barrel, and turned the handle. Steaming hot water poured into the bucket, and Red grinned like a child with a new toy. "Damn, this is even better'n those hot springs we usually bathe in. The water don't smell of sulfur at all."

"Enjoy yourselves, gentlemen," Van Horne said as he turned to go.

"Uh, Bill," Bear Tooth said.

"Yes?"

"Could you have that Willard bring us in a bottle of whiskey an' some glasses. If'n I'm gonna dunk myself in one of those contraptions, I'm gonna need some whiskey to see me through it."

"And you might want to bring in a couple of extra brushes," Red said, looking over at Bear Tooth. "If you want all the dirt off'n Bear, it's gonna take more'n one brush to do the job."

Bear Tooth grimaced and threw a bar of soap at Red. When it sailed over his head and into a far wall, Bear laughed. "Red, I bet that's the closest you ever came to soap."

# Chapter 10

The snow that until a few days before had been knee-deep in the center of the main street of Noyes was melting under the rays of the spring sun, and Sheriff Luke McCain stood on boardwalk in front of his office with his hands on his hips, surveying the mess it was making. Main Street was now not much more than a river of mud, and the mosquitoes and black flies were already beginning to swarm.

McCain slapped his neck with a grimace. If there was any time of the year he hated worse than winter it was spring, with its mud, bugs, and temperatures still cold enough to freeze the balls off a mule at night. He vowed for perhaps the thousandth time to move south where he could hold up a snowball and the people would say, "What's that?"

He smiled to himself, thinking that if he did that, he might have to get a real job and work for a living. Noyes, with its population made up mainly of people of Swedish descent, was a very law-abiding town. About the worse thing that McCain had to face was the occasional fight when the farmers from the surrounding area would come to town and get a load of whiskey on, and that, thankfully, was about as rare as hen's teeth. He put his hand on the butt of his pistol as he thought about this, trying to remember the last time he'd had to draw his gun. Not able to remember such a time, he shook his head and decided yet again to stay where he was. After all, when the temperature hit eighty or so, the black flies would disappear for another year and the glorious summer would make it all worthwhile.

As he turned to go back into his office and get a cup of coffee and a cigar, hoping the smoke from the stogie would keep the mosquitoes at bay, he heard the sound of a large number of horses coming into town.

He shaded his eyes from the sun with his hand and cursed softly to himself. Damned if it didn't look like that asshole John Hammerick leading a large group of men into his town. Now what would a lowlife like Hammer be doing up here? he thought. There ain't nobody up here in this godforsaken wilderness with anything worth stealing. And from what McCain remembered about his old acquaintance, stealing from other people was about all old Hammer did other than strut around like the cock of the walk with his chest stuck out.

As Hammer and his men walked their horses through the muddy street and stopped in front of his office, McCain nodded. "Hello, Hammer," he said, his voice flat and unfriendly. "What kind of trouble are you in and is it going to visit my town?"

Hammer gave him a look, his eyes hard for a moment, and then they softened and he grinned. "Now what kind of welcome is that for an old friend come to visit?" he asked.

"Sharing a cell with me in the Tucson State pen don't make us exactly friends, Hammer," McCain replied. He looked around at the group of men sitting in their saddles behind Hammer and he sighed. "Why don't you send your men on over to the saloon for some drinks while you come on in to my office and tell me just what's going on?"

Hammer nodded. "Bull, take the men with you and go get something to cut the trail dust. I'll meet you there in a while."

Hammer got down off his horse, stretched and rubbed his butt, and then followed McCain into his office.

"Coffee?" McCain asked, moving toward the Franklin stove in the corner that had a tin coffeepot sitting on top.

"Don't you have anything stronger?" Hammer asked as he took a seat in one of the two straight-backed chairs in front of McCain's desk.

McCain shook his head. "Not in the office I don't." He stared at Hammer for a moment, wishing the man were anywhere but here. "If it's whiskey you want, you're welcome to go on over to the saloon with your friends."

Hammer shrugged, as if the coldness of McCain's welcome didn't bother him at all. "Coffee it is then."

McCain handed him a large cup, and took his with him as he sat behind his desk. "So?" he asked, peering at Hammer over the brim of his cup as he drank.

"I've got a proposition for you, Luke," Hammer said after sampling his own coffee and making a grimace at the bitter taste.

"In case you hadn't noticed, Hammer, I got me a job already, and I'm far too old and too smart to take off riding the owlhoot trail with you."

"This ain't exactly a job offer, Luke. In fact, all you got to do to make yourself quite a bit of change is to ignore me and my men for the next few months."

"Oh, and you'll be doing what exactly while I'm ignoring you?" McCain asked, thinking ten minutes was too much time to spend with Hammer, let alone several months.

"We'll be staying here in your town, behaving ourselves, and every now and then taking a little ride up into Canada. When we come back here, you'll get a full share of any proceeds we've gotten from our trip."

McCain pursed his lips as he drank his coffee and stared at Hammer without speaking for a couple of minutes. "And just how are you planning on making any money up in Canada, Hammer?" he asked. "Hell, the only place big enough to call itself a town within riding distance is Winnipeg, and there ain't nothing up there but trappers and miners who for the most part don't have two dollars to rub together."

Hammer grinned. "I guess you ain't heard 'bout the railroad they're gonna be building up there then."

McCain shook his head. "They've been talking about doing that for the last five years, but I didn't know they were actually going to start on it anytime soon."

Hammer nodded. "Yep. Matter of fact, I hear they've already got over fifteen thousand men shipped in to do the dirty work of laying the tracks."

McCain stroked his jaw and finished his coffee. "I see. You're thinking the payroll for that many men is going to be easy pickings, huh?"

Hammer shrugged. "I don't know how easy it's gonna be, but I'm damned sure gonna find out."

"And all I gotta do is just look the other way while you and your men run back and forth and rob the railroad?"

"Yep, an' for that, my friend, you'll get the same share as all of my men are getting."

A slow grin curled McCain's lips. He couldn't for the life of him see any problem with this arrangement. If Hammer was still as stupid and greedy as he had been back when McCain knew him, he thought, he wouldn't last a week in Canada. "Well, now, I think I can manage that, friend," McCain said, his manner decidedly friendlier now that he knew what Hammer wanted. He reached across the desk and shook Hammer's hand.

"In fact," he added, "I'll do better than that. There's a boardinghouse here that's been closed all winter, and it isn't due to open for another week or two, but I'll put in a word for you and your men and I think I can have you a place to stay where you won't be bothered by a lot of questions."

"Excellent," Hammer said. He looked at his coffee cup, which was still almost full. "Now, what do you say we head on over to the saloon and seal our deal with something a little stronger than this coffee?"

McCain smiled. "One thing I've learned being sheriff. With the low pay and all the bullshit I have to put up with, I never refuse the offer of a free drink."

"Who said I'd be paying?" Hammer asked, grinning.

"It's your proposition, Hammer, so you get to do the buying," McCain said as he grabbed his hat from a rack next to the door.

# Chapter 11

By the second day on the train, washed and scrubbed and with their beards trimmed, Rattlesnake and Bobcat were right at home riding in the fancy parlor car with the other men. No longer afraid they'd mess the place up with their dirty boots and clothes, they, along with Bear and Red, acted like seasoned travelers who'd never been afraid of the infamous Iron Horse at all.

After several days of this luxury, and changing engines three times, the group finally arrived in Winnipeg, Canada. Sore and stiff from sitting down for most of the time, the men could hardly wait to get off the train and stretch their legs.

"I'll have one of the porters take your horses to the livery stable, and another one will take our bags to the hotel we'll be staying in until we get organized for the surveying trip," Van Horne said as they stepped down out of the railcar and onto the wooden platform next to the tracks.

Louis Longmont walked out from the tracks and stood with his hands on his hips staring at the outskirts of Winnipeg, a wry smile on his lips.

Smoke moved up next to him and followed his gaze. "What are you grinning at, Louis?"

Louis raised his nose in the air and took a deep sniff. "I'm amazed at the appearance of this place, Smoke." He turned his eyes to Smoke. "It takes me back to my first days out West, more years ago than I care to think about."

Smoke looked around and nodded. The streets were full of men wearing buckskins and canvas miners' trousers, and the air was filled with the smells of horse droppings, mud, leather, and wood smoke. The streets were little more than mud baths, but due to the colder temperatures this far north, the mud in places was still frozen patches of black ice.

"You're right, Louis," Smoke responded with a smile. "Winnipeg reminds me of the way towns looked when I first came out to Colorado Territory with Preacher—rough, rowdy, and full of the excitement that comes with knowing you're on the very edge of civilization."

"That's right, Smoke, the kind of place where anything can happen and usually does, especially after the sun goes down and the town really comes to life," Louis agreed. "One of the first gambling halls I owned was in a place exactly like this, and I had the most fun I've ever had in my life there."

Cal and Pearlie were standing wide-eyed just behind them. Neither of them had ever seen a town like this, both being much too young to have been around in the glory days when Colorado Territory was being formed.

"Jiminy," Cal said as he stared at the number of men wearing beards who were moving about the town, all of whom were armed to the teeth and looking like they'd just as soon shoot someone as look at him. There didn't seem to be anyone who had less than two or three weapons arrayed on their persons.

"I ain't never seen anything like this before," Cal added.

Van Horne overheard his comment, and stepped up between Cal and Pearlie. "You're right about that, son," he said. "Canada is the last frontier, that's for sure."

"An' damned if men like us ain't gonna ruin it forever," Bear Tooth said grimly, leaning his head to the side to spit a stream of tobacco juice into the mud swelling up over his boots.

Van Horne looked at him. "What do you mean, Bear Tooth?" he asked.

"He means, once you got that iron horse of yours making regular trips back and forth 'crost the wilderness, it won't be wilderness no more," Red Bingham answered scowling as he stood with his hands on his hips looking around at the swirling bustle of activity in front of them.

"That's right," Rattlesnake Bob agreed. "Pretty soon you'll have pilgrims an' women an' snake-oil salesmen travelin' here on your trains an' crowdin' out all the men like us who like the town the way it is now."

Van Horne shrugged. "Well, gentlemen, you can't stop civilization, and if I don't build the rail lines someone else will." He didn't mention that James Hill's plans were exactly as they'd said, to flood the area with tourists and settlers and in so doing, make himself yet another fortune by building inns and hotels and restaurants all along the hundreds of miles of tracks.

Bobcat Bill put his hand on Van Horne's shoulder. "Oh, we ain't blaming you none, Bill," he said. "It's just that we're old coots who'd like life to stay wild an' hairy a mite longer so's we can enjoy our last days without havin' to put up with what you call civilization."

"Who're you callin' an old coot, you sumbitch?" Bear Tooth growled, trying to look fiercely at his friend.

"For a man who's older than dirt, you're awful touchy

'bout bein' reminded of it," Bobcat Bill said, leaning to the side to spit tobacco juice in the mixed snow and mud at their feet just as Bear Tooth had a moment before.

Smoke stepped between the men, laughing at their antics. "Come on, men," he said. "From what I can see from here, about every other building is either a saloon or a restaurant. What say we try a few of them out while Mr. Van Horne gets our rooms ready at the hotel."

"You think they'll let an old relic like me into one of those places, Smoke?" Bear Tooth said sarcastically, casting his eyes at Bobcat Bill.

Bobcat laughed and clapped Bear on the shoulder. "Hell, yes, Bear. Since you smell so nice and sweet now, they wouldn't dare turn you away."

"Yeah, an' with the amount of that there toilet water you put in your hair, you're liable to be real popular with these miners I see walking around too," Red Bingham added.

With that final comment, the mountain men all licked their lips and hitched up their pants, and began to walk rapidly toward the main street of the town, talking excitedly among themselves about how the town reminded them of this place or that place from the old days.

"Masterfully handled, Smoke," Louis said, smiling as he moved to follow the mountain men.

Smoke turned to Van Horne. "Bill, I think the men need a little time to unwind and get the kinks from the trip out of their systems. We'll meet you over at the hotel after a while."

Van Horne nodded. "That's a good idea, Smoke. I'll just check in with my men at the construction site and make sure everything's on track for starting the surveying, and I'll meet you and the other men at the hotel in a couple of hours." He turned and pointed to a three-story building at the end of the street. "It's the Rooster's Roost down there on Main Street."

He reached in his pocket and pulled out a stack of bills. "Here's some Canadian money to pay for your drinks and food."

Smoke eyed the bills. "That's a lot of money just for food and drinks, Bill."

Van Horne grinned. "Well, prices are a mite high, this being a frontier town and all. Don't worry, you and your men are going to earn every cent of it before I'm through with you."

He paused and added with a wink, "And if I know men like Bear Tooth and the others, you might end up having to pay for some damages if things get a bit too rowdy."

Smoke laughed and looked at the backs of the mountain men as they walked down the center of the street. "You mean you think gentle, peaceable men like those might get into trouble, Bill?"

Van Horne laughed and shook his head as he walked off mumbling, "Gentle, peaceable, in a pig's eye!"

The group entered a saloon appropriately called the Dog Hole, a common euphemism for drinking establishments of the time, and pushed two tables together in a corner to accommodate the eight of them.

While they were waiting for a waiter to come to the table, Louis leaned over to Smoke and said, "It's like I've been here before. Remember that gambling hall I said I owned? This could be its twin."

Smoke nodded. He too had been in hundreds of places like this one back in his early days on the frontier. "I know what you mean," he said, glancing around at the rough plank bar with brass spittoons every few feet along its length, handmade wooden shelves behind it holding a myriad of bottles, many of them without labels, showing they were home-brewed.

The clientele reflected the time and the place, with about half the patrons being rough-hewn trappers and explorers and railroad workers and the other half being miners, with a few well-dressed men who were obviously cardsharps and other characters who preyed on the first two groups.

There were no Chinese in the place, however, probably due to the fact that a large hand-painted sign was on the wall behind the bar saying NO CHINEE ALLOWED!

There were, though, a few men dressed in various types of garb with pistols slung low on their hips and tied down in the manner of gunfighters. Their hard eyes were never at rest as they continuously scanned the patrons and stayed on the alert for danger.

Pearlie leaned across the table toward Smoke and whispered, "I'll bet you at least half those men over there with their guns tied down low are on wanted posters back in the States."

Smoke nodded his agreement. He knew the look of a man on the run well, having been one for several years in his youth himself.

Finally, a young man with an acne-scared face, a pronounced limp, and a dirty apron tied around his waist approached the table.

"What can I get for you gents?" he asked in the flat accent of the home-born Canadian.

"Do you serve any food here?" Smoke asked, realizing it was just past noon and they hadn't eaten yet.

The young man smirked and flicked his head at the bar. "Yeah, if you call boiled eggs and pickled pig's feet food."

Bear Tooth grinned. "Hell with that! You got any bourbon from Kaintuck?"

The bored young man just shook his head. "Mister, we got whiskey, rye, and something the barman made up in his basement he calls brandy. As for where the shit is from, your guess is as good as mine."

"Bring us a couple of bottles of whiskey," Smoke said, and he glanced at Louis, knowing he preferred brandy.

Louis sighed. "And a bottle of the barman's brandy too, if you don't mind."

The waiter shrugged. "I don't mind, but you might," he said, smiling for the first time since he came to the table.

A few minutes later, when he put the bottles on the table, all without labels, Louis asked, "Don't you have any with labels on them?"

The young man grinned again and leaned over to whisper, "Sure, but they cost twice as much and to tell you the truth, they got this same liquor in them as these do. The barman just refills the bottles every night outta the same barrel as these other bottles."

"I take it you don't much care for the barman," Louis said, smiling.

"Not a whole lot," the boy said, looking over his shoulder toward the bar. "He's my father."

"That explains it," said Smoke, being well aware of the anger some boys felt against their parents from back when Sally used to teach school in Big Rock. In fact, he could remember when his father had dragged him out West from their hardscrabble farm in Missouri and how he'd thought his father was a relic from days gone by.

"You think maybe we ought'a order some sarsaparilla or lemonade for the kid here?" Pearlie asked, inclining his head toward Cal sitting next to him.

"Who you callin' a kid, yahoo?" Cal asked, elbowing Pearlie in the ribs as the other men around the table laughed.

"Just kiddin' with you, Cal boy," Pearlie said. "It's just that I know you can't handle hard liquor hardly at all, an' I don't want you getting in no trouble or nothin'."

"I guess if I'm gonna be ridin' out in the wilderness with you fellows, I'm big enough to drink what you drink," Cal said, his cheeks burning red at the laughter.

"Cal's right, boys," Smoke said, coming to his defense. "Cal's old enough to decide when and how much he drinks, just like he's old enough to do a man's work for a man's wages. Besides, if his stomach can take that mountain man coffee Bear Tooth makes every morning, it can stand just about anything."

Cal nodded defiantly and reached over, poured a large jolt of whiskey into his glass, and upended it, drinking it down in one large gulp. His eyes widened and his face turned even redder and he coughed violently several times.

Bear Tooth took a similar drink and grimaced. "The boy's right, fellers. This stuff ain't long outta the barrel, that's for sure."

Red Bingham nodded after taking a sip of his whiskey. "Yeah, but it'll sure get the job done," he said, refilling his glass. "It tastes just like Bear Tooth's horse liniment," he said, and took another long swallow.

Louis, the only one trying the brandy, took a tentative sip and sucked in his breath, his eyes watering. He looked around the table at the men who thought that, being a saloon owner, he would grouse about the local brew. "I've had worse, and in far better establishments than this," he said with a grin.

Cal shook his head, his face still red from the whiskey. He got to his feet. "I think I'll go and get some boiled eggs from the bar to cut the taste of that stuff from my mouth," he said.

Red Bingham commenced to tell a story about having nothing to eat one winter except boiled quail and dove eggs, while Cal made his way toward the bar.

Smoke was smiling at the story when he heard a commotion from across the room, and looked up just in time to see Cal flying backward as one of the men wearing a low-slung pistol on his hip smacked him backhanded in the face.

The man was well over six feet tall and had about fifty pounds on the slim Cal.

Smoke got to his feet, along with Pearlie, and walked rapidly over to stand between Cal and his assailant. "What's going on here?" he asked, his face neutral.

The gunny, who was standing over Cal with his hand on the butt of his pistol, glared at Smoke. "Who asked you to butt in, mister?" the gunny said, scowling. "This ain't none of your business."

Smoke ignored the man and glanced down as he helped Cal to his feet. "What happened, Cal?"

Cal rubbed his bleeding lip with the back of his hand. "I went to get me a couple of eggs, and this man said they was his eggs and to keep my damned hands off," Cal replied. "And then he hauled off and hit me without any warning."

Smoke looked over at the bar at the stack of eggs, noting there were at least twenty eggs on the platter.

He raised his eyebrows as he turned his gaze back to the man. "You planning on eating all of those eggs by yourself?" he asked.

The man grinned sourly. "What if I am?"

Smoke smiled. "Then I suggest you get to it. I for one would like to see you do it."

"Like I said before, what business is it of your'n?" the man asked, moving his fingers over the butt of his pistol.

Smoke squared around and faced the man from two feet away, his face suddenly going flat and his eyes turning as hard as flint. "If you're planning on drawing that smoke wagon, I suggest you get to work," Smoke said. "Otherwise, I'm going to hit you so hard you'll be gumming your food for the rest of your miserable life."

The man growled and grabbed iron, but before he could clear his holster, Smoke's Colt was drawn, cocked, and the barrel was poking the man in the nose.

His eyes widened and his face paled as he slowly took his hand from the butt of his pistol.

"Now," Smoke said, holstering his own gun. "Let's see you get to work on those eggs."

The man's eyes narrowed and he looked over at Cal. "This is all your fault, you young pup," he growled.

Cal edged Smoke aside and stood in front of the angry man, his face set. "Is that right?" he asked. "Well, why don't you try to hit me again, now that I'm ready for it?" Cal asked, standing with his feet apart and his fists hanging at his sides, his jaw muscles bulging.

The man yelled an obscenity as he made a clumsy swing at Cal's head with his right fist.

Cal leaned to the side, easily ducking the blow, and slammed his right fist into the man's gut, doubling him over and dropping him to his knees. As he knelt there, gasping for breath, Cal squatted in front of him.

"I'm going to teach you to keep your goddamned hands to yourself and your big fat mouth shut from now on, mister," he said. He grabbed the man by the collar of his shirt and lifted him to his feet as if he weighed only a few pounds, and then he marched him over to the platter of eggs, every eye in the place on him.

As one of the gunny's friends, seeing Cal and Smoke were distracted, went for his gun, Pearlie drew quickly and slashed the man backhanded across the face with the barrel of his Colt, knocking him out cold and spreading his nose all over his face in the bargain.

The loud metallic click of the hammer of a Sharps Big Fifty being eared back came from Smoke's table, and the men in the bar turned to see Bear Tooth standing there, his Sharps cradled in his arms. "Anybody else want to dance?" he asked, staring around the room, his eyes narrow. "If'n you do, let's strike up the band an' git to it!"

When he got no answer from the crowded room, he sat back down and laid his rifle on the table, his finger still on the trigger as he watched Cal and the man at the bar.

"Thanks, Pearlie, Bear Tooth," Smoke said. He stepped back from Cal and grinned. "It's your show, Cal."

Cal leaned the man up against the bar. "Start eating, asshole, and if you stop before every egg on that plate is gone, I'm going to beat you within an inch of your life," the young man said.

The man groaned and began to stuff boiled eggs in his mouth as fast as he could, looking out of the corner of his eyes at Cal, his face burning red at being handled so easily by such a thin, wiry young man.

Smoke picked up two of the eggs off the platter and handed them to Cal. "You might want to give the man a break and eat a couple of these for him," Smoke said, smiling.

Cal took the eggs, returned the smile, and then he stuck his face next to the man's. "I'm gonna be watching you from over there, and I better not see no eggs left on that platter or I'll be back."

And then he and Smoke walked back to their table, smiling at the expressions on the faces of the men in the bar.

Bear Tooth put the Sharps back under the table and grinned at Cal. "For a boy without no meat on his bones, you pack a mean punch, son," he said approvingly.

Cal inclined his head. "Smoke taught me and Pearlie how to fight a couple of years back, but I ain't hardly had to use none of it till now."

"I'd say you a good learner, young beaver," Red said, paying Cal the highest compliment he could by calling him a beaver, a mountain-man term of respect.

Bobcat Bill clapped Pearlie on the shoulder. "An' you're pretty quick with that hogleg too, boy," he said.

"Yes," Smoke said, "they do make quite a pair, don't they?"

"I guess they'll do to ride the river with," Rattlesnake said, and then he held up his glass to the two young men and added, "To the young beavers, may they give us old beavers a little more time 'fore they take over the river."

Everyone laughed and joined in the toast, yelling at the waiter to bring more whiskey because they were just getting started.

# Chapter 12

Hammer Hammerick picked up Bull Bannion from the room next to his in the boardinghouse Luke McCain had provided, and told him to get the gang together, they were going for a ride.

Soon, Hammer and Bull, followed by almost thirty men, rode out of Noyes and headed for Winnipeg.

"What're we gonna do when we get there, Hammer?" Bull asked as his horse trotted next to Hammer's.

"We're gonna look the situation over an' see what the lay of the land is," Hammer answered around a long, black cigar stuck in the corner of his mouth. "When the time comes to hit the payroll trains, I want to be sure we know every road in and out of Winnipeg, as well as finding some likely spots to hole up if the posses they send after us get too close."

"Posses?" Bull asked, his eyebrows raised. "You think they're gonna have posses ready for us?" He'd never thought of that, because the trains they'd robbed together before had never had enough money on them to be well guarded. In fact, most of the time they'd had to be content to just take watches and pocket money from the passengers.

Hammer sighed. Bull was a good man with a gun and he was loyal to a fault, but he was dumber than a skunk. "No, probably not the first time, Bull. On that one, we'll probably get a free ride, since they won't be expecting anyone to try and rob them. But I don't expect the railroad to take the loss of thousands of dollars lying down. After we take the first payroll, I expect they'll have more guards on the second one, so we're gonna have to take different routes to and from the railroad each time we hit it, an' I want to make sure we know the country as well as we can before we start taking the railroad's money."

"Oh," Bull said, "that's a good idea."

Hammer smiled grimly. "That's why I'm ramrod of this outfit, Bull, 'cause of good ideas like that."

They spent the next few days traveling back and forth along the tracks of the railroad into and out of Winnipeg, making notes on a hand-drawn map Hammer had made showing the best trails along the way and where they could stop and set up ambushes against any posses or guards that happened to get onto their tails.

They spent the nights camped out in the open, sleeping under small tents and eating campfire food, with the men complaining bitterly about the bugs and the cold and just about everything else, until finally Hammer had had enough.

Once he had what he wanted, Hammer told the men to divide up and head into Winnipeg. "Go into town in groups of two and three," he said. "Don't act like we know each other while we're in town. I don't want the sheriff or marshal or whatever they have up here in the way of law to know we're all together. Find rooms at different hotels and let me know where you're staying, so I won't have any trouble getting in touch with you when the time comes to hit the train," he told his men.

"What are you gonna be doing?" Bull asked.

"I'm going to be mixing it up with the railroad men in the saloons around town and trying to find out the schedule of payroll payments, so I'll know when to plan to rob the trains coming into town." Hammer smiled. "I wouldn't want to hit an empty train, now would I?"

As the men dispersed, riding off at intervals of five or ten minutes, Hammer lit up another cigar and sat in the saddle thinking of how he was going to spend all the money he planned to take from the men who owned the railroad. Slapping at his neck where a mosquito as big as a bumblebee had dug in, he decided the first thing he was going to do was to move south away from the insects and the cold of the north.

Finally, when only he and Bull were left, he spurred his mount toward Winnipeg, just visible in the distance.

Hammer and Bull reined in their horses in front of a saloon named the Dog Hole just in time to see a large, heavyset man run out of the batwings holding his stomach, his face a pale shade of green. The man stopped on the boardwalk and bent over with his hands on his knees, vomiting into the dirt of the street.

Bull glanced at Hammer as he stepped down off his horse. "Mayhaps we'd better not order any food in here, Hammer," he said, staring at the mess the big man was making on the boardwalk.

Hammer shook his head as he dismounted. He hated men who couldn't hold their liquor. He and Bull went into the saloon, and found most everyone in there laughing and howling.

Hammer made his way to the bar and as he leaned on

it, he asked the barman what they'd missed that was so funny.

When the bartender told him the story of the big mountain man and his young friend who'd made the gunny eat almost two dozen eggs, Hammer turned to stare at Smoke Jensen, his lips pursed.

That might be the kind of man I'd like to have in my gang, he thought, wondering what would be the best way to approach the subject.

As he was preparing to make his way to the table, he saw a large, portly man in a three-piece suit walk into the saloon and join the mountain man at his table.

"Who's that sitting with him?" he asked the bartender when the man brought him and Bull their drinks.

"Oh, that's William Cornelius Van Horne," the bartender said. "He's in charge of building the railroad from here to the West Coast." As he continued to wipe down the bar, the bartender shook his head. "A damn fool idea if you ask me," he said.

Hammer nodded. "Then those men must work for him," he said, glad he'd held off on making his offer to the big man wearing buckskins.

"That'd be my guess," the barman said as he moved off to serve another customer.

As he sipped his whiskey, Hammer thought of another ploy he might use to get the information he needed. "Stay here, Bull. I'll be back in a few minutes."

Hammer finished his drink and made his way over to the table with Smoke and his friends.

When they looked up, Hammer spoke to Van Horne. "I hear you're in charge of building the railroad, Mr. Van Horne," he said.

Van Horne leaned back, his thumbs stuck in the armholes of his vest. "That's right, mister. Are you looking for work?" he asked.

Smoke's eyes examined Hammer, noting the way his

gun was tied down low on his thigh, and also noting his hands had no calluses on them. "I don't think he's interested in working on the railroad, Bill," Smoke said. "He doesn't look like a laborer to me."

Hammer cut his eyes to Smoke and nodded. "You're right about that, mister," he said. "I'm more interested in . . . ah . . . security work if there is any."

"Security work?" Van Horne asked.

Hammer shrugged. "You know, like keeping men in line if they get too rowdy, or perhaps guard work if you have anything to guard," Hammer said.

Van Horne pursed his lips, taking in the confident manner Hammer had about him. He slowly nodded. "There might be some way I could use you. Let me talk to my foreman about it and ask me again in a day or two."

Hammer nodded and touched the brim of his hat. "Thank you kindly, Mr. Van Horne," he said, and he walked slowly back to the bar to order another drink.

Bear Tooth leaned to the side and spat onto the floor. "That galoot smells like trouble to me, Bill," he said. "I ain't one to tell nobody their business, but I'd steer clear of that sort if'n I was you."

Van Horne laughed. "Bear Tooth, if I failed to hire men simply because they looked a little rough around the edges, I wouldn't have more than a dozen men working for me instead of almost twenty thousand."

"In this case," Smoke said, "I agree with Bear Tooth, Bill. That man's eyes were dead. I have a feeling you'd be sorry if you hired him."

Van Horne stared at Smoke for a moment, his face thoughtful.

"One thing I've learned over the years, Bill," Louis said. "Smoke Jensen is the best judge of character I've ever met. If he tells you a man is bad, you can take that to the bank."

"You know I respect your opinion, Smoke, so if he does come back, I'll turn him down."

He got to his feet and said, "Now, come on over to the railroad yard. There are some people I'd like you all to meet before we start work on the surveying."

"Uh, Mr. Van Horne," Pearlie said.

"Yes, Pearlie?"

"We ain't had no lunch yet"—he grinned—" 'cepting Cal an' his boiled eggs, an' it's way past noon, an' I was wondering if you had any grub over at the railroad yard."

Van Horne laughed, his ample stomach shaking. "Sure, Pearlie. As soon as we get there, I'll have Cookie make you all up something to take the edge off your appetite until we can get dinner tonight."

Cal laughed. "The only thing that'd take the edge off Pearlie's appetite, Bill, is to feed him an entire cow."

When the group arrived at the railroad yard, about a mile and a half out of town, they were all amazed to see over a thousand tents set up and thousands of men milling around a large compound that contained several odd-looking machines that Van Horne told them were used to travel down the tracks as they were laid and bring supplies to the men working the lines.

"Jiminy," Cal said, staring around wide-eyed. "How many men you got workin' for you, Bill?"

"Over twenty thousand so far," Van Horne replied.

"How come most of 'em seem to be staying out here in tents 'stead of in town?" Rattlesnake Bob asked.

Van Horne grinned. "Well, most of the men are of Chinese descent," he said, "and as you saw by the sign in the saloon, the town folk don't exactly welcome Chinese." He gave a slight shrug as he looked around the expanse of tents. "As for the others, most are men like you, Rattlesnake. They're used to living out in the open and feel cooped up when they're in a hotel room."

Louis, ever the pragmatist, glanced over at Van Horne. "You say you've got over twenty thousand men, huh, Bill?"

"That's right."

"And I suppose most of them are being paid about a dollar a day or so?"

"Well, the Chinese don't make that much, but I suppose that's about the average."

"So, when payday comes around, you're paying out almost half a million dollars a month, I guess."

Van Horne nodded. "Probably about that much, but I really don't know for certain, Louis. My job is to get the track laid. Paying them for doing it is someone else's headache."

Smoke knew Louis was trying to make a point. "What are you getting at, Louis?"

Louis shrugged. "I don't know really. It's just seeing that hard-eyed fellow at the saloon asking about security made me think that half a million dollars would make an awfully tempting pie for someone to try and cut himself a piece of."

Van Horne laughed. "Oh, well, you don't have to worry about that, Louis. The payroll train is heavily guarded, and the money is kept in a large safe in a boxcar that is bolted to the floor and is much too heavy to carry off."

"What if some robbers held a gun to the guards?" Cal asked. "Couldn't they make them open it up?"

"Not a chance," Van Horne said. "No one on the train has the combination to the safe, so even if they wanted to, they couldn't get into it."

"That makes me feel a lot better," Pearlie said, "'cause now I know I'm gonna get paid for all this work we're gonna be doing." He sighed. "Now, if we could just get fed, I'd feel even better!"

Van Horne laughed again and slapped Pearlie on the back. "Well, then, come on, men. I'll introduce you to Cookie and see if he can find you all something to eat."

"That's good," Pearlie said with a grin. "If there's one man on a crew I like to know personally, it's the cook."

"That's a fact!" Cal said. "And I can tell you one thing for sure, he's gonna get awfully tired of your face hanging around asking him when the next meal's gonna be ready."

# Chapter 13

Later that evening, Hammer sent Bull off to have supper with some of the men at a local restaurant while he went back to the Dog Hole to see if perhaps the man named Van Horne was there. He wanted to see if the man had considered his request for security work.

He stood inside the batwings for a minute, looking around the place, but didn't see either Van Horne or any of the other men who'd been with him at noon.

As he was glancing around, he saw a portly man in a dark suit and bowler hat having a drink at a table by himself. The man had the cold, calculating eyes of a star-packer of some sort, so Hammer decided to approach him and see what he could learn.

He walked over to the table and said, "Howdy."

The man looked up from his drink and turned his black eyes on Hammer, no expression of welcome in them.

"Do I know you?" he asked coldly.

Hammer shrugged and shook his head. "I don't think so, but you have the look of a lawman about you," he said, forcing his lips into an innocent smile. "And since I used to carry a badge myself, I thought if I was right, I'd offer to buy you a drink."

The man's expression softened a little, though his eyes remained suspicious. Lawmen weren't always welcome in frontier towns, and it was wise to be cautious when talking to strangers, especially in saloons. The man leaned back and let his hand drop to his waist, and Hammer could see the butt of a pistol in a shoulder holster under his coat.

"You're partially right," the man said. "I carry a badge, but it's private. I work for the Pinkerton Agency."

"Close enough," Hammer said, signaling to the bartender to bring them another round. "My name's John Brody," Hammer said, picking a name out of the air. "I used to work for the hanging judge over to Fort Smith, Arkansas, a while back."

"Oh, Judge Isaac Parker," the man said. "I met him once. He's as hard as a granite boulder."

"You got that right," Hammer said, grinning. All he really knew about Judge Parker was what he'd read in the *Grand Forks Gazette*.

"My name's Albert Knowles," the Pinkerton man said.

After the bartender's limping son brought their drinks, Hammer said, "By the way, I thought the Pinkertons only worked in the States."

"That's changing," Knowles said, upending his drink and draining it in one swallow. After he wiped his mouth with the back of his hand, he continued. "Now that Canada is getting strongly into the railroad-building business, James Hill, who we've done a lot of work for in the States, has decided to use us for his security force." He added, "That's how the Pinkertons got started in the first place, working as railroad detectives."

Hammer nodded encouragingly. "More business is always good, I expect."

"Damn right," Knowles said, and this time he was the one that signaled the bartender for another round.

"I saw all those men camped out by the rail yard," Hammer said. "There must be thousands of them."

Knowles nodded. "Almost twenty thousand," he said, "though most of 'em are Chinee."

"Damn, that must mean a huge payroll."

Knowles leaned forward and said in a low voice, "You have no idea, John."

"That's a big responsibility, guarding that much money," Hammer said in an offhand manner, as if he were just making small talk. "I handled some pretty big jobs as a marshal, but I don't know as I'd want to take that on."

"Naw, it's not so hard," Knowles said, beginning to slur his words a bit as he took another large drink of whiskey. He whispered, "I got ten men hiding in the boxcar with the safe, all armed with the latest Henry repeating rifles and Winchesters, and I got another ten riding in the car behind, with horses all saddled and ready just in case they need to take out after some would-be robbers." He leaned back and grinned. "A few men tried to rob us on the first run last month, but we took care of them."

Hammer grinned, one lawman to another. "What'd you do, Al?"

"The ones we didn't kill outright, we strung up to the nearest telegraph pole and watched 'em dance till they was deader than yesterday's news. Then we brought them into town and set them up in caskets in front of the local undertaker's office, with a sign on them that said this is what happens to train robbers."

"I guess a man would have to be crazy to try and hit

one of your payroll trains after seeing that," Hammer said, waving the waiter over for another round.

"Yeah, that's why we haven't had no more trouble since that first time," Knowles said. "And if it was up to me, those bodies'd still be there, though I suspect they'd be a mite ripe by now," he said, chuckling drunkenly at his joke. "But Mr. Van Horne ordered them taken down and buried over in Boot Hill," Knowles added. "Shame too, it was some of my best work."

"So this Mr. Van Horne don't appreciate you, huh?" Hammer asked, trying to get a rise out of Knowles.

"No, no, it ain't that," Knowles said. "It's just that Mr. Van Horne is a real decent man, though he's hard as nails if you don't do your job."

He finished off his drink and got unsteadily to his feet. "Thanks for the drinks, John. Be seein' you."

Hammer nodded as Knowles walked off, veering to one side as he went through the batwings. A slow smile spread across his face. "You're right about that, Al," he said in a low voice to himself. "You'll be seeing me again, and a lot sooner than you think."

Hammer leaned back in his chair and sipped his drink, trying to figure a way around twenty Pinkerton men so he could get the gold they were guarding.


While Hammer was pumping the Pinkerton man for information, Van Horne was treating Smoke and his friends to dinner at the restaurant attached to the Rooster's Roost Hotel.

Van Horne noticed Bear Tooth and Red Bingham glancing nervously around the room and whispering to one another.

"Bear Tooth, Red," Van Horne asked, "is anything wrong?"

"Uh, Bill, it's just that we're not used to eatin' in-doors," Bear Tooth answered.

"Yeah," Red added, "it don't seem natural somehow."

"But you ate in the car on the train," Pearlie said.

"That was different," Bear said. "Then it was just us eating, kind'a like being in camp with your partners." He looked around. "Here there's a whole passel of strangers around watchin' us eat."

Louis, who was holding a glass of real brandy in his hands, not the homemade variety he'd had at the Dog Hole, looked up as he swirled the amber liquid around the snifter. "Oh, you'll get used to it, boys. The only difference from eating outdoors is there are far fewer bugs to bother you while you eat."

Van Horne laughed. "Yes, but don't get too used to it, men. We're going to be taking off in a day or two for the wilds of Canada to do some surveying."

He looked up as a tall, slim man wearing buckskins entered the door to the restaurant and looked around. Van Horne held up his hand and waved him over.

As he approached their table, Smoke noticed he had the sun-wrinkled face and observant eyes of a mountain man, but unlike most of those he'd known in the past, the man's beard was short and well trimmed.

"Gentlemen," Van Horne said, getting to his feet and holding out his hand to the newcomer, "this is Tom Wilson. He's the leader of our surveying crew."

"So, you're to be our new boss, huh?" Smoke said with a smile as he got to his feet and held out his hand.

Wilson returned the smile, though it looked like it was an effort. "Yeah, I guess so," he said, taking Smoke's hand.

"I'm Smoke Jensen," Smoke said, and then he introduced the others at the table, who all nodded and then went back to their food and drink.

Wilson's eyes took in the other mountain men at the table, and then moved over Smoke's broad shoulders and muscled arms. "You boys all look like you got some hair on you," Wilson said, and then he hesitated, glancing at Louis and his fancy clothes and at Cal and Pearlie. "At least, most of you do," he added with a half smile.

Smoke took his meaning. "Oh, by the way, Tom, don't let Louis's clothes or the boys' young years fool you," Smoke said. "They've all been tested by fire, and I'll guarantee you they're up to the job."

Wilson stared at Smoke for a moment, his eyes narrowed, and then he snapped his fingers. "I've been trying to remember where I've heard the name Smoke Jensen before," he said.

"Oh?" Smoke inquired.

"Yeah. It was last year, right after the spring thaw, and I was up in the mountains just north of here checking out the elk herds, fixin' to do some hunting, when I ran across one of the oldest men I've ever met who wasn't sitting in a rocking chair on a porch somewhere."

Smoke's heart began to beat rapidly, knowing what was coming. "He give you a name?"

Wilson grinned. "Yeah, the old beaver said he was called Preacher."

The name Preacher got the immediate attention of all of the mountain men at the table, Preacher being a legend among them.

Wilson reached behind him, took a chair from a nearby table, and pulled it around, sitting on it backward with his arms folded over the back of the chair. "Well, one thing led to another and we made a camp together up there in the High Lonesome. This Preacher, he made me some coffee that'd take the hair off a bear hide, and then he proceeded to tell me he'd come all the way up here to Canada from down Colorado way 'cause it was getting too crowded in the mountains down there. He said you couldn't hardly trap any beaver for tripping over pilgrims and such all the time."

"Jesus," Bear Tooth whispered, staring at Wilson. "Ol' Preacher must be in his eighties at least by now."

"I'd just assumed the old codger had holed up somewheres an' died," Red Bingham said, equally awed by Wilson's story.

Wilson nodded. "You're right, men. Preacher had to be at least eighty, and he looked like he'd been rode hard and put up wet besides. Anyway, some of the tales he told me I put down to typical mountain-man exaggeration, especially the ones about a young pilgrim he'd met years ago who was fast as greased lightning with a handgun and, to hear Preacher tell it, as hard as an anvil."

Rattlesnake Bob nodded. "Well, sonny boy, if'n he was talking about Smoke here, you can take what he said to heart, no matter how outrageous it sounded."

Smoke smiled and shook his head. "I wish I'd been here to see him. We had some fun times in the old days, hairy as hell, but fun nevertheless."

Wilson pulled a canvas pouch out of the pocket of his buckskins and began to build himself a cigarette. When it was done, he screwed it into the corner of his mouth and lit it with a lucifer he struck on his pants leg.

As he let the smoke drift out of his nostrils, he looked at Smoke. "If half of what he said about you was true, Smoke, it's gonna be a pleasure to ride the peaks with you."

Smoke laughed. "And if it's not?"

Wilson shrugged. "Then you probably won't make it across the mountains, and neither will the rest of you." He took a deep drag, leaving the cigarette in his mouth as he talked around the smoke. "Boys, the mountains in Colorado ain't nothing compared to what you're gonna see up here. Besides the Stony Indians, who'd just as soon scalp you and eat your heart as to look at you, we got just about ever kind of wild creature ever born with fangs and claws up here. There ain't been more'n a handful of whites to even try to cross the territory where we're going, an' half of them never lived to tell about what they'd seen."

"If the surveying job is so difficult and dangerous, why did you agree to ramrod the team?" Louis asked, a bit angry at the way Wilson was talking down to them as if they'd never been in dangerous situations before.

Wilson shrugged. "Hell, I was gonna be up in the mountains anyway, since that's what I do, so why not take the railroad's money for doing what comes natural?"

He hesitated, looking around the table. "The question is, since you all seem to have at least most of your senses, why have you agreed to take such a job on?"

Smoke stared at Wilson, wondering why the man had so little regard for others. "Probably for the same reason Preacher told you he was up here," Smoke said. "Colorado's getting crowded and most of the Indians have been either wiped out or beaten into submission. And like you say, we'd be up in the mountains anyway, so why not see some new country and get paid for it?"

Wilson nodded as he stubbed the cigarette out in an ashtray on the table. "Good enough then. I'll see you men 'bout sunup in the morning, and we'll get started going toward the mountains to see if we can find a pass for Mr. Van Horne to drive his iron horse through."

"By the way, Tom," Smoke said, "whatever happened to Preacher after your camp together?"

Wilson shook his head and smiled. "Hell if I know. When I woke up the next morning, the coffee was made and there was no sign of the old man. He'd vanished into the woods as if he'd never even been there. I tried to track him, and believe me when I say I can track a fart in a windstorm, and I couldn't even tell which way he'd gone."

Smoke smiled. "That's Preacher, all right. He once told me he could walk across mud without leaving a print, and damned if I don't believe it."

# Chapter 14

The next morning, Smoke got up and dressed and went to wake the rest of the group just before dawn. After collecting Cal and Pearlie and Louis, he knocked on the doors to the other four mountain men's hotel rooms and received no answer.

Cautiously, he opened the door to Bear Tooth and Red Bingham's room and entered, his hand near the butt of his pistol. There was no telling what trouble the men might have gotten into during the night. They were, after all, not used to city life and its many dangers. As he looked around, he was surprised to find that the beds hadn't been slept in. He moved further into the room, and he heard the sound of voices coming in through the open window.

He slipped his pistol out of its holster and eased over to the window and peered out, finding Red and Bear Tooth just getting out of sleeping blankets they'd set up on the balcony running alongside the building.

He shook his head, smiling as he stuck his Colt back into its holster on his right hip. It was just like mountain men to prefer sleeping outside on a balcony under the stars to a soft, comfortable bed inside.

"Morning, boys," Smoke said, leaning his head out of the window.

Bear Tooth looked up, yawning and stretching. "Howdy, Smoke. Looks like it's gonna be a humdinger of a day," he said, peering up at a clear sky still full of stars.

"I reckon it does," Smoke agreed. "Didn't you boys find it a mite chilly out here last night? The temperature must've been well below zero."

Bear looked over at Red and shrugged. "I didn't notice it being particularly cold. Did you, Red?"

Red didn't bother to answer, just shook his head and yawned.

Smoke leaned a little further out of the window and looked to the side. Just down the balcony, in front of the window to their room, lay Rattlesnake Bob and Bobcat Bill. At least Smoke thought it was them. It was hard to tell, for they were burrowed deep in heavy blankets and only their outlines could be seen.

He jerked his head to the side. "Better go wake up those slugabeds down the way, or before long we'll be burning daylight," he said to Bear Tooth.

Bear Tooth grinned. "Them always were lazy layabouts, ever since I knowed 'em," he said as he got to his feet and walked down the balcony.

He stirred the sleeping form of Rattlesnake Bob, and was rewarded with the barrel of an old Walker Colt poking out of the blankets at his face.

He chuckled and pushed the gun aside with his foot. "Don't go pointin' that hogleg at me 'less'n you want it shoved where the sun don't shine, Rattlesnake."

"Then don't go kickin' at me with them dirty boots of your'n, you polecat!" Rattlesnake growled in a phlegmy voice as he struggled up out of his blankets.

"Hell, somebody's got to do it, else you'd likely sleep till noon, an' Smoke says breakfast is waiting."

"Did I hear somebody say breakfast?" Bobcat Bill said, jumping up out of his blankets and onto his feet. He was instantly awake, a trait soon learned by mountain men, else they didn't survive long in the wilderness.

As usual, all of the mountain men had gone to sleep in their clothes, as they did out in the High Lonesome.

Rattlesnake grimaced. "Just like in camp, boys," he said to Bear. "Bobcat don't hardly ever stir from his blankets till I've got breakfast on the fire."

Bobcat looked over at his partner and grinned. "An' I do so appreciate the fine cuisine you fix too, podna," he growled. "Especially that stew you make that's just got to have skunk meat in it."

In less than an hour, they were all sitting around a table in the huge mess tent in the rail yard, stuffing down flapjacks and eggs and bacon and beans as fast as they could. Pearlie had even taken a few sinkers and slathered thick white gravy over them, and was eating them as well.

Van Horne appeared, unshaven, his clothes rumpled and untidy.

"What happened to you, Bill?" Smoke asked as Van Horne grabbed a mug of coffee and drank it down.

"This is a mite too early for me, Smoke. I usually wait until at least dawn to crawl out of bed"— he smiled— "but then, I also usually work until after midnight when I'm in the middle of laying track."

"Where's Tom Wilson?" Smoke asked. "I figured he'd have his tent here near the camp."

Van Horne shook his head. "Not Tom. He's not exactly what I'd call the most sociable fellow I've ever met.

He usually makes his own camp a ways away from the rest of the crew. Says it's just about all he can do to stand other people's company all day without having to listen to them snore all night."

"You mean he just ups and heads off when the day's work is done?" Cal asked, his mouth full of bacon.

"That's about the size of it," Van Horne answered. "Ol' Tom's a real loner."

"It ain't that I'm a loner," Wilson said from the tent door as he entered and picked up a plate. "It's just that I ain't found all that many people I enjoy being around much is all."

Cal watched wide-eyed as Tom piled on even more food than Pearlie had. When the mountain man sat down, Cal said, "Jiminy, Mr. Wilson, I ain't never seen nobody eat more'n Pearlie here."

Wilson looked up from pouring a half quart of maple syrup on his pancakes. "One thing you learn out here in the High Lonesome, young'un," he said, "is to eat as much as you can whenever you got the chance, 'cause you never know when you'll get your next chance to eat."

Cal laughed. "Heck fire, my friend Pearlie's been following that advice as long as I've knowed him, an' he don't even live up in the mountains."

While they finished their breakfast, Van Horne pulled out a wrinkled hand-drawn map from his coat pocket. He handed the map to Smoke. "I've drawn a rough sketch of what we know about the mountain ranges to the north and west of Winnipeg, and I've penciled in a rough line where I want the tracks to go, with provisions, of course, for any detours we might have to make around peaks or valleys in the mountain range."

Tom Wilson glanced up from his food long enough to pull several sheets of paper from his breast pocket and pass them over to Smoke. "Here's some more maps for you, Smoke. They detail several routes explored by others some years back."

Smoke looked at the maps. They were labeled with the names Dawson, Palliser, and Fleming. "Which of these do you think is the best bet to try, Tom?" he asked.

"Won't know till we get out there, but from what I've read in the journals of the men involved, I think Fleming's more northern route offers the best chance of finding some passes through the Selkirk and Caribou Mountains."

Smoke grinned. "Then I guess we'll try the northern routes first, assuming we can get through the snowpacks."

Wilson grunted. "And assuming we can find suitable portages across the rivers that dot the area."

"Rivers?" Pearlie asked, looking up from his breakfast for the first time since he sat down. "You mean we're gonna have to cross freezing rivers on this trip?"

"'Less you can fly, boy, that's about the size of it," Wilson replied dryly.

"Just how many men are you planning on taking with us on this little jaunt?" Louis asked as he sipped his after-breakfast coffee and smoked a long black cigar.

Wilson paused in his eating. "Just three in addition to us here at the table. William and Thomas McCardell and Frank McCabe will be good men to have with us, I think. They're experienced surveyors, and if we run into the Stony Indians, we're gonna need every gun we can carry to get us through."

"Do you think there's much chance of that?" Pearlie asked, a worried look on his face.

Wilson looked at him and grinned. "Do you think there's much chance of it snowing up here in the winter?" he asked in answer to Pearlie's question. When Pearlie didn't answer, he added, "It's not a question of whether we run into the Indians, Pearlie, but of when it's gonna happen."

"The trick to fightin' Injuns, young'un," Bear said around his food, "is to see them 'fore they see you, 'cause if'n it's the other way 'round, there won't be much fightin' goin' on, just a lotta dyin'."

While Smoke and his men were eating breakfast, Hammer Hammerick and his gang were stationed alongside the railroad tracks leading into Winnipeg, about ten miles out of the town.

He'd worked out a plan to deal with the Pinkerton men stationed on the train as guards, and he was anxious to see if it would work.

He had his thirty men lined up in wooded areas on either side of the track. As the rails made a long, sweeping curve to the right, he'd had his men loosen the tracks just enough to derail the train, but leave them in place so the engineer wouldn't see anything amiss. Each of his men had been supplied with several sticks of dynamite with fuses attached.

As the engine made the curve, its wheels jumped the track and the cars following began a crazy dance, waving back and forth and tipping first to one side and then to the other as they ran off the tracks and onto the soft dirt alongside. The train soon completely derailed, sliding to the side and plowing twin furrows in the soft earth for over a hundred yards, before the engine and the cars immediately behind it slowly toppled to the side, rupturing the boiler with a loud explosion and great plumes of steam billowing into the chilly air.

When the rest of the cars had come to a stop, Hammer and his men rode their horses out of the woods and galloped toward the disabled train, lighting fuses from cigars in their mouths and pitching them toward the cars containing the Pinkerton men, many of whom could be heard screaming in pain and terror from the piles of wreckage alongside the tracks.

The wooden cars exploded into pieces, and men and horses on the train screamed in further agony as their bodies were ripped apart by the force of the explosions.

Hammer reined his horse in next to the boxcar containing the large iron safe and the dead and wounded bodies of the Pinkerton agents lying scattered all around the ruined car amid body parts, blood, and dead horses.

As he dismounted, he looked around at the men on the ground. There were over twenty men, some still alive, partially buried in the splintered pieces of wood from the car.

He, like all of his men, had covered his face with a bandanna, so he didn't feel the need to execute the wounded men, but he was careful to make sure none were in any shape to take a shot at him with the rifles most had nearby.

"Bull," he called over his shoulder to Bannion, who was just behind him. "Make sure you and the men pick up the weapons, especially from the wounded men. We wouldn't want them taking potshots at us while we get the safe open."

Ignoring the pitiful crying and moaning of injured men all around him, he climbed up on the stack of broken lumber, pulling boards aside until he was standing next to the big iron safe lying on its side in the wreckage.

After examining the safe's door for a moment, he saw that it had a combination lock on it, just as Albert Knowles had said it did.

He reached into the gunnysack he was carrying, and took out a stack of dynamite sticks he'd tied together with a piece of twine. He wedged the dynamite under the door, just next to the dial on the lock, and took his cigar out of his mouth.

"You ready, Bull?" he called.

Bull, who was standing nearby with several other members of the gang with their arms full of new rifles, took one look at the large stack of dynamite and began to walk rapidly away from the car.

"Yeah, Boss, just let me get a little bit farther away 'fore you light that bundle."

As Hammer put the bright orange tip of the cigar against the fuse, a wounded man lying a few yards away croaked, "No, mister, please don't." The man struggled to hold out his right arm, which was bloody and mangled from the explosions.

"Sorry, pal," Hammer said as he began to trot away from the dynamite. "Guess this'll teach you not to work for the Pinkertons no more."

Hammer crouched down behind a nearby overturned car with his men, and covered his ears with his hands, waiting for the explosion.

A few moments later, the dynamite blew, with a resounding clap of thunder that shook the ground and raised a cloud of dust that billowed out and engulfed Hammer and his men.

Broken boards, body parts, and even one of the wheels of the car were blown into the air and rained down around them like hailstones.

"Jesus, Boss," Bull said as the heavy iron wheel of the car landed a few feet away from them with a loud thud. "Maybe you shouldn't've used so much dynamite."

Hammer grimaced. Bull was right, but he knew he'd had to be sure the amount was enough to open the safe.

He stepped out around the edge of the car they'd been hiding behind, and walked through the dust cloud toward what remained of the boxcar. Hammer was surprised to see a large crater over three feet deep where the safe had been. The wounded man who'd been near the safe was nowhere to be seen. He'd been blown to bits by the explosion.

The safe was lying open, its door bent and twisted with one hinge completely off. Piles of paper were burning, small bits of the bills rising on heat waves into the air, glowing like fireflies on a summer night.

"Damn it!" Hammer said, running over to try and salvage what he could of the payroll. Knowles hadn't told him the railroad was using paper money to pay the railroad workers their salaries. He'd just assumed it would be in gold or silver coin.

"Where's the gold, Boss?" Bull asked, standing behind Hammer as he knelt and tried to snatch some of the bills out of the safe before they all burned up. Ignoring the fire, he stuck his hands in the remains of the safe and pulled out several tightly wrapped bundles of hundred-dollar bills.

"There isn't any, Bull," Hammer said disgustedly. "Those assholes are paying the men with Canadian paper money, not gold." He glanced down at the packets of money in his scorched hands and made a quick calculation.

"Aw, shit," Bull said. "You mean we did all this for nothin'?"

Hammer stood up, smiling and holding up the bundles of bills he'd been able to salvage from the fire.

He took a deep breath. "Not exactly for nothing," he replied. "It looks like we got about fifty thousand dollars here, boys, give or take a few thousand. Not exactly bad pay for one day's work."

Juan Sanchez, one of the gang members, scowled. "*Sí,* but you said there would be over five hundred thousand in it for us," he groused.

Hammer turned hard eyes on Sanchez. "You don't

want your share, Juanito, that's fine by me. Course, I'll bet you can't remember the last time you had over a thousand dollars cash in your hands at one time, can you?"

When Sanchez shrugged and grinned, Hammer turned and looked at the bodies scattered around the wreckage, saying to Bull, "Send the man out to search the bodies. Take anything of value, including watches and any guns they're carrying."

Bull made a face. "But Boss, some of them bodies have been torn apart. We'll get all messed up with blood and guts an' stuff."

Hammer glared at Bull. "Just do it, Bull. You've had blood on your hands before, and after all, you're being paid pretty damn good for it." He took a deep breath, trying to calm down and hide his disappointment at the small amount of money they'd gotten. He added, "Pretty soon they're gonna realize this train is behind schedule and they're gonna be sending a posse out here to see where it is. I'd kind'a like to be long gone by then."

"Sure thing, Boss," Bull said, an expression of distaste on his face as he glanced around at the bodies lying all around them. "I'll get the men right on it."

# Chapter 15

Xiang Chang walked slowly through deep forest on top of a hill. His head was bent down and he stared at the ground, searching for the big, brown mushrooms his friends loved so much when chopped and fried in his ancient wok and mixed with rice and fish heads.

So far today, he had found almost three pounds of the mushrooms. Dinner tonight would be special indeed.

In the distance, he heard the mournful-sounding cry of the large steam engine coming toward him. He paused in his search to stand and peer through the trees to watch it approach, billowing huge clouds of steam from the turret on the top of the engine.

Xiang ducked as the engine suddenly lurched to the side and slid slowly off the tracks, plowing up twin furrows of earth with its wheels until it toppled to the side and slid to a stop.

Huge flames leaped from the engine as the boiler exploded and tore the engine to pieces.

His hands went to his mouth when he saw dozens of men rush from the underbrush on either side of the rail tracks and begin to throw smoking sticks at the cars that had followed the engine off the tracks.

Several more explosions boomed across the valley between the ruined train and Xiang as the rail cars jumped and came apart in the air under the influence of the dynamite wielded by the men swarming toward the train.

Xiang winced at the sight of so many bodies being thrown into the air, and he dropped his precious sack of mushrooms and ran toward the mule that had carried him from the rail camp. He had to get back and warn the big boss man about what had happened to his shiny new train.

Tom Wilson had the men lined up and ready to depart, along with several packhorses loaded with supplies, extra ammunition, and tents, when Bill Van Horne came running toward them, waving his arms and shouting for them to wait.

Wilson pulled his horse's head around and sat in the saddle, leaning forward with his arms crossed over the pommel as he waited to see what was so all-fired important as to hold up the surveying party.

Van Horne stopped running when he got to them and leaned over, his hands on his knees, breathing heavily.

"Slow down a mite, Bill," Wilson said with a smile. Van Horne was much too fat to be exerting himself like this. "You're gonna kill yourself runnin' like that."

Two smallish Chinese men were close behind Van Horne, and stood patiently, waiting for him to ask them to tell their story.

Finally, after Van Horne had caught his breath, he straightened up. "We got trouble, Tom. Bad trouble with the payroll train."

Wilson grinned. "What else is new, Bill? There's always something goin' on out here. What happened? Didn't they send enough money from headquarters?"

"It's not that, Tom," Van Horne said, his face serious and grim. "The payroll train is overdue and this man has some information about it."

Wilson and the others turned their gaze to the two Chinese men. One, who looked older than the other, spoke. "This man is Xiang Chang," he said, inclining his head toward the other man. "He speaks no English, so I will translate his story for you. He was out a few miles from town picking wild mushrooms to use in the camp cooking, when he saw a group of men attack the payroll train. He says there was a large explosion, as if many sticks of dynamite were used, and it caused the train to run off the tracks and turn onto its side. Soon, further explosions occurred and several of the train cars were blown up into many pieces."

"Tell them about the men on the train," Van Horne said, his eyes tortured and sad.

The first man spoke to the other in Chinese for several seconds, and then replied in English, "He says there were very many bodies lying on the ground among the wreckage. It was his opinion that few survived the attack."

"How many men were in the attacking party?" Smoke asked, joining in the discussion.

After a few more words between the two in Chinese, the interpreter answered, "He didn't count them, but said more than two dozen."

Van Horne said, "That's enough, Chiu. We won't need you any longer."

After the two Chinese left, he turned to the group. "Almost every one of my security men was on that train," he said.

"Why are you telling us this, Bill?" Wilson asked. "We're a surveying party, not part of your security forces."

Van Horne took a deep breath and turned his attention to Smoke. "Uh, I was wondering if you'd be willing to head out there and see what you could do, Smoke. You have a certain . . . reputation for handling men like this, and since my Pinkertons are probably out of commission, I'm in desperate need of someone who knows his way around a gun to take charge of this mess."

Smoke pursed his lips, thinking for a moment. "How about if I take Louis and Cal and Pearlie with me, leaving the mountain men to help Tom with the survey until we can get back and catch up to them?"

Van Horne glanced over at Wilson. "That all right with you, Tom?"

Wilson shrugged. "Sure. We ain't gonna get into any hairy areas for at least a week. The first part of Fleming's trail is pretty straightforward until we get up into the mountains, an' I'm gonna be leaving a blazed trail for the railroad workers to follow anyhow. I don't see where it'd be a problem, long as they catch up to us 'fore we get into Stony Indian territory."

Smoke nodded. He looked around. "That all right with you?" he asked his friends.

Louis grinned. "Hell, yes. I'm ready for a little excitement, so this will be a pleasure."

Cal and Pearlie nodded. "We're with you, Smoke, an' where you go, we go," Pearlie said, his jaw tight and set, while Cal just nodded his agreement.

Smoke looked back down at Van Horne. "Get me another packhorse and load it up with plenty of ammunition, some extra firearms, a Sharps if you have one, and enough food and supplies for two weeks. By then, we'll either have them, or they'll be long gone."

"All right," Van Horne said. "You and your men head on out to the wreckage site, and I'll be right behind you with some wagons and our medical people to see how many of the Pinkertons we can save."

Tom Wilson walked his horse over to Smoke's mount. He stuck his hand out. "Ride with your guns loose and loaded up six and six, Smoke," he said. "Anyone who'd kill that many men just to steal some payroll ain't to be trifled with."

Smoke nodded. "I've met plenty of that kind before, Tom," he said, his eyes flat and dangerous-looking. "I know how to handle them."

Bear Tooth called, "Don't give 'em no quarter, Smoke boy. Just shoot 'em down like the animals they is."

Ten minutes later, Van Horne had two packhorses loaded with what Smoke had asked for, and Smoke, Cal, Pearlie, and Louis put their spurs to their mounts, the pack animals following on dally ropes wrapped around Cal and Pearlie's saddle horns.

Van Horne told them to just follow the tracks out of town and they'd come to the ambush site within a few miles, according to the Chinese man.

They rode on the cleared area right next to the train tracks so they wouldn't have to slow down to weave through the forests and woods that were thick in the area.

It took them less than an hour, pushing the horses as fast as they could, before they could see dark smoke rising on afternoon air currents to cover the sky like storm clouds ahead of them.

Smoke slowed his mount and loosened the hammer thongs on his pistols as he pulled his Winchester '73 from its saddle boot and jacked a shell into the chamber.

Cal wrinkled his nose as he checked the loads in his own rifle. "Jiminy, what's that godawful smell?" he asked no one in particular.

Pearlie looked at Smoke before he replied, "That's the smell of burning flesh, Cal, an' once you smell it, it's a smell you never forget."

Smoke and the others walked their horses around a turn in the tracks just in time to see a group of men mounting up onto horses and beginning to ride off in a direction away from them.

Pearlie jumped off his horse, pulled the Sharps Big Fifty from its scabbard on the packhorse, and laid it across the rear of the animal, taking aim at one of the fleeing outlaws.

"Hold on, Pearlie," Smoke said.

"But I can get one or two 'fore they get out of range," Pearlie protested, his eye still on the raised sights of the Sharps.

"Yeah, but then they'll know we're on their trail," Smoke said. "Let 'em go for now. We'll follow them until they make camp, and then we'll be able to set up an ambush and take out more than one or two before they know what hit them."

"Oh," Pearlie said, putting the Sharps back in its rifle boot. "I never thought of that."

"Smoke's right, Pearlie," Louis said, a pair of binoculars to his eyes. "It appears they have us outnumbered five or six to one, so we're going to have to outthink them as well as outfight them if we're to have any chance of bringing them to justice."

As the robbers disappeared from sight, Smoke said, "Let's head on down there and see if there's anyone left alive that we can help until Bill gets here with the doctor."

Louis moved his binoculars as he surveyed the scene down by the rail tracks.

"I think I can see a few men moving, but they all look like they're in a bad way," he said. As he surveyed the extent of the wreckage, he added, "It'll be a miracle if more than a handful are still alive."

"I wonder why they didn't kill all of the wounded men when they had the chance," Pearlie said.

"They probably wore masks and didn't think it was necessary," Smoke said. "But hopefully, some of the wounded may have heard or seen something that will help us as we track the bastards down."

Cal shook his head as he followed Smoke down the rise toward the wrecked train.

"I gotta tell you, Smoke," he said, his voice low. "I ain't lookin' forward to this job."

Smoke nodded. He knew the boy had probably never seen anything like what they were about to experience down below, and truth to tell, he wasn't much looking forward to dealing with this many casualties either.

# Chapter 16

Hammer and his men, their horses loaded down with rifles, handguns, and the personal property of the men they'd robbed on the train, made their way up slopes still partially covered with snow toward the higher elevations of the hills around the ambush site.

Bull Bannion twisted in his saddle and looked at the trail behind them. "We're leaving a pretty easy trail for a posse to follow, Hammer," he said.

"Don't worry about it, Bull," Hammer replied, glancing at the sky, which was full of dark, roiling clouds. "Looks to me like we got us a spring storm coming 'fore too long. By the time it clears enough for a party to catch up with us, we'll be across the border and back in Noyes."

Bull shivered in his heavy overcoat. "Yeah, an' with the temperature being so cold for this time of year, it'll probably be snow rather than rain."

"That should take care of any tracks we leave," Hammer said. "And judging by the number of Pinkertons on that train, I don't expect the railroad men are gonna have too many security people left to take off after us anyhow."

"So, you're plannin' on headin' straight on back to Noyes?" Bull asked as he pulled his coat tighter around him to ward off the blast of frigid air coming from the north.

"That's right. We need to lay low for a couple of days, but I plan to come right back here within the week," Hammer replied.

"How come?"

"Think about it, son. We just destroyed the entire payroll for the railroad workers back there. They ain't gonna take kindly to being told there won't be no pay this week."

"So?"

Hammer sighed. Bull was dumber than a stump for sure. "Well, Bull, they're gonna have to send another train right away, just as soon as they can get those tracks fixed. I thought when they do, we might just set up another ambush, maybe a mite further back up the line, and see if this time we can get the money outta the safe without burning it up."

"But Boss, won't they be expectin' us to do that very thing?"

Hammer shook his head. "No, I 'spect they'll think we took off for parts unknown, especially if they follow the direction of our tracks and see we headed back across the border. But even if they do, where are they gonna get another carload of guards so fast?" he asked. "Pinkerton men don't exactly grow on trees around here."

"Maybe they'll just use railroad workers as guards," Bull offered.

"Yeah, you're probably right, Bull. But railroad workers ain't exactly experienced gunmen, now are they? Once we blow up that car and commence to shootin', my guess is they'll hightail it for the nearest cover, leaving the safe to us."

Bull nodded at this expression of wisdom from his boss. "So, I guess that means we're gonna be camping out tonight in this storm that's fixing to hit."

"That's right, since there's no way we can make it all the way back to Noyes today. Once we get far enough away from the tracks and back in these thick woods, we'll fix us a big fire and pitch our tents real close to it. This time of year the storm shouldn't last overly long."

"I hope you're right, Boss, 'cause I don't relish sitting through a real winter norther out in the open." Bull said, shivering in his coat.

Hammer grinned. "Just keep thinking of fifty thousand dollars, Bull," he said. "That ought'a warm you up better than a campfire."

As soon as the outlaws were out of sight, Smoke and his men came down off the hillock overlooking the railroad tracks and approached the wreckage site.

"Jesus!" Louis whispered at the number of bodies lying scattered on the ground.

They got down off their horses and began to move among the dead and wounded. Their horses snorted and shied at the smell of so much blood and at the sight of so many horses and men torn apart by the explosions.

When the group would find men still alive, the boys would try to make them comfortable, covering them with blankets against the cold and telling them help was on the way.

If the men weren't too badly injured, they would move them over closer to the pile of boards that was all that was left of the boxcar to get them out of the wind and elements, for Smoke had told them a storm was on the way and they needed to get the men under cover if at all possible.

The final tally was eighteen dead, six injured so badly it was doubtful if they would survive, and five with non-life-threatening wounds.

When they had done all they could to stop the bleeding and get the wounded covered, Smoke asked Cal to start a fire near where the men lay to give them some warmth and to get some coffee brewing. The more seriously wounded he gave small drinks of water and whiskey mixed together to help ease their pain.

While Cal and Pearlie gave the others coffee when it was ready, Smoke and Louis stood nearby, smoking cigars as they drank some coffee in tin mugs, cradling the mugs in their hands to keep them warm.

Louis glanced back over his shoulder at the bodies lying dead all around them. "I've seen a lot of bad men in my time out West, Smoke, but I don't know as I've ever seen anyone who could do this and just ride away as if nothing had happened," he said, a look of deep disgust on his face.

"I know what you mean, Louis," Smoke said, his expression grim as he sipped his coffee. It burned all the way down, and made his already upset stomach burn like it was on fire.

He took a deep breath, trying to get the stench of burnt flesh out of his throat, and turned to look at the dead bodies. "I want you all to remember this sight when we finally catch up with the men that did this, 'cause I do not intend to give them any quarter or mercy." He turned his eyes to Louis. "And if any of you have any reservations about what I'm going to do, you'd better head on back to the rail yard with Van Horne and the wounded men when he gets here."

Louis shook his head. "Don't worry about me, Smoke. Whatever you've got planned for the bastards that did this is too good for them." Louis's cultured face had turned grim and his eyes looked like those of a hawk, black and ferocious and unforgiving.

Smoke's lips curled in a savage grin of anticipation. "Just remember you said that, pal, when the blood starts to flow and the outlaws' bodies start to pile up."

Within an hour, Van Horne showed up with ten covered wagons and a doctor and nurse, along with ten hard-looking men, to take care of the dead and wounded.

As the doctor and nurse began to examine and care for the wounded, Van Horne and the other men moved among the dead bodies of the Pinkerton agents who'd been killed by the outlaws.

Two of the men helping put the bodies in a wagon stopped and bent over, vomiting on the cold ground in response to the carnage around them. Many of the dead were in pieces; body parts blown off by the force of the explosions that tore the train apart. Blood was everywhere, staining the mounds of snow scarlet, and the smell of burning flesh was making everyone edgy and nervous.

Van Horne, a man not unused to violence, stood looking around with tears in his eyes. "I cannot imagine the depth of evil of the men who did this," he muttered, shaking his head as the stack of bodies in the wagon grew higher.

He turned to Smoke and Louis, who stood next to him with Cal and Pearlie behind them. "The railroad will offer a ten-thousand-dollar bonus to you and your men if you capture or kill the bastards responsible for this outrage, Smoke," he said, his voice low and grim.

Smoke glanced at the others, who all shook their heads. "No, Bill, that's not necessary. My men and I will track the sons of bitches down for you and do whatever is necessary to bring them to justice without any thought of reward or payment," Smoke said, his voice equally serious.

"Yes, Bill," Louis agreed. "There are some things money cannot buy, and justice for the dead is one of them."

"Thank you, men," Van Horne said with feeling, shaking each of their hands in turn.

From over near where the wounded lay, the doctor raised his head and called, "Mr. Van Horne, one of the men wants to talk to you."

The group walked over and stood next to the man the doctor was kneeling next to.

It was Albert Knowles, the chief detective assigned to head the Pinkerton contingent on the train. His left leg was lying at a funny angle and there were cuts and smoke burns on his face and hands.

Van Horne squatted next to him. "Albert, how are you doing?" he asked gently, smoothing Knowles's hair back with his ham-sized hand.

Knowles grimaced as he tried to shift position. "I'm all right, Mr. Van Horne," he said, his eyes moving over to the wagon being filled with dead bodies. "At least, I'm in better shape than most of my men," he added in a strangled, hoarse voice full of remorse.

"Don't blame yourself for this, Al," Van Horne said. "There was nothing you could have done against an attack like this."

"No, Mr. Van Horne, I'm afraid I *am* to blame for this," Knowles said, his voice filled with self-disgust.

"How's that, Al?" Van Horne asked. "How can you possibly blame yourself for this atrocity?"

"I think I recognized the voice of the leader of the men who blew up the train," Knowles said, his eyes shifting around, unable to meet Van Horne's.

"Oh?"

"Yes, sir. While I was eating lunch at a saloon in town, a man approached me and told me he was an ex-marshal from down Fort Smith way. We got to talking and he asked a lot of questions about the security arrangements on the payroll trains." Knowles sighed. "I didn't think much about it, and he did it in such a way as not to arouse my suspicions, but I can see now he was pumping me for information on where my men would be stationed on the train to use against us."

"What was his name?" Van Horne asked grimly.

"He said his name was John Brody, but I doubt he was telling the truth," Knowles said. He went on to describe the man he'd talked to in detail, as only an experienced detective could.

Van Horne had started to shake his head when Smoke spoke up. "Bill, doesn't that sound a lot like that man who came up to us the other day while we were in town eating, who inquired about a security job?"

Van Horne snapped his fingers. "Damn, Smoke, I think you're right." He pursed his lips, thinking back to that day. "Now what was his name?" he said, almost to himself.

"He didn't give a name, as I recollect," Louis said. He glanced at Smoke. "But I think Smoke had him pegged from the get-go."

Smoke nodded. "That's right. He sure as hell didn't look like he'd spent much time using his hands for manual labor, and he wore his side arm like a man who knew how to use it, tied down low on his hip."

"Well, whatever the hell his name is and wherever he goes to try and hide, I want him brought down," Van Horne said. "One way or another!"

# **Chapter 17**

Hammer and his men rode hard for the rest of the day to put as much distance between them and the railroad as they could, until just before dusk they came to a large lake.

The edges of the lake were still rimmed with ice, with large patches out away from shore showing brilliant blue water where the ice was beginning to melt. About twenty yards from shore, the dead body of a large elk floated in an open hole in the ice where he'd evidently fallen through the ice pack.

"Looky there, Hammer," Bull said, pointing to the elk. "That sumbitch must weight over a thousand pounds."

"Yeah, an' that elk meat would taste mighty good if we cooked it over a fire," Sam Johnson, one of the gang members said, licking his lips at the thought.

Hammer glanced around. The place where they'd stopped had a good cover of trees growing by the edge of the lake, and was moderately well protected from the frigid north wind blowing across the lake toward them.

"That's a good idea, Sam," he said. "Why don't you

see if you and the boys can get a rope around his horns and drag him into shore. We'll make camp here and see about cooking up some hot food."

"It's 'bout time," Shorty Wallace observed as he sat shivering in his saddle, his coyote-fur coat pulled tight around his shoulders. "I'm 'bout frozen clear through."

Hammer grinned. "Good. Then a little work pulling that elk in will warm you up, Shorty," he said. "Go on, get to it so we can eat 'fore it gets dark."

"You think that ice will hold a hoss?" Shorty asked as he tried to figure out a way to get the elk to shore.

Hammer laughed. "Well, it sure as hell didn't hold that elk, did it, Shorty?"

"Yeah, an' if you fall in that water, you'll be frozen solid 'fore we can get you out," Bull added, shaking his head at the thought.


By the time Shorty and Sam and a couple of other gang members had managed to rope and drag the elk to shore using long ropes tied to their saddle horns, Bull had a roaring fire going in the center of the copse of trees they were camping in.

Coffee had been brewed in several pots, and the men were mixing it with generous dollops of whiskey and brandy to ward off the chill as the temperature continued to fall and large, wet flakes of snow began to drift downward from the dark clouds overhead.

The wind, instead of dying at dusk as it usually did, was freshening as the storm built to its full force and the snowfall intensified.

"Damn," a half-breed Indian named Spotted Dog said, rubbing his hands together in front of the fire. "I thought Minnesota was cold, but this land is even worse."

"Shit," Jerry Barnes said, edging closer to the fire

and turning his back to it to warm up his rear. "I thought Injuns don't feel the cold like us white men do."

Spotted Dog laughed. "That's right, Jerry, they don't. But I'm only half-Indian, and my white half is freezing its balls off."

"Well, why don't you squat over that there fire, Dog?" Sanchez asked, laughing. "That'll warm them *cojones* right up for you."

Shorty looked up from where he was working on the elk with a long-bladed skinning knife. "Damn, Hammer. This beast is near frozen solid. I can't hardly cut no steaks off'n it with this knife."

Hammer shook his head in disgust. "Dog, go on over there an' show Shorty how to skin an elk."

"Yeah, Dog," Jerry Barnes said. "It's just like scalpin' a man, only you got to cut deeper."

Spotted Dog glared at Barnes, who had only a fringe of hair around the side of his head, the top being completely bald. "There are times when I'm tempted to try scalping you, Jerry, but with the sparseness of your hair, I figure it would be a waste of time."

With that parting shot, which made the other men around the fire laugh, Spotted Dog stepped over to the elk and with expert flicks of his wrist, stripped the skin off and cut several large steaks off the back strap. "The trick to cutting meat, Shorty," Dog said as he held up the bloody steaks, "is to have a knife that's sharper than your thumb."

Soon, the charred meat was being cut up and passed out among the men, who were eating it with large plates of pinto beans and hard biscuits that had to be dunked in their coffee before they could be chewed.

As the men ate, they also drank a great deal of whiskey, trying to get warm. Before long, they were all in a festive, half-drunk mood, and were all talking about how they planned to spend the money they'd stolen from the train.

Smoke and Louis and Cal and Pearlie lay on their stomachs, peering through binoculars over a ridge at the outlaws' camp two hundred yards away. They'd laid their ground blankets down so the dampness of the ground wouldn't get their clothes wet, a sure way to freeze to death in this weather.

The snow was falling heavier now, and the brims of their hats and their shoulders were becoming covered with ice. Though the others were shivering from the cold, Smoke didn't even notice it, the fires of vengeance burning in his gut keeping him warm.

"I make it about thirty men, give or take a couple," Smoke said, speaking in a low voice even though he knew the snow and wind would muffle any sounds they made.

"Me too," Louis said, peering through his own set of binoculars.

"I wonder why they've made that fire so big," Pearlie whispered from his position next to Smoke. "It's like they ain't afraid of nobody seein' it."

"They probably think that since they killed most of the Pinkertons, there ain't nobody on their trail yet," Cal said, his voice quivering from the chattering of his teeth.

"You're right, Cal," Smoke said. "That and the storm that's come up to cover their tracks gives them a false sense of safety. They probably have no idea that the Chinaman who saw the robbery would have gotten us on their trail so fast."

Louis glanced at Smoke. "You planning on hitting them tonight?" he asked.

Smoke thought about it for a moment and then he

nodded, his eyes flashing in the reflected light from the campfire down the slope. "Yes, but not just yet. Let's pull back a mile or so and build us a fire. We'll eat and feed the horses and get warm and wait until just before dawn to attack. That way the sentries, if they bother to post them, will be tired enough that they won't be effective."

They followed him as he eased back off the ridge and got up on his mount. He walked the horse away from the outlaws' camp for a half hour and found a good spot for a camp, nestled in a thick grove of tall pines and maple trees in a small depression surrounded by heavy boulders that would hide the light from their campfire.

As he dismounted, he told Cal and Pearlie, "Gather up as many pinecones as you can carry. They'll light easy and burn hot to get the wet wood going for our fire."

While the boys were gathering pinecones and sticks of wood, Smoke set about making coffee and fixing a camp supper that would give them the energy they were going to need later on that night. Louis saw to the horses, getting them covered with blankets and setting out piles of grain for them to eat. Once the fire was going, he would melt some snow for them to drink.

After they'd eaten and filled their bellies with plenty of hot coffee, Smoke showed them how to gather tree limbs covered with pine needles and lay them in piles up against the trunks of some of the larger pine trees. They put their ground blankets down, crawled into their sleeping blankets near the fire, and pulled the tree limbs over them. The pine needles on the limbs kept both the snow and the cold away from them, and they slept snug as bugs in rugs.

At almost exactly three in the morning, Smoke came awake. Years of living in the High Lonesome had helped him develop an internal alarm clock that rarely failed to waken him whenever he wanted.

He crawled out from under his blankets and pine limbs to find almost two feet of snow had fallen. He threw some pinecones on the red-hot embers of the fire and prepared another large pot of coffee before waking the others.

By the time Louis and Cal and Pearlie were up and awake, he was sitting next to a roaring fire, sipping steaming hot coffee from his mug and planning his next move.

As Louis filled their mugs, he glanced over at Smoke. "All right, Smoke, what's our next move?"

Smoke spoke while staring at the fire. "There's too many of them to just go into their camp with our guns blazing. We could probably get most of them, but sure as hell they'd manage to get a couple of us before we finished them off."

"So, what should we do?" Pearlie asked. "Maybe we could surround them and shoot down into their camp from a distance," he offered.

Louis shook his head. "No, son, it's too dark for accurate fire, and even then, there's so many of them that they'd be able to mount an attack on us before we could get them all."

Smoke looked up at them, his eyes full of reflected flames from the campfire, his grin fierce. "You're right Louis, so here's what we're going to do, men . . . "

Cal and Pearlie and Louis squatted down on their haunches next to the fire and listened as Smoke outlined his plan of attack.


Squatty Lyons was leaning back against the bole of a ponderosa pine, his arms crossed over his chest and his chin tucked into the collar of his rawhide coat against the north wind. "Damn that Hammer for giving me the dog watch," he mumbled to himself, his teeth chattering against the cold. "You don't see him out here in the dead of night freezing near to death keeping watch when no one's within a hundred miles of us," he complained to the night air.

He glanced over at the long line of horses tied one after the other to a rope strung between two trees as he fumbled in his coat and tried to keep his hands from shaking while he built himself a cigarette. Hammer had told him it was his responsibility to keep watch on the horses during the night. "Huh, as if someone's gonna sneak up here in the middle of nowhere an' steal 'em," he growled, sticking the cigarette into the corner of his mouth and pulling out a lucifer to light it with.

Suddenly, he sat up straighter and reached for the new Winchester he had between his legs when he saw a shadow moving over near the horse string. "What the . . . " he began to say when he felt a sharp sting followed by the sensation of someone dragging ice across his throat.

He had time to turn his head and see a hulking figure behind him before the blood from his severed throat gushed into his mouth and choked him. His eyes opened wide as the Winchester fell from his hands and he toppled over onto his face in the snow at his feet.

"*Adios,* pond scum," Louis whispered to the dead man before he moved silently off looking for another sentry. Louis fought the nausea the killing had caused in his stomach. He was used to standing face-to-face with men he was up against, and the thought of sneaking up on a man and killing him from behind went against his grain. Of course, these dirty bastards deserved no mercy, he told himself, and he steeled his conscience for the next man he was going to kill.

Cal and Pearlie, watching from behind some nearby bushes, moved to the rope holding the horses when they saw the guard fall. A quick flick of Cal's knife at one end and of Pearlie's at the other, and the rope parted. Being careful not to spook the animals into whinnying, Pearlie and Cal took the ends of the rope and slowly led the horses away from the camp and deeper into the forest.

On the other side of the camp, Roy Woodson was walking in small circles and flapping his arms against his chest trying to keep warm as he kept watch over the packs and supplies that'd been stacked there earlier. He'd left his rifle sitting on the ground leaning up against one of the packs so he could put his hands in the pockets of his coat to keep them warm.

He turned rapidly, his heart beating fast as he heard a small splash from the edge of the nearby lake. He peered into the gloom at the ghostly whiteness of the ice and snow, wishing like hell the moon were out so he could see what had made the sound.

He whirled back around at the sound of a soft voice behind him. "Hey, did you forget this?" Smoke asked, holding the forgotten Winchester in his hands as he walked toward Roy.

Roy opened his mouth to shout for help, and Smoke swung the rifle as hard as he could. The front sight on the barrel tore through Roy's cheek, knocked three of his teeth out, and snapped his jaw to the side, dislocating it. Roy fell as if he'd been poleaxed, unconscious before he hit the ground.

Smoke crouched and waited to see if anyone had heard the sound of the sentry hitting the ground. When there was no response, he straightened up and moved over to the stack of supplies. He took two sticks of dynamite out of his coat pocket and placed them under the stack of packs and boxes and supplies the man had been guarding.

Striking a lucifer on his pants leg, he lit the two-minute fuse. As he moved toward the campfire in the middle of camp, he gave a low whistle that sounded remarkably like the call of a night hawk, the signal to the others they had two minutes to get clear of the explosion.

As he walked quickly by the embers of the campfire, he reached out and dumped the contents of a cardboard box into the coals, along with a burlap sack full of pinecones, and kept moving, making no sound at all. It was as if he were walking on cotton, he was so silent.

A sleepy voice from a pile of blankets near the fire mumbled, "Roy, is that you?"

Smoke grunted what might have been an answer, but he didn't slow down until he was fifty yards from the camp.

A low whistle from off to the side alerted him to the position Louis and Cal and Pearlie had staked out while waiting for him.

He moved to join them, and Cal handed him his Henry repeating rifle. The four men settled down behind the trunk of a large pine tree that had been felled by lightning, and aimed their rifles across its bark.

"Remember, fire only until your rifles are empty, and then hightail it out of here towards the horses," Smoke said, never taking his eyes off the campfire that was now burning brightly from the pinecones.

Twenty seconds later, the dynamite among the supplies exploded with a tremendous roar, shredding the outlaws' supplies and gear and extra ammunition and blowing it into the night sky in a huge fireball.

Shouts and screams of fear and pain rang out as men were literally blown out of their sleeping bags by the force of the explosion.

Dark figures could be seen outlined in the firelight as

they scrambled for their boots and weapons, shouting at each other, trying to figure out what had happened.

Suddenly, the boxful of ten gauge OO-buckshot shells Smoke had put into the fire began to explode, sending molten balls of lead in every direction, rending flesh and bone like a buzz saw as they ripped into the outlaws.

"Now," Smoke said quietly, and the four of them began to fire into the crowded camp as fast as they could pull their triggers and jack new shells into their firing chambers.

More screams of pain rang out as the outlaws dropped like flies from the onslaught of .44-caliber rifle bullets spraying into their midst. Dark figures could be seen crawling and scrambling on hands and knees trying to find cover from the withering rifle fire.

As Cal fired his last bullet, Pearlie grabbed him by the collar and jerked him to his feet. "Come on, Cal boy, 'less you want to be left behind!" he urged.

The four men jogged to their horses tied a dozen yards away, and swung up into their saddles just as answering fire from the camp began to whine over their heads and slap into nearby trees.

"Shag your mounts, boys," Smoke said as he leaned over his saddle horn and put the spurs to his horse. "It's about to get real exciting around here before too long!"

As they rode off into the night, they took the time to scatter the outlaws' horses ahead of them. Few if any of the animals would be able to be tracked down by the men they'd attacked.

Once they were out of rifle range, Smoke slowed his horse and stopped long enough to take out a handful of cigars and pass them around to the others. As they all lit up, he said simply, "A good night's work, men."

Louis nodded. "There's at least of few of those

treacherous bastards who won't be killing any more men again," he said.

"Amen to that, Louis," Smoke replied, drawing the smoke from his cigar into his lungs.

Cal coughed a couple of times getting his cigar lit, and then he looked back toward the outlaws' camp. "That'll teach you sorry sons of bitches," he muttered, remembering the dead men at the train wreck.

# Chapter 18

When he heard the sound of their attackers' horses riding off into the darkness, Hammer came out from behind the tree he'd hidden behind and surveyed the damage to their camp. Blood was running down his face from a wound on his forehead where a slug from a shotgun shell had creased his skin, and he had a hole in his trouser leg where a piece of wood from the dynamite explosion had torn through it, barely missing his thigh.

Four men lay dead near the campfire where the exploding shotgun shells had torn them apart. Two more had died in the explosion of the dynamite that had destroyed all of their supplies and extra ammunition, and Bull walked up telling him the two sentries were also dead.

"Eight men dead," Hammer said, talking to himself as he took stock. "That leaves us with twenty-one, twenty-two counting me."

"An' some of them are wounded," Bull said, glancing around the ruined camp, "though none so bad they can't ride."

One of his men, named Little Joe Calhoun, got up off the ground and dusted snow off his britches. "You think they'll be coming back soon, Boss?" he asked. His face was scorched black and he was limping from a flesh wound in his right leg, blood slowly oozing onto his boot.

Hammer thought about it for a few moments, then shook his head. "Not tonight, Little Joe. There must not be too many of them in the party or they would've finished what they started." He glanced around at his men, who were slowly coming out of hiding, some nursing superficial wounds, others miraculously untouched. "This has more the feel of a lightning raid to me." He clamped his jaws shut tight when he realized his voice was shaking from the fear and terror he'd felt during the onslaught earlier.

Shorty Wallace came running into the camp. "They've scattered the hosses, Boss. It'll take hours to try and round 'em up."

Hammer sniffed at the acrid smell coming from Shorty, and realized the man had shit his pants. He turned away to get away from the smell and considered his options, which weren't very many as he figured it.

"No, we're not gonna try for the horses, men."

"But what're we gonna do then, Boss?" Bull asked. "Just sit around here and wait for them to hit us again?"

"No," Hammer replied, looking off to the south. "We're gonna start walking as fast as we can toward the border."

"Walking?" Spotted Dog asked. "But Hammer," he argued, "the snow's almost two feet deep."

"That's all right," Hammer replied. "I figure it's less than ten miles to the border and only another five to Noyes. We've got at least another three or four hours until daylight, and on foot we won't leave much of a trail if we're careful. We should be across the border just after sunup if we make tracks now and don't hang around here jawin' about it all night."

"What good's being across the border gonna do, Boss?" Bull asked.

"If the men who're after us are Canadian lawmen, they won't be able to cross the border to come after us, at least not legally, an' if we can get to Noyes, the sheriff there will swear we were there during the time of the train robbery, so we'll be safe."

"I don't relish walkin' no ten miles in these boots," Juan Sanchez said.

Hammer shrugged as he bent to pick up a Winchester rifle he'd stolen from one of the dead Pinkerton men. "Then sit here on your ass, Juan, and you can give our regards to those bastards when they come back here to finish the job they started."

Juan gave a lopsided grin. "Well, when you put it that way, I guess walking ain't so bad after all."

"Leave everything behind except your weapons and let's make tracks," Hammer said.

Bull gave a sarcastic laugh. "Hell, there ain't nothin' left 'ceptin' our saddles, an' we sure as hell don't need those." He rubbed his hands together and added, "One good thing, walking ten miles in this weather is gonna keep us warm at any rate."

"Now, follow me, men," Hammer said, glancing at the sky, from which snow continued to fall. "And walk in single file so the snow will cover our tracks. That should give us a few more hours while the men who attacked us try and figure out which way we went."

His men picked up their weapons and strung out in a line behind Hammer as he began walking rapidly to the south, cursing under his breath the bastards that'd killed his men and messed up his plans for a leisurely ride to Noyes.

As he walked, he silently gave thanks that he'd kept

the bag full of money in his blankets with him instead of packing it with the other supplies, or it'd be ashes by now.

Back at their camp, Smoke and his men sat near the fire, warming up after their raid. Cal had made more coffee, and they were drinking it and eating the last of the food they'd fixed the night before. Louis passed around a small bottle of brandy he had in his saddle-bags.

"Here you go, boys, add a little of this to the coffee. It'll warm your insides a bit."

"What are we gonna do now, Smoke?" Pearlie asked as he poured a tablespoon of brandy into his coffee. "Go back and hit 'em again?"

"No," Smoke said, a thoughtful look in his eyes as he recalled the number of Winchesters he'd seen stacked around the fire when he ran through the enemies' camp. "They're pretty well armed, and even counting the men we killed, they've still got us outnumbered over five to one."

"Yes, and without any food or supplies left, they are going to be getting awfully hungry before too long, especially in this cold weather," Louis said.

"We scattered their mounts pretty good," Cal said, "so they won't be going nowhere until they can manage to gather 'em back up."

Smoke grinned. "Which we don't intend to let them do, Cal. We'll keep them on foot and let them get good and hungry before we go after them again. By tomorrow afternoon, I think they'll be softened up enough for us to take another shot at them."

He dumped his coffee out into the fire. "I don't think they'll venture out into the darkness for the rest of the night, not knowing how close we are, so let's get a few hours sleep so we'll be fresh and ready for them tomorrow morning."

Smoke woke up just after sunup, and stoked the coals from the campfire into a fire large enough to cook them some breakfast. The storm had abated, and there were only isolated snowflakes falling gently on a soft breeze.

As they filled up on fatback and beans and biscuits made fresh by Pearlie, they discussed their plan of attack against the outlaws.

"First, we'll find out what the bastards are up to," Smoke said as he chewed the crunchy bacon he'd put between two halves of a biscuit. "I suspect they'll be scattered out trying to run down their horses. If that's the case, we should be able to take out a few more of them from a distance without too much trouble."

"What if they're still bunched up in their camp?" Cal asked.

"Then we'll surround them and use our long guns to pick them off one at a time until they decide to surrender," Louis said.

"That's right, Louis," Smoke agreed. "We should be all right if they try to mount a counterattack since we'll have our horses and they'll still be on foot. But one way or another, they're going to be in our custody by this afternoon, or they're going to be dead."

When they were finished with breakfast, Cal and Pearlie struck the camp while Smoke and Louis got extra ammunition off the packhorses and made sure all of the rifles and pistols were fully loaded.

Once they were ready, Smoke took the lead and they moved out toward the outlaws' camp, keeping a close watch to make sure they didn't come up on any of them unexpectedly.

As they breasted the rise where they'd observed the enemy camp the night before, Smoke and Louis took out their binoculars and took a long look at the deserted camp below.

"That's strange," Louis said as he swept the area with his binoculars. "I don't see any sign of life in the camp."

"You're right, Louis," Smoke said. "I see several bodies lying where they fell, but there's no sign of other men in the area."

Pearlie shook his head, a disgusted look on his face. "They didn't even bother to bury their dead," he said angrily.

"I guess they figure coyotes and wolves need to eat same as worms," Louis said dryly.

"You think they might be out lookin' for their mounts?" Cal asked.

Smoke shook his head. "No, I don't think so, Cal. We would've seen them on our way here if that were the case, since we scattered the horses toward our camp."

"Maybe they're hiding in the woods nearby," Pearlie offered. "Just waiting for us to show ourselves so they can ambush us."

Smoke nodded. "That's possible." He sat up in his saddle and looked all around the camp through his glasses, but could see no sign of the outlaws.

"I guess we'll have to split up and check out the area on all sides of the camp, but I want you to go slow and be very careful. If you see any sign of them, fire off a shot and the rest of us will come running," Smoke said.

The four men each took off in separate directions, walking their horses slowly with their guns in their hands, ready in case of an ambush.

Two hours later, they met up at the outlaws' camp, having seen no sign of the outlaws.

Smoke got down off his horse and walked slowly around the perimeter of the camp, bending over and staring at the ground as he walked.

After a while, he straightened up and looked off to the south. "Look here," he said, squatting and pointing at the fresh layer of snow.

"I don't see anything," Louis said as he peered over Smoke's shoulder.

"This snow is an inch or so shallower than the surrounding snow is," Smoke said. He stood back up. "And the depression seems to run toward the south."

"What's that mean, Smoke?" Pearlie asked, staring in the same direction as Smoke.

"I think the outlaws took off walking to the south, and they walked in single file hoping the snow would cover their tracks," he answered. "But the depression their feet caused in the snow caused the new snow to be several inches shallower than the surrounding snowfall."

"How long ago?" Louis asked.

"From the depth of the snow, I'd say they've got five or six hours on us at least," Smoke said.

"Why would they head south?" Cal asked. "There ain't nothing that way for miles and miles."

Smoke glanced at him, his eyes thoughtful. "Nothing except the Canadian border," he said.

"Well, they can't have gone far on foot," Pearlie said, grinning.

Louis shook his head as he made a mental calculation. "The average man can walk at two to four miles an hour, Pearlie. That means if they've been going steady for five or six hours, they could have made ten to fifteen miles . . . farther if they're hurrying."

"It'd be hard to keep up that pace in this weather and with no food or warm drinks," Smoke said. "But you're right, Louis, they could be pretty close to the border by now."

"What difference does that make to us?" Cal asked.

Smoke grinned. "None, Cal. They're probably figuring we're Canadian authorities and won't be able to cross the border after them, and that's where they've made a big mistake, one that's going to cost them either their freedom or their lives, depending on how stupid they are."

He turned toward his horse. "Now, let's mount up and see just how far they've gotten."

"I hope they get frostbite on their feet," Cal said. "It'd serve 'em right."

Smoke grinned. "Frostbite's the least of their worries, Cal. I'm planning on giving them some lead poisoning to worry about."

# Chapter 19

Hammer and his men had made better time than they'd figured, both the cold weather and fear spurring them on to push themselves as hard as possible. They stopped only once, to build a small fire and fix a couple of pots of hot coffee to drink to help ward off the cold. Hammer wouldn't let them stop long enough to cook any food, and he didn't even let them rest to enjoy the coffee, but made them put it in canteens to drink as they walked.

They passed the Canadian border an hour or so after dawn, and were within a mile of the outskirts of the town of Noyes when they heard hoofbeats coming up fast behind them.

Hammer looked over his shoulder and saw four men on horseback bearing down on them in the distance, rifles in their hands.

He glanced around, and saw a line of boulders over near a small draw containing a tiny stream of water off to their right.

"Spread out, men," he called, jacking a shell into the

firing chamber of his Winchester. "Take cover in that draw over there."

As the men dove over the banks of the stream and lined up with their rifles pointing toward the approaching men, bullets began to pock the dirt and snow around them as the horsemen fired on them.

Hammer and his men began to return fire, causing two of the men chasing them to rein in, jump down off their mounts, and take cover behind some boulders in the open spaces near them. The other two split up, going in opposite directions as they rode in a flanking maneuver to either side of the outlaws.

"Shit!" Hammer exclaimed, knowing that soon they'd be taking fire from behind as well as in front. Without horses of their own, they were trapped like rats in a barn full of cats.

"Bull," he shouted, "take half the men and get them on the opposite side of the stream. They're coming around behind us!"

Bull spat out a curse word and shouted at some of the men to join him on the opposite bank of the stream.

The two men in front of the outlaws lay on their stomachs, firing over the rocks and not giving the gang a suitable target to shoot at as they rained shell after shell on the trapped men.

Hammer fired a couple of quick shots, but knew there was almost no chance of hitting their attackers since all he could see was the tops of their heads.

"Maybe we should rush them," Jerry Barnes yelled from his place down the line to Hammer's right.

Hammer shook his head. He's as dumb as Bull, he thought. "You go right ahead, Jerry," he called back, "and I'll be right behind you."

Jerry stared at him for a moment, and then he turned back to the front and continued shooting, wasting valuable ammunition without even coming close to the men firing at them. He did manage to hit the rocks a time or two, but the slugs ricocheted harmlessly off to the side.


Smoke and Louis, after leaving Cal and Pearlie to attack from the front, made their way around the outlaws' position to either side, staying just out of rifle range, riding bent low over their saddle horns.

Twenty minutes later, they were behind the gang, and took positions on the ground in a small depression as they aimed and fired into the draw.

Two of the outlaws screamed and collapsed under their fire as Smoke and Louis began to find the range, the dead outlaws rolling down the sides of the draw and out of sight.

"I wonder how many we'll have to kill before they decide it's time to give up," Louis said, a fierce grin on his face as he levered the rifle and fired as fast as he could.

"It wouldn't bother me if they never gave up and we killed all of the pond scum," Smoke said. "That'd save us the trouble of having to take them back to Winnipeg to stand trial before they're hung."

Smoke was about to fire again when he heard a shot from behind him and Louis, and he turned to see five men riding out toward them from the town off in the distance. All of the men were holding rifles and they were aimed straight at Smoke and Louis.

"Put down your weapons," the man in the lead shouted as he peered down the barrel of his Winchester.

Smoke got to his feet and ran crouched over toward the horsemen, noticing the man who'd shouted had a tin star on his chest.

As Smoke got closer to him, the man lowered the barrel of his rifle until it pointed at Smoke's chest. Smoke lowered his rifle and held his hands out in plain sight away from his sides, but he didn't put the rifle down.

"What the hell's going on here?" the sheriff asked, scowling down at Smoke.

"I'm Smoke Jensen," Smoke said. "And my friends and I have tracked those men all the way from Canada. They held up a train there and killed almost twenty Pinkerton agents."

The sheriff's eyes narrowed as he stared over Smoke's shoulders at the men in the draw, who'd quit firing at his arrival. "You got some papers saying you're a lawman, or a warrant or wanted sheet on those men?" he asked finally, after thinking it over for a couple of minutes.

"I'm not a lawman," Smoke said. "I was hired by the railroad to bring these men in."

"Well, we'll see about that," the sheriff said. "I'm Sheriff Luke McCain, and Noyes there is my town," he said, pointing over his shoulder at the town nearby.

"Tell your friends to cease firing and to throw down their weapons, Mr. Jensen."

Smoke looked back over his shoulder at the outlaws. "What about them?" he asked in frustration. "If we throw down our guns, what's to keep them from rushing us?"

"I'll take care of them, you just do what I say!" McCain ordered, raising the barrel of his rifle until it pointed at Smoke's head.

Smoke turned and yelled, "Cal, Pearlie, Louis, stop firing and put down your weapons. This is the sheriff."

McCain, once he'd seen Smoke's men comply, said, "Keep an eye on this one, boys. I'm gonna ride up there and take those men in the draw into custody."

"You be careful, now, Sheriff," one of his deputies warned. "They're liable to blow you outta the saddle if you ride straight on in there."

"Not likely," McCain said. "Not with all of us out here on horseback and them on foot."

He spurred his horse forward until he got to the draw where the outlaws were still lying in cover.

Hammer grinned. "Luke, it's good to see you."

"Keep your mouth shut and do what I say," McCain said in a low voice so no one else could hear. "And maybe we'll all get out of this alive. You and your men put your guns down and pretend you don't know me. I'm going to have to arrest you and take you to jail."

"What?" Hammer asked, gripping his rifle tighter as his face turned red. "Why don't you just shoot hell outta those hombres and let us go on our way?"

McCain shook his head. "Don't be a damned fool, Hammer. There're too many witnesses around. Those deputies of mine aren't in on this with us. Just do what I say and don't worry. I've got the judge in my pocket, but we have to play this out like it's real."

Hammer's lips curled into a smile. "You wouldn't be trying to fool me, would you, Luke?" he asked.

"Not a chance, Hammer. You got too much on me for me to try that. Now do what I say and everything will be all right, as long as you and your men keep your heads."

"All right, Luke, but if you try to double-cross me, you'll live to regret it."

Luke's eyes got hard. "Hey, pal, if you want I can just leave you and your men here and let those fellas behind me pick you off one by one . . . how would that be? Then I wouldn't have to put my ass on the line trying to save yours."

Hammer glanced over Luke's shoulder at Smoke and Louis, standing near Luke's deputies a hundred yards away, and he shook his head. "No, all in all, I think I'd rather go with you and your men."

"Then shut the hell up and put your weapons down

and climb outta that draw," Luke ordered, turning his back on Hammer and walking his mount away.

Hammer turned to his men and gave the order to drop their guns and come with him. "And," he added, scowling, "keep your mouths shut and let me do all the talking or we'll end up swinging from a rope!"

"But Boss," Bull argued, "he said he was gonna put us in jail."

"Bull," Hammer said, his voice harsh, "you say one more word and you won't go to jail, 'cause I'll kill you where you stand!"

An hour and a half later, with all of Hammer's men crowded into the small jail cells in Noyes, Sheriff Luke McCain had a meeting with Smoke and his men and Hammer in his office.

Luke sat canted back in his swivel chair behind his desk, while Hammer and Smoke sat in straight-backed chairs in front of the desk. Louis and Cal and Pearlie stood nearby, with two of Luke's deputies keeping watch on them. All of their guns had been confiscated on Luke's orders—until he could get the stories straight, he'd said.

"Now, Mr. Jensen," he began, "tell me your side of the story."

Smoke glanced at Hammer, and if looks could kill, Hammer would have fallen over dead. "This bastard and his men robbed a payroll train near Winnipeg, Canada, yesterday. In so doing, they killed or severely injured over twenty-five Pinkerton agents who'd been hired as security on the train. My men and I were hired by William Cornelius Van Horne to track them down and bring them to justice."

Luke nodded, and then he turned his attention to

Hammer. "Mr. Hammerick, what have you got to say for yourself?"

Hammer shook his head, trying his best to look innocent. "Me and my men don't know nothing 'bout no train robbery. We were up in Canada mining for gold, and once we'd cashed out our ore, we were on the way back here when this man and his friends ambushed us. They killed eight of my friends in Canada last night and ran off all our horses." He shrugged. "So, we began walking as fast as we could trying to get back here to Minnesota, where we hoped to find some lawman to protect us from these killers." He paused and stared at Smoke. "And then they attacked us again right outside your town and killed two more of my men while we were trying to hide from them." He looked back at McCain. "Personally, I think you should arrest Jensen and his men for murder, instead of bothering us innocent miners who ain't done nothing wrong."

Smoke snorted. He glanced over at a canvas bag sitting on a nearby desk. "What about that money you found on them?" Smoke asked the sheriff.

Luke looked at Hammer, his eyebrows raised. "Yes, what about the money, Mr. Hammerick?"

Hammer grinned insolently. "I told you, we sold our ore and that's the money we got for it. It's my guess these men found out about it and were trying to rob us of it when we managed to sneak off in the middle of the night and escape from them."

"I'm told there's fifty thousand dollars in that sack, and all of it in new bills," Smoke said, this time addressing Hammer. "Are you trying to get us to believe you were paid in brand-new currency for your gold?"

Hammer shrugged again. "That's what the assayer's office gave us. I don't know anything about where he got it from or if it's new bills or old. All me and my men cared about was getting paid for our ore and heading back down south to get away from the cold up there."

Smoke got to his feet, went over to the bag, and pulled out several stacks of bills. "And these burn marks on some of the bills," he said, "how do you explain that?"

Hammer's eyes narrowed. "That happened when you and your men blew up my camp with dynamite. We were lucky to save the money from the fire you started." He looked over at McCain. "You can backtrack us to our camp, Sheriff, and you'll see I'm telling the truth. There's plenty of evidence of the dynamite explosion there, along with eight dead men these men killed last night."

Smoke shook his head and went back to his seat. "He's lying through his teeth, Sheriff. If you'll wire Winnipeg, you can get the straight story from Mr. Van Horne," Smoke said, glaring at Hammer.

Hammer leaned forward, speaking earnestly to McCain. "What will that prove, Sheriff?" he asked. "I don't know, but maybe these men here were hired to find the train robbers, and maybe they made an honest mistake and attacked my men and me thinking we were the ones." He smiled slyly. "But why don't you ask Mr. Jensen here if he or his men actually saw us rob this train or if he's just guessing about who did it."

"What about that, Mr. Jensen?" Luke asked. "Did you see this man or any of his companions rob the train?"

Smoke shook his head. "No, sir, we didn't," he said through tight lips.

"There, you see, Sheriff? He has no proof that me and my men were even involved in a train robbery."

"Oh, I wouldn't say that, Mr. Hammerick," Smoke said, smiling. "There was a witness. A man you wounded but left alive who will testify that he knows you and recognized you at the robbery site."

"There couldn't be!" Hammer exclaimed. "We wore . . . " he began, and then he stopped himself and clamped his mouth shut before he could implicate himself anymore.

Smoke laughed at the man's gaff. "You were about to say you wore masks, weren't you, Hammerick?" he asked.

Hammer shut his lips tight, his face flaming red.

"Well, the fact is you did wear masks," Smoke said, "but the lead Pinkerton detective, Albert Knowles, recognized your voice and your clothes from a conversation you had with him the day before the robbery, and he's willing to testify to that in court."

Luke sighed and shook his head at Hammer. "Well, that changes things, Mr. Hammerick. I find Mr. Jensen's story to have enough substance to hold you and your men here until I can check out the facts for myself."

"How about you just put them in our custody and let us take them back to Winnipeg to stand trial?" Smoke asked.

"I can't do that, Mr. Jensen," Luke said. "First, I'll have to wire this Van Horne fellow, and then, if he backs your story, we'll have to go before Judge Harlan Fitzpatrick here in Noyes to see if Mr. Hammerick and his men will be tried here or in Canada."

"But that could take days," Smoke argued. "And my men and I have to be back in Winnipeg as soon as possible."

Luke shrugged. "You're welcome to leave, Mr. Jensen, and if the judge says they can be sent back to Canada to stand trial, I'm sure the Canadian government can send some lawmen down here to collect them."

Smoke looked over his shoulder at Louis, who just shrugged. "It won't hurt to give them a couple of days," Louis said. "I know I can use the rest."

"All right," Smoke agreed. "We'll get some rooms in a

hotel and wait for you to contact Mr. Van Horne, and then we'll see what happens."

As he got to his feet, Smoke saw Hammer smirking at McCain. "Don't get your hopes up, killer," Smoke said. "I promised Van Horne I'd see you dead or in jail, and if truth be told, I'd just as soon it be dead." He paused and stared into the sheriff's eyes. "And that goes for anyone who stands in my way too."

"Are you threatening me, Mr. Jensen?" McCain asked with some heat.

"No, sir, not if you're just doing your job. But something smells funny here, and it's not just these men."

# Chapter 20

Smoke and his friends left the sheriff's office and took their horses to the livery stable, where they arranged for them to be fed and curried and taken care of for a few days.

As they left the livery, Louis had a thoughtful expression on his face, and Smoke noticed him glancing toward the sheriff's office as they walked down the street toward the town's only hotel.

"What's on your mind, Louis?" Smoke asked.

"I was just thinking how strange our conversation with the sheriff was," he answered. "He seemed to be leaning over backwards to take Hammerick's side in all this."

Smoke realized Louis had the same doubts he did. Both of their instincts were trying to tell them something, and Smoke had found over the years that he should trust his instincts.

Sheriff McCain had acted a little strange in their meeting, but in the beginning Smoke had just put it down to the fact that they were all strangers to the sheriff, nothing more. Now that he found Louis had the same suspicions, he wasn't so sure that was all it was.

"You may be right, Louis, but I guess we'll just have to wait and see what the judge says after they contact Bill and he verifies our story."

"When you men get through taking about how strange the sheriff was, do you think we could find someplace to eat?" Pearlie asked. "My stomach's done shrunk up to the size of a walnut, it's been so long since it's been fed."

Smoke laughed. "Sure, Pearlie. We wouldn't want you fainting from hunger out here in the middle of Main Street, now would we?"

Pearlie lifted his feet from the muck and mud in the middle of the street. "Hell, Smoke, if'n I did faint, I'd probably drown in this here mud."

They stopped at a small restaurant with MA'S DINER over the door, and went in to take a table in the corner so Smoke could watch the door, as was his habit.

"Three things I've learned over my many years out West," Louis said after they'd given their orders to a rather rotund woman wearing a gravy-stained apron who had a dusting of flour in her hair and on her cheeks.

"What's that, Louis?" Cal asked, eager to glean some knowledge from a man as well traveled and as cultured as Louis Longmont was.

Louis held up his hand and raised one finger at a time as he spoke his words of wisdom: "One, never get in a shooting match with Smoke Jensen; two, never play cards with a man who uses the name of a city as his first name; and three, never eat in a place called Ma's."

Smoke and Cal and Pearlie laughed, enjoying the first peace and quiet they'd had since they set off on the trail of the train robbers. Cal stretched his neck and let his shoulders relax, enjoying the feeling of not having to worry about some outlaw drawing a bead between his shoulder blades.

After their meal, which even Louis had to admit was quite good, though he put it down to the fact they were all about half-starved to death, they walked down the street to a small, two-story hotel named WINSTON'S.

Smoke took three rooms on the second floor facing the street, another precaution he'd learned over the years. The second floor made it harder for someone to sneak up on them or fire through an open window, and the windows facing the street let him monitor what was going on in town without exposing him to gunfire from an adversary.

Over at the jail, McCain held up his hand when Hammer argued about having to spend the night locked up with his men. "Now, hold on, Hammer," Luke said. "First off, I don't want Jensen getting suspicious about us having an arrangement. I don't want him trying to telegraph any U.S. marshals until after we've seen the judge and gotten things fixed up."

Hammer sullenly agreed McCain was probably right, though he did insist on the sheriff leaving the cell door unlocked and their guns out where they could get to them if Jensen or his men tried anything during the night.

McCain told him not to worry about that, and that he was going to have a deputy keep watch on Jensen's hotel rooms through the night.

"Now, I'm gonna take five thousand dollars of your money and pay a little visit to Judge Fitzpatrick over at the courthouse," Luke said.

"Five thousand dollars?" Hammer blurted out. "Hell,

back where I come from, you could buy an entire town for that much money."

Luke shook his head, disgust on his face. "Listen, Hammer. You and your men did kill over twenty Pinkerton agents in cold blood. That's a lot for a judge to overlook, even one whose nose is always in a bottle. He and I are both gonna catch a lot of heat on this when you and your men end up walking out of here free and clear. I'm sure he won't think it's too much money when the federal marshals and the circuit court judge ream his ass out for finding for you in the upcoming trial, so pay him the money and keep your mouth shut!"

"You haven't said what your share is gonna be yet," Hammer said warily, his eyes narrowed and suspicious.

McCain smiled. "I think five will do me nicely, and at that you're getting a bargain."

"But that only leaves me and my men a little over two thousand dollars each, and we did all the work," Hammer argued from his jail cell.

"Yeah, well, I could always let Jensen and his men have another go at you," McCain said. "If he managed to kill most of your men, your share would be even bigger, Hammer. Is that what you want?"

Hammer looked down at his feet and shook his head.

"And don't forget, it was you and your men who killed a lot of Pinkertons and then managed to let yourselves be followed to my town," Luke said, his voice hard. "Just be glad you'll be walking out of here and able to rob another train rather than taking a short trip on a rope followed by a long dirt nap."

"All right, all right," Hammer said, tired of arguing with the sheriff. After all, he reasoned to himself, there was time enough after Jensen and his men had been taken care of to see about making a better deal. Hell, they'd killed over twenty men to get that money. Another couple, like a judge and a sheriff, wouldn't be too hard.

The next morning, after McCain had visited Judge Fitzpatrick at his home the previous night and given him more money than he could make in two years on the bench, the sheriff summoned Smoke and his friends from the hotel. He walked with them over to the county courthouse, and ushered them into Judge Harlan Fitzpatrick's courtroom at precisely nine o'clock in the morning.

Of the outlaws, only Hammerick was present in the courtroom when they entered. He was being watched over by one of the deputies from the day before.

After a moment, the judge entered from his chambers and proceeded to take his seat behind a high desk in the front of the room.

A bailiff advised everyone to rise and said the county court was now in order.

After everyone took their seats again, Louis leaned over and whispered into Smoke's ear. "Look at the judge's red nose and take a whiff. I can smell the whiskey on his breath all the way back here."

Smoke nodded and whispered back, "It sure looks like he drank his breakfast, that's for sure."

The judge cleared his throat, and then he went into a coughing fit that turned his face red and made the veins on the side of his neck bulge out. For a moment, Smoke was afraid he was going to go into a fit of apoplexy right in front of them and die before he could hear the case.

"This court will come to order," Fitzpatrick said in a

gravelly voice once he'd gotten control of his breath. He dropped his eyes to a sheet of paper in front of him and studied it.

After a moment, he looked up over the half-glasses perched on the end of his bulbous, vein-lined nose. "The sheriff has provided me with a telegram from a Mr. William Cornelius Van Horne, who is in charge of the Canadian Pacific Railroad. This telegram does say there was a train robbery in which many Pinkerton agents were killed and that you"—he cut his eyes to Smoke— "Mr. Jensen, and your companions were hired to apprehend the perpetrators of said robbery."

Smoke turned his head and looked into Hammerick's eyes, as if to say, "Got you."

"However," the judge went on in his deep voice, "the telegram does not state the name of any of the robbers, and the description given of the leader of said band of thieves could fit most any man here."

"Your Honor," Smoke said, standing up and addressing the judge.

"Yes, Mr. Jensen? You have a statement you'd like to make to the court?"

"Yes, sir," Smoke answered. "Mr. Van Horne's message doesn't give a name because until we caught up with the robbers we did not know any of their names. However, there is a Pinkerton agent who can make a full identification of Mr. Hammerick here as the leader of the outlaws."

Judge Fitzpatrick cleared his throat again and made a show of looking out at the courtroom over his spectacles. "And is this witness here in the court ready to make such an identification?" he asked. "If he is, let him come forward and be heard."

"No, Your Honor," Smoke said. "The Pinkerton agent, a Mr. Albert Knowles, was rather severely injured in the attack on the train, and will not be able to travel for several weeks at least."

The judge pursed his lips and pretended to contemplate this turn of events. After a few moments, he spoke. "And you yourself and your companions were not witnesses to this alleged train robbery, and therefore cannot say with absolute certainty that Mr. Hammerick and his associates were the men who committed this dastardly crime?"

Smoke hesitated. This was not going well at all. Finally, he answered, "No, Your Honor, but—"

The judge banged his gavel on his desk, cutting Smoke off before he could explain. "Well, then." The judge shook his head sadly, as if he were performing an arduous task against his will. "In that case, I see no alternative but to postpone this hearing until such time as this Mr. Knowles can be brought down here to make his identification." The judge paused, and then he added, "I will reset the preliminary hearing for one month from today, at which time the circuit court judge and any necessary federal marshals can be present for the hearing."

"But Your Honor—" Smoke again began.

The judge banged his gavel again. "The court has ruled," he said quickly, staring at Smoke intently. Suddenly, the judge's face paled and his eyes changed, as if seeing Smoke for the first time. He shook his head, got ponderously to his feet, and gathered his robes around him and disappeared through the door to his chambers with as much dignity as a man half-inebriated could manage.

The sheriff looked over at Smoke and shrugged his shoulders as he got to his feet and approached him. "I'm sorry about that, Jensen," he said. "I'll try to keep Hammerick and his men locked up until you can get your witness here, but I don't know if the judge will allow it. He may release them on bail until the time of the trial."

Smoke just shook his head, his eyes boring into McCain's. "Well, we can't wait around here for a month, so I guess we'll head on back to Canada and see what we can do about getting Mr. Knowles back here in time for the trial."

"I think that would be best, Jensen," Luke said. "And I'll make sure that Hammerick and his men aren't released until you've left town, just so there won't be any . . . uh, altercations or disagreements."

"But you will make sure they stay here in town until we get back, won't you, Sheriff?" Louis asked suspiciously.

"Oh, I'm sure Judge Fitzpatrick will set bail high enough to insure they show up for the trial," Luke said, smiling a completely insincere smile.

"I hope so, Sheriff," Smoke said, his voice hard, "because as soon as we get back to Winnipeg, I'm going to make sure the governor of Minnesota as well as the U.S. marshals' office is notified of what happened here today."

"That's certainly your right, Mr. Jensen," the sheriff said, though there was an element of uncertainty and fear lurking behind his eyes at Smoke's threat.

"And we'll also make sure the Pinkertons know where to find the men who killed so many of their agents," Louis added, staring at the sheriff. "And I'll tell you one thing, Sheriff McCain, I sure as hell wouldn't want to have the entire Pinkerton organization mad at me. Those boys are known to play rough, if you get my meaning."

McCain looked nervously over his shoulder at Hammerick, and then he nodded his head. "I certainly do get your meaning, Mr. Longmont, and I'll be sure to pass it along to the judge just as soon as I can."

"Be sure that you do, Sheriff," Louis said. He turned abruptly, and he and Smoke and the boys started to walk out of the courtroom. Then Louis stopped and turned. "Because if something happens and those men aren't here to stand trial next month, I wouldn't give even odds on a bet that you or the judge live to see the summer."

As McCain started to protest this attitude, Louis smiled and held up his hand. "No threat, Sheriff, just stating the plain facts."

As they saddled up their horses at the livery, Smoke said, "The more I see of this town, the more I can't wait to leave it."

Louis looked at him over his saddle. "You think the sheriff and judge are in cahoots with the outlaws?" he asked.

"I wouldn't go that far yet," Smoke answered. "But then again, I wouldn't be too surprised to find out that was the case either."

# Chapter 21

After Smoke and his men left their hotel and went to the livery to get their horses, Sheriff McCain followed them at a distance to make sure they left town, and to make sure they didn't stop at the telegraph office to send any telegrams to the U.S. marshals' office.

Once he was sure they were on their way, he stopped back by the jail and picked up Hammer, and they headed for the judge's chambers to thank him for what he'd done in court.

When they entered, they found Judge Fitzpatrick leaning back in his chair, sipping from a glass of amber liquid, an almost empty bottle of bourbon on the desk in front of him. The judge's eyes were unfocused, and his thoughts seemed to be a thousand miles away.

In spite of the fact that the judge was clearly well on the way to being drunk, he had a worried look on his face, and a small sheen of sweat covered his brow in spite of the coolness of the room.

"Hey, Judge," Luke called as they took seats in front of his desk. "Why the frown? Everything went just as we'd planned it, and Jensen and his men have already left town."

Fitzpatrick turned bloodshot, bleary eyes on the two men sitting in front of him. He gave a sad, half grin and sighed heavily. "Dear Luke, you have no idea what you've done, do you, dear boy," he asked grimly.

"What do you mean, Judge?" Luke asked, plainly nonplussed by the judge's attitude. He'd thought everything went extremely well in the courtroom and that by the time Jensen and his friends returned from Canada, it would all be over.

Fitzpatrick leaned forward and slowly refilled his glass from the bottle on his desk. Then he sat staring at the liquor as he slowly swirled it around in the glass. Finally, he looked up, and Luke had the irrational thought that the judge was about to cry, so mournful was his expression.

"Why didn't you tell me one of the men we were going up against was Smoke Jensen?" he asked.

Luke shrugged. "I didn't think it mattered who it was as long as you made sure the letter of the law was on our side," he replied. And then, after a moment when the judge didn't say anything, he added, "And I did tell you one of the men's names was Jensen, don't you remember?"

The judge nodded slowly. "Yes, but you didn't say his first name was Smoke," he said in a voice so low McCain could barely hear him.

McCain asked, "What does that matter, and just who is this Smoke Jensen anyway that he's got you so spooked?"

The judge grinned again, but there was no mirth in his smile. McCain thought it had the appearance of the smile on a corpse that the undertaker fixes before a funeral.

"Let me tell you men a story," the judge began, his

eyes staring into his drink as if he might find some solace there, "and then maybe you'll understand why I'm not jumping with joy about the fact that I took five thousand dollars to betray my robes."

He hesitated and shook his head, "In fact, I doubt very seriously if I'll live long enough to spend a tenth of it."

McCain looked at Hammer and shrugged, wondering what was going on.

"What are you talking about, Judge Fitzpatrick?" Hammer asked. "This Jensen fellow is just another of those old coots they call mountain men that like to live up in the mountains and kill beaver and such for a living."

Fitzpatrick snorted and downed his drink, immediately pouring himself another one. "You couldn't be more wrong, Mr. Hammerick." The judge leaned back and held his glass with both hands, resting it on his paunch as he slowly rocked in his swivel chair.

"Now, as I said, let me tell you a story, and then maybe you'll understand." He hesitated and stared at the ceiling for a moment, as if gathering his memories.

"Many years ago," he began, "I was just out of law school and my first job was working in a small town in Idaho named Rico. It was mainly a mining camp, and I kept myself busy filing claims for miners and settling disputes over who filed first and elementary things like that. Then one day, two men drifted into town, one older and the other barely out of his teens. Their names were Preacher and Smoke Jensen. I was in a bar, just making conversation, and asked them why they'd come to Rico, since they didn't look like miners. The young one, Smoke, said they were looking for the men who'd killed and robbed his brother and then killed his father when he went looking for them."

The judge paused in his tale to take a sip of whiskey, and to take a cigar out of the wooden box on his desk and light it. And then, with smoke trailing from his nostrils, he continued. "Well, I didn't have much to say to that since at that time Rico was plumb full of outlaws and brigands, and the old man named Preacher asked me where the nearest general store was. I told him we didn't have a store, but there was a trading post down the street a ways and that I'd be glad to point it out to him.

"After a while, we finished our drinks and he and the young fellow got on their horses and rode down the street, me walking alongside to show them the way. When we got there, I pointed the place out to them and stopped to build myself a cigarette, and the damnedest thing happened . . ."


Smoke and Preacher dismounted in front of the combination trading post and saloon. As was his custom, Smoke slipped the thongs from the hammers of his Colts as soon as his boots hit dirt.

They had bought their supplies and turned to leave when the hum of conversation suddenly died. Two rough-dressed and unshaven men, both wearing guns, blocked the door.

"Who owns that horse out there?" one demanded, a snarl in his voice, trouble in his manner. "The one with the SJ brand?"

Smoke laid his purchases on the counter. "I do," he said quietly.

"Which way'd you ride in from?"

Preacher had slipped to his right, his left hand covering the hammer of his Henry, concealing the click as he thumbed it back.

Smoke faced the men, his right hand hanging loose by his side. His left hand was just inches from his left-hand gun. "Who wants to know—and why?"

No one in the dusty building moved or spoke.

"Pike's my name," the bigger and uglier of the pair said. "And I say you came through my diggin's yesterday and stole my dust."

"And I say you're a liar," Smoke told him.

Pike grinned nastily, his right hand hovering near the butt of his pistol. "Why . . . you little pup. I think I'll shoot your ears off."

"Why don't you try? I'm tired of hearing you shoot your mouth off."

Pike looked puzzled for a few seconds; bewilderment crossed his features. No one had ever talked to him in this manner. Pike was big, strong, and a bully. "I think I'll just kill you for that."

Pike and his partner reached for their guns.

Four shots boomed in the low-ceilinged room, four shots so closely spaced they seemed as one thunderous roar. Dust and bird droppings fell from the ceiling. Pike and his friend were slammed out the open doorway. One fell off the rough porch, dying in the dirt street. Pike, with two holes in his chest, died with his back against a support pole, his eyes still open, unbelieving. Neither had managed to pull a pistol more than halfway out of leather.

All eyes in the black-powder-filled and dusty, smoky room moved to the young man standing by the bar, a Colt in each hand. "Good God!" a man whispered in awe. "I never even seen him draw."

Preacher moved the muzzle of his Henry to cover the men at the tables. The bartender put his hands slowly on the bar, indicating he wanted no trouble.

"We'll be leaving now," Smoke said, holstering his Colts and picking up his purchases from the counter. He walked out the door slowly.

Smoke stepped over the sprawled, dead legs of Pike and walked past his dead partner in the shooting.

"What are we 'posed to do with the bodies?" a man asked Preacher.

"Bury 'em."

"What's the kid's name?"

"Smoke."

The judge let his eyes settle on Hammerick for a moment as he took a long drag from his cigar. "Anyway," he continued through a cloud of blue smoke swirling around his head, "that was the first time I met the man named Smoke Jensen. A few days later, I went to visit a friend in a nearby town, and I heard how everyone was talking about how a friend of Preacher's told Smoke that two men, Haywood and Thompson, who claimed to be Pike's brother, had tracked him and Preacher and were in town waiting for Smoke to show up . . ."

Smoke walked down the rutted street an hour before sunset, the sun at his back—the way he had planned it. Thompson and Haywood were in a big tent at the end of the street, which served as a saloon and cafe. Preacher had pointed them out earlier and asked if Smoke needed his help. Smoke said no. The refusal came as no surprise.

As Smoke walked down the street a man glanced up, spotted him, then hurried quickly inside.

Smoke felt no animosity toward the men in the tent saloon, no anger, no hatred. But they'd come here after him, so let the dance begin, he thought.

Smoke stopped fifty feet from the tent. "Haywood! Thompson! You want to see me?"

The two men pushed back the tent flap and stepped out, both angling to get a better look at the man they had tracked. "You the kid called Smoke?" one said.

"I am."

"Pike was my brother," the heavier of the pair said. "And Shorty was my pal."

"You can't do anything about your family, but you should choose your friends more carefully," Smoke told him.

"They was just a-funnin' with you," Thompson said.

"You weren't there. You don't know what happened."

"You callin' me a liar?"

"If that's the way you want to take it."

Thompson's face colored with anger, his hand moving closer to the .44 in his belt. "You take that back or make your play."

"There is no need for this," Smoke said.

The second man began cursing Smoke as he stood tensely, legs spread wide, body bent at the waist. "You're a damned thief. You stolt their gold and then kilt 'em."

"I don't want to have to kill you," Smoke said.

"The kid's yellow!" Haywood yelled. Then he grabbed for his gun.

Haywood touched the butt of his gun just as two loud gunshots blasted in the dusty street. The .36-caliber balls struck Haywood in the chest, one nicking his heart. He dropped to the dirt, dying. Before he closed his eyes, and death relieved him of the shocking pain by pulling him into a long sleep, two more shots thundered. He had a dark vision of Thompson spinning in the street. Then Haywood died.

Thompson was on one knee, his left hand holding his shattered right elbow. His leg was bloody. Smoke had knocked his gun from his hand, and then shot him in the leg.

"Pike was your brother," Smoke told the man. "So I can understand why you came after me. But you were wrong. I'll let you live. But stay with mining. If I ever see you again, I'll kill you on sight."

The young man turned, putting his back to the dead and bloody pair. He walked slowly up the street, his high-heeled Spanish riding boots pocking the air with dusty puddles.*

When the judge paused in his story, Hammer cleared his throat and asked, "You mind if I have a shot of that whiskey, Judge?"

Fitzpatrick grinned and shook his head. "No, not at all, Mr. Hammerick. How about you, Luke? You want a taste too?"

Luke didn't answer, but just reached out and poured him and Hammer drinks, emptying the bottle.

"Not to worry, there's plenty more where that came from," the judge said, and got another bottle out of his desk drawer and placed it on the desk between them. "I have a feeling we're all going to need another one soon," he said as he refilled his glass yet again.

"Anyway," the judge went on, "after Smoke shot and killed Pike, his friend, and Haywood, and wounded Pike's brother, Thompson, he and Preacher went after the other men who had killed Smoke's brother and stolen the Confederates' gold. They rode on over to La Plaza de los Leones, the Plaza of the Lions. It was there that they trapped a man named Casey in a line shack with some of his friends. The way I hear it, Smoke and Preacher burned them out and captured Casey. Smoke took him to the outskirts of the town and hung him on a telegraph pole for the entire town to see."

McCain almost choked on his drink. "He just hung him? No trial or anything?"

The judge took his cigar out of his mouth and stared

*The Last Mountain Man

at the half-inch-long ash on the end before scraping it off into an ashtray. "Yes, Luke, but you've got to realize that's the way it was done in those days. That town would never of hanged one of their own on the word of Smoke Jensen." He snorted. "Like as not, they'd of hanged Smoke and Preacher instead. Anyway, after that, the sheriff of that town put out a flyer on Smoke, accusing him of murder. Had a ten-thousand-dollar reward on it too."

"Did Smoke and Preacher go into hiding?" asked Hammer, thinking that would have been what he would have done.

"With a ten-thousand-dollar reward on his head?" McCain said. "He must've, 'cause most men would turn in their mother for that kind of money."

"No, sir, he didn't," the judge replied. "Seems Preacher advised it, but Smoke said he had one more call to make. I didn't see this, you understand, but a man who was there told me all about it shortly after it happened. They rode on over to Oreodelphia, looking for a man named Ackerman. But, and this is the funny part, they didn't go after him right at first. Smoke and Preacher sat around doing nothing for two or three days. You see, gentlemen, Smoke was smart, as well as fast with his guns. He wanted Ackerman to get plenty nervous. He did, and finally came gunning for Smoke with a bunch of men who rode for his brand . . ."

At the edge of town, Ackerman, a bull of a man, with small, mean eyes and a cruel slit for a mouth, slowed his horse to a walk. Ackerman and his hands rode down the street, six abreast.

Preacher and Smoke were on their feet. Preacher stuffed his mouth full of chewing tobacco. Both men had slipped the thongs from the hammers of their

Colts. Preacher wore two Colts, .44's. One in a holster, the other stuck behind his belt. The old mountain man and the young gunfighter stood six feet apart on the boardwalk.

The sheriff closed his office door and walked into the empty cell area. He sat down and began a game of checkers with his deputy. He wanted no part of this blood feud, no part at all.

Ackerman and his men wheeled their horses to face the men on the boardwalk. "I hear tell you boys is lookin' for me. If so, here I am."

"News to me," Smoke said. "What's your name?"

"You know who I am, kid. Ackerman."

"Oh, yeah!" Smoke grinned. "You're the man who helped kill my brother by shooting him in the back. Then you stole the gold he was guarding."

Inside the hotel, pressed against the wall, the desk clerk listened intently, his mouth open in anticipation of gunfire.

"You're a liar. I didn't shoot your brother; that was Potter and his bunch."

"You stood and watched it. Then you stole the gold."

"It was war, kid."

"But you were on the same side," Smoke said. "So that not only makes you a killer, it makes you a traitor and a coward."

"I'll kill you for sayin' that!"

"You'll burn in hell a long time before I'm dead," Smoke told him.

Ackerman grabbed for his pistol. The street exploded in gunfire and black-powder fumes. Horses screamed and bucked in fear. One rider was thrown to the dust by his lunging mustang. Smoke took the men on the left, Preacher the men on the right side. The battle lasted no more than ten to twelve seconds. When the noise ended and the gun smoke cleared, five men lay in the street, two of them dead. Two more would die from their wounds. One was shot in the side—he would live. Ackerman had been shot three times: once in the belly, once in the chest, and one ball had taken him in the side of the face as the muzzle of the .36 had lifted with each blast. Still, Ackerman sat in his saddle, dead. The big man finally leaned to one side and toppled from his horse, one boot hanging in the stirrup. The horse shied, and then it began walking down the dusty street, dragging Ackerman, leaving a bloody trail.

Preacher spat into the street. "Damn near swallowed my chaw."

"I never seen a draw that fast," a man said from his storefront. "It was a blur."

"The editor of the local paper walked up to stand next to the man who told me this story, where he'd been standing watching the show," the judge said. "He watched the old man and the young gunfighter walk down the street. He said he'd truly seen it all. The old man had killed one man, wounded another. The young man had killed four men, as calmly as picking his teeth.

"'What's that young man's name?' the editor asked him.

"'Smoke Jensen,' the man said. 'But he's not a man, he's a devil.'"

The judge finished his story and drained his glass, his face pale at the memory of such a dangerous young man.

McCain watched the judge finish his drink, and he felt nauseated in the pit of his stomach. He could tell Jensen was a dangerous man, that was evident from the way he handled himself, but he'd had no idea he was crazy as well. He would have to be to have done half the things the judge had said he had.

He glanced at Hammer, whose face was as pale as the judge's. I don't blame him, McCain thought. That's not a man you want on your trail with blood on his mind.

# Chapter 22

Hammer drained his drink and glanced over at Luke McCain, who had a thoughtful expression on his face. "So, Judge," Hammer said, trying to appear nonchalant. "I appreciate your story about this Smoke Jensen and what a tough hombre he was, but what was your point in telling us all this?" He smirked, trying not to show how afraid he was.

The judge smiled sadly at Hammer. "Do you know how old Jensen was when all this happened?" he asked.

When Luke and Hammer both shook their heads, the judge chuckled, though there was little mirth in his face. "He was only eighteen years old," he said. "And I remember thinking to myself I'd never seen eyes so cold except on a diamondback rattlesnake."

Luke and Hammer remained silent, their eyes fixed on the judge.

"And my point in telling you this, Mr. Hammerick, was to let you know that you've got us all in a hell of a mess."

"Why didn't you say something when I came to you and we made our plans on how to handle this?" Luke asked.

The judge shook his head. "I'd forgotten all about it," he answered. "After all, that was over thirty years ago, and Jensen is a rather common name."

"So, how do you know this Jensen is the same one in your story?" Hammer asked, hoping the judge was mistaken.

"I said Jensen is a common name, Mr. Hammerick, but Smoke is definitely not."

The judge sighed, and put his empty glass down and stubbed out his cigar. "But it really only came back to me when Jensen stared at me at the end of the trial and said he'd be back. When I looked into those eyes as black as obsidian, I knew I was looking at death incarnate." The judge looked at his empty glass, as if wishing it were full so he could drain it again and put the thought of those eyes out of his mind.

"I think you're overreacting, Judge," Hammer said, trying once again to put up a brave front, though he felt as if his insides were full of ice.

The judge shook his head. "No, Hammer. The story I told you illustrates that Smoke Jensen is a man who neither forgets nor forgives. When he finds out you and your men were set free and that Luke and I were in this with you, he will come after all of us, and God help us, he'll kill us all as sure as the winter up here brings snow."

"Maybe we'll get him first when he comes," Hammer said, though his voice was uncertain and he felt as if his bowels were turning to water.

The judge shook his head again. "If you think any of us has the slightest chance against such a man when he's on the prod for us, then you are sadly mistaken, my boy," the judge said with conviction. "But even if by chance you or Luke get lucky and do finish him before he kills all of us, by then it won't matter. Jensen will have already contacted the governor and the U.S. marshals, so even if by some fluke of luck you do survive his attack, there will be a price on all of our heads that will make us a target for every bounty hunter in these territories."

"So, what do you propose?" Hammer said, sweat beginning to form on his brow. He had a wild urge to get up and bolt from the courthouse and run as far and as fast as he could in any direction as long as it was away from Smoke Jensen.

"Your only chance, and Luke's and my only chance, is if you and your men go after Smoke Jensen and kill him and his companions before they find out you've been released and he has cause to contact the governor and the marshals. Then, and only then, will we be safe."

"But Judge," Luke argued, "you just said we wouldn't stand a chance against Jensen. So why are you recommending we go looking for him?"

"I said you could not defeat him once he's on your trail and looking for you, Luke. I think the only chance anyone has of killing Smoke Jensen is if he doesn't know they're after him. If he's not expecting an attack, perhaps he can be ambushed and killed before he's on his guard."

Hammer interrupted. "But Judge, Jensen and his men are going up into the Canadian wilderness to survey for the railroad. There's no telling where they'll be or even if me and my men can find them."

The judge held up his hand. "Yes, there is a way, Mr. Hammerick. When you survey for a railroad, you leave trail marks to show the men coming behind you where to lay the tracks. Jensen and his men will be leaving a trail even a child could follow."

He looked back and forth between McCain and Hammer. "All you and your men will have to do is stay clear of the railroad authorities so you won't be identified before you can find and eliminate Jensen and his men."

Hammer nodded slowly, thinking it through. "Yeah, and while we're up there, I'll make sure to take care of that Knowles fellow who's the only witness to my being at the robbery site."

"Good thinking," the judge said. "If there are no witnesses against you, then Luke and I will not have to explain why we let you out of jail."

Hammer got to his feet. "If I hurry, maybe my men and I can catch them before they get back to Winnipeg."

The judge held up his hand. "No, give them a good lead. It'll be much better if they're killed in the Canadian wilderness rather than on the trail back to Winnipeg. That way, if you're careful, you can blame it on the Indians or some other brigands up there and no suspicion will fall on you."

"Also," Luke added, "you need to take care of this Knowles man first so that if Jensen does call the governor, he won't have a witness who can testify against you."

Hammer glanced at McCain. "So, I take it you're not planning on coming with us up to Canada?"

Luke shook his head. "No. Inasmuch as you got yourself and the judge and me into this mess, I think it's only right you should get us out of it on your own."

Hammer smiled evilly. "That will be my pleasure."

The judge smiled, and reached over to pour them all fresh drinks. "In that case, I think we should drink to a successful conclusion to all our troubles."


Smoke and his friends took their time riding back to Winnipeg. They were still tired after the long, hard ride to catch up with Hammer and his men, and decided an extra day or two on the journey back wouldn't make any difference to Van Horne.

When they finally arrived in Winnipeg, they went immediately to see Van Horne, only to find he'd already left town. He was pushing his tracklaying laborers harder than he ever had and according to the men still in Winnipeg, he was managing to stay only a few miles behind the surveyors as they blazed a trail through very heavily wooded countryside.

"How far out of town has he managed to lay the tracks?" Smoke asked.

"Close to twenty miles already," the man answered.

Smoke looked at Louis. "Twenty miles? That'll take us several days to catch up with them on horseback," he said, dreading even another day in the saddle without resting first.

The station man smiled and shook his head. "Oh, Mr. Jensen, there's no need for you to try and follow him on horseback. With the tracks laid, we can send you by train with no problem. Hell, we have to go back and forth almost every day with supplies for the laborers anyway."

"But what about our horses and equipment?" Pearlie asked, looking at Smoke. "We're gonna need 'em when we catch up with Wilson and his crew."

The station man answered with a negligent wave of his hand. "That's no problem either, my friends. We'll just attach an extra boxcar to the train, and your animals and supplies can be carried along with you. When you reach the end of the track, you can talk with Mr. Van Horne and then be on your way to join up with Tom Wilson and the other surveyors up ahead."

"When's the next train leaving?" Smoke asked.

"Yeah, and do we have time to eat first?" Pearlie added, rubbing his stomach.

The man pursed his lips and glanced at the pocket watch he pulled from his vest. "Sure, I'll tell the cook to fix you up something right away, and by the time you're done eating, the train should be loaded up and ready to go."

"You boys go on over to the cook tent," Smoke said. "I'm going to drop by the hospital tent and see how Albert Knowles is doing and let him know what happened in Noyes."

Louis and the boys headed for the cook tent, while Smoke made his way over to the tent where injured workers were kept until they healed enough to be put back on the line. Knowles had elected to stay there rather than in town so he could better supervise his few remaining men in their guard duties, and to be on site when the replacement agents he'd sent for arrived in Winnipeg.

Smoke pulled back the tent flaps and walked down the aisle between the rows of beds, amazed at how many men were in the tent recovering from injuries suffered while laying track or blasting rocks from the rail bed. "This must be a hard life for these men," he muttered to himself. "And they sure as hell don't get paid enough for the dangers they face every day."

When he got to the end of the aisle, he saw Albert Knowles, his broken left leg propped up on a wooden device that kept it elevated so the swelling would stay down while he healed. Most of his burns were scabbed over, and Smoke was glad to see there was no sign of infection, the thing that killed most men with bad burns.

"Hey, Albert," Smoke called, giving the man a nod of his head.

"Why, Smoke. When did you get back?" Knowles asked, putting an extra pillow behind his back so he could sit up and talk better.

"Just a little while ago," Smoke answered.

"Did you catch those sons of bitches that killed my men?" Knowles asked, his smile fading.

Smoke nodded. "Yes. We had to kill a few, but the rest are in custody in Noyes, Minnesota."

"Noyes?" Knowles asked. "Why the hell did they head down that way?"

Smoke shrugged. "I don't really know, unless they were trying to get across the border thinking we wouldn't be able to go after them there."

"But you fooled 'em, huh?"

Smoke smiled. "Yeah. Anyway, the sheriff and judge down there promised to hold them for at least a month, until you're well enough to go down there and make a positive identification of the leader, a man named Hammerick."

"So that's the bastard's name, huh?"

"Yes, and he's as hard a case as I've ever come across," Smoke said. "It won't be any loss when you identify him and he and his men are hanged."

Knowles patted his broken leg. "Good. The doc says another two or three weeks and I'll be able to travel. I'll see if Van Horne will arrange for me to go part of the way down there by train, so I should be able to be there within a month if there are no complications."

Smoke reached over and shook his hand. "Well, I'll be seeing you, Albert. You take care of yourself, and let me know what happens at the trial."

"I will, Smoke, and thanks for what you did for my men and me."

"Think nothing of it. Those men deserve what they're going to get. I just wish I could be there to see it happen when they hit the end of their ropes."

Smoke turned and went to the cook tent, hoping he'd have time to eat before the train got ready.

As it turned out, Smoke had just finished his meal

when the station man came into the cook tent and told them the train was loaded and ready to leave. Just as he'd promised, their horses and supplies were loaded in a boxcar that'd been added to the train.

As they boarded the short train, Pearlie looked at the almost empty passenger car. "Good, there's plenty of empty seats," he said. "I think I'll take me a short nap to help me digest my food."

"When did you ever need any help digestin' your food, Pearlie?" Cal asked, grinning.

"Well, I don't often get steaks as thick and as good as the railroad cook fixed us," Pearlie said defensively. "Especially if you're doin' the cookin', Cal."

"Huh, I never heard you complain when I cooked," Cal said. "You always had your mouth too full to even speak, let alone complain."

"That's 'cause the bellyaches always came later," Pearlie rejoined, "when you weren't around."

"A nap sounds good to me too," Louis said, interrupting the argument between Cal and Pearlie.

"Yeah, it might be good if we all got some sleep," Smoke said. "I have a feeling once we join up with Tom Wilson and the mountain men, we're gonna be working from daylight to dark most every day."

"That's right," Louis said. "And the country we're going to be surveying is among the wildest in North America, from what I heard around the rail yard."

"It's hard to believe it's any wilder than the High Lonesome north of Colorado," Pearlie said, covering a wide yawn with the back of his hand.

"Well," Smoke said, "the country's about the same, but since the Rocky Mountains in Canada are so much farther north, the weather is even worse than in Colorado."

"I find that hard to imagine," Cal said, remembering some of the winters they'd spent up in the mountains with Smoke in the past.

As the train pulled out of the station on its two- or three-hour journey, the four men stretched out on seats in the car, pulled their hats down over their eyes, and dropped off to sleep before the train got up to full speed.

# Chapter 23

The men were so tired that they had to be woken up when the train finally reached the end of the tracks. Van Horne himself performed the task, standing in the front of the car and banging a knife against the side of a bottle of fine brandy.

When the bell-like tones brought the men to their feet, he had a Chinese boy pour generous drinks into brandy snifters for them all, then sat among them, demanding to be told in detail of their exploits on the trail of the train robbers.

Smoke left the telling of the tale to Louis, who was much the better speaker, and he had Van Horne in stitches laughing at how Smoke had blown up the outlaws' supplies and then killed them by dropping shotgun shells into their campfire.

His expression sobered when he heard how the sheriff and judge had acted as if Smoke and the rest of them were the criminals instead of the outlaws.

"Those dumb sons of bitches," Van Horne exclaimed. "Just wait until I get back to camp. I'm going to wire the governor of Minnesota, who by the way is a personal friend of mine, as well as the United States marshals' office in Grand Forks, and see if I can't light a fire under those boys."

He sniffed and adjusted his vest. "They'll be sorry they ever messed with William Cornelius Van Horne before I'm done with them."

Smoke and the others had to laugh at Van Horne's expressions of rage, and soon they had him laughing too, and pouring more brandy into their glasses.

"Whoa there, partner," Smoke said after the second glass, when Van Horne tried to fill his glass for the third time. "You keep that up and we won't be able to sit a saddle when we head on up ahead to join Tom Wilson and his crew."

"Nonsense," Van Horne said, continuing to pour. "You'll spend the night here with me, of course. I've got my private rail car at the head of the tracks. You boys have been on the trail almost continuously. It's time you had a good night's sleep and some decent food."

"Did you say food?" Pearlie asked, even though it had been a mere three hours since his last meal back in Winnipeg.

Van Horne laughed. He'd forgotten Pearlie's penchant for fine food, and lots of it. "Yes, Pearlie. In addition to bringing my private car with me whenever I'm out laying track, I also bring my own private chef along as well."

He reached down and patted his more-than-ample stomach. "As you can well see, I believe in living as well as one can, no matter the circumstances or the geography."

"How about them copper bathtubs?" Cal asked. He looked at Pearlie and sniffed elaborately. "Some of us could use a bath and another go-round with that brush and soap we used on the way up here."

Van Horne nodded, smiling. "Yes, I think hot baths and a good shave will make all of you feel better," he said, and after a moment's hesitation, added with a grin, "as well as making those who sit near you more comfortable as well."

When they got out of the passenger car and walked up the tracks toward Van Horne's private cars, Smoke was amazed at the number of men he saw working alongside the tracks up ahead. He figured there must have been several thousand men stretched for almost a mile on either side of the tracks, emptying fist-sized chunks of gravel from a rail car onto the ground to be a base for the tracks.

Two other cars contained large wooden ties, which Van Horne said were being cut a few miles over and brought to the building site by wagons, and iron rails. Up ahead of these men were even more men cutting down trees, blasting boulders and rocks into fist-sized pieces, and generally transforming a heavily wooded area into a flat road upon which the men behind would lay the tracks.

Van Horne followed Smoke's gaze, saying proudly, "We can make between three and five miles a day, weather permitting, if the terrain isn't too hilly and we don't have to cross too many rivers."

"Damn," Pearlie said, his eyes wide, "I'll bet Wilson and his men don't do much more than that."

Van Horne grinned. "You're correct, Pearlie," he said. "In fact, we usually manage to stay just a few miles behind him."

"That's amazing," Louis said.

"Well, of course, he's doing the really hard work of finding a suitable path for the tracks, and sometimes he'll have to backtrack for miles if he comes to an area that cannot be tunneled through or swung around, and I've got the benefit of thousands of men, each doing one particular job, so we can move very fast indeed."

After an evening of fine conversation with Van Horne, wherein he told them of some of his exploits building other railroads in the past, and an even finer dinner, the boys were treated to steaming hot baths, and finally, exhausted, they went to sleep in his sleeping car.

Just before he fell asleep, Pearlie asked the Chinese attendant to put more wood in the potbellied stove at the end of the car. "I've been cold for so long, I don't hardly remember what it's like to feel warm," he mumbled as his eyes closed.

They awoke the next morning to a sumptuous breakfast of eggs, bacon, thinly sliced fried steak, flapjacks, and, with Smoke wondering where in the world Van Horne got it at this time of year, freshly squeezed orange juice.

As he finished his third cup of coffee topped off with a cigarette, Smoke thanked Van Horne for being such a gracious host, and he and the men prepared to leave.

Van Horne escorted them out to their horses, and showed them how Wilson was marking the trail he was leaving for Van Horne's tracklayers to follow.

"See how he not only blazes the trees to either side of the trail," Van Horne said. "He also has several rolls of bright red cloth that he ties high up in trees on either side, so the trail will be easy to find."

"Thanks, Bill," Smoke said. "We shouldn't have too much trouble locating him."

"Just be sure to give him a signal when you get close," Van Horne said. "Tom's been out here in the wilderness many times, and he's been known to shoot first and ask questions later if he feels his men are being threatened."

"Will do," Smoke said, and after they'd all shook Van Horne's hand, he and his friends hit the trail.

# Chapter 24

Much refreshed by their rest with Van Horne, Smoke and his men set off along the trail ahead of the tracks that had been blazed by Tom Wilson and his crew. Even though the air was chilly and carried a hint of frost, the sky was clear and there were no signs of any spring storms in the offing.

As Van Horne had said, it was remarkably easy to follow the blaze marks and the swatches of red cloth tied to nearby trees along the way. As they rode, Smoke would occasionally check his compass, and he found they were heading generally north by northwest, along the route discovered and advocated by Fleming back in 1877. Of course, Fleming wasn't trying to find a level course a train could follow, so they occasionally had to deviate from his path due to natural obstructions he had ignored on his journey.

Soon, they came to the edge of a large lake, and Smoke consulted the rather crude map Wilson had given him weeks before. "This must be Lake Manitoba," Smoke said.

"I don't understand it," Louis said as he rode his

horse to the very edge of the lake. "The blaze marks lead right up to the water's edge."

"You don't suppose he means for Van Horne to build a bridge across this lake, do you?" Pearlie asked.

"I suppose so, but it looks like an awfully long way for a bridge to be built," Smoke answered, scratching his head. "And I just can't imagine how men could stand to work in water that's just a few degrees above freezing."

"Hold on a minute," Cal called from off to the left. "Here's a note under this red cloth on this tree. You want me to pull it out and read it?"

Smoke nodded, and Cal stretched up in his stirrups and pulled out the paper, which was encased in waxed paper to prevent it from getting wet in case of rain. He unfolded the paper and read to himself for a moment, his lips moving as he scanned the letter. "Oh," he said, refolding the letter. "Wilson is giving Van Horne a choice, it says here."

"Well, go on, Cal boy, tell us what it says," Pearlie said impatiently.

"Wilson says it's only about a mile across the lake and it's not very deep, and that it's another fifteen miles to go southwest and cut around the lake. I guess he's leaving it up to Van Horne whether to build the bridge or to detour around the lake the longer way."

Cal stuck the note back under the red cloth and turned back to Smoke. "What do you want to do, Smoke?"

"Well," Smoke said, grinning, "unless you want these horses to swim us a mile across a lake where there's almost more ice than water, I guess we'll take the route around the lake."

As they turned their horses to the southwest, Pearlie said, "If it's really fifteen miles around the lake, that's gonna take us another day or two to catch up with Wilson and the others."

Smoke glanced at the terrain they'd be going through, which was fairly heavily wooded, though, thankfully, flat without much slope. "Yes, I think you're right, Pearlie." He looked up at the clear sky overhead. "However, with the moon out tonight, if it doesn't cloud in, we may be able to ride pretty late and make up five or six hours on them."

"Smoke," Pearlie said, "if we're gonna be riding half the night, I suggest we take our nooning now."

"Oh, hungry, are you?" Louis asked, smiling, for he knew Pearlie was always hungry.

"It's not that," Pearlie argued, his face red. "It's just I think we need to give the horses a rest if we're gonna be working 'em all night."

Smoke and Cal both laughed, seeing through Pearlie's excuse. "All right, I guess you're right, Pearlie. Let's make a short camp here and let the horses eat."

Cal glanced at the lake, a dozen yards away. "Smoke, you think there might be fish in that lake?"

"I don't see why not," Smoke replied.

"Fried lake trout would sure go down nice for lunch," Pearlie said.

"But we didn't bring any fishing poles," Louis said, though the sound of fresh fish appealed to him too.

"Oh, Smoke don't need no fishin' poles, Louis," Cal said. "Last year, up in the mountains above Big Rock, he showed us how the mountain men caught their fish."

"Well," Louis said, stepping down off his horse. "This I've got to see."

"Come on, Louis, I'll make a mountain man out of you yet," Smoke said. "Boys, take care of our horses and get a fire and some mountain-man coffee going while I show Louis how to catch our lunch."

Smoke walked among the birch and maple and ash trees near the water's edge until he found a fairly straight young tree that was about two inches in diameter.

He pulled out his knife and with a couple of swings, cut the tree down and skinned off the small branches. He then whittled a sharp point onto the end and walked over to the lake. He moved down the bank until he came to where a maple was leaning out over the water.

"The shadow of the tree makes you able to see down into the water better," Smoke said as he squatted down on his haunches. "It cuts the reflection from the sun and sky. In fact, you can sometimes see shore birds standing in shallow water with their wings held out to make a similar shade," he added. He looked back at Louis. "Squat down," he said. "Otherwise, the fish will see your shadow and it'll spook 'em."

A few minutes later, Smoke struck out with the homemade spear and brought it out of the water with a three-pound lake trout wiggling on the end.

"Hey, that's great," Louis said. "Can I try it?"

"Sure, but remember, the water distorts your vision. You have to aim a little bit under where you think the fish is or you'll miss it."

Sure enough, it took Louis three or four tries before he got the hang of it. But the lake was full of fish and since the water was so cold, they were moving slowly. In no time at all, Smoke had a pan full of fish filets cooking in bacon grease on the fire.

As Louis sampled the fish, he smacked his lips and moaned, rolling his eyes. "Smoke, I've never tasted anything better than this."

"I wouldn't tell Andre that," Smoke said, smiling.

Louis assumed a horrified look, "Oh, heavens, no. The man would quit instantly were I to admit anyone else could cook as well as he."

"Course," Smoke said, "there's something about eating food cooked outdoors over a campfire that makes whatever it is seem to taste even better. You'd probably turn your nose up at these fish if you'd ordered them in a fancy restaurant."

"Oh, I'll agree the location has something to do with it," Louis said, "but these fish would meet with anyone's approval in any restaurant in the world, no matter how fancy."

When they finished eating, and Cal and Pearlie had washed the plates and coffeepot out, Smoke said, "Now, unless you think you need an after-lunch nap, Pearlie, we can be on our way."

Pearlie blushed. "No, I think I'll be all right for a while, Smoke."

"I wished you hadn't put the idea in his head, Smoke," Cal said, grinning. "Now he'll be dozing in his saddle an' we'll have to stop ever so often to pick him up when he falls on his butt."

"That'll be the day," Pearlie retorted, smiling at the picture Cal painted.

"So I guess you're saying you can stay awake then, at least until dinnertime anyway," Cal said, swinging up into his saddle.

Pearlie took a swat at the young man with his hat, but missed.

They rode as hard as they could push the horses through the rough terrain, Smoke electing to hold off stopping for supper until just past ten o'clock that night. The half-moon cast enough light so that they could easily follow Wilson's blaze marks, and other than stopping for a quick pot of coffee and to let the horses rest, they continued riding until late that night.

Smoke decided to stop after Cal had fallen asleep in the saddle twice and almost fallen off his horse, much to the delight of Pearlie, who teased him unmercifully about being the one who almost fell off his horse.

"All right, men," Smoke finally said. "Enough is

enough. Let's make camp, eat, and get some sleep. Dawn's gonna come awfully early."

"Thank God," Louis said, getting down off his horse and rubbing his buttocks with both hands. "I didn't realize how sitting in my saloon all day had made me unused to the saddle. I think my blisters have blisters on them."

"I still got some of that liniment Bear Tooth gave me," Pearlie said, a malicious grin on his face. "Want to give it a try?"

Louis shook his head quickly. "No, thanks, Pearlie. I saw how it affected you, so I'd just as soon live with my blisters if you don't mind."

"I may be too sleepy to eat, Smoke," Cal said. "Mind if I just crawl into my blankets now?"

"Hang on for a little while, Cal," Smoke said. "You need to put some food in your stomach. I wrapped up some of the fish from lunch, so it won't take long to heat them over the fire."

As Pearlie got the fire going and Louis made sure the horses were fed and watered, Smoke threw some fish on a skillet and began to heat it over the fire.

While they were eating, Smoke suddenly cocked his head to the side and held perfectly still, his fork halfway to his mouth.

Louis, noting his actions, whispered, "What is it, Smoke? You hear something?"

"Keep on eating, boys," Smoke said, putting his plate down on the ground. "Just act like nothing's wrong. I'm gonna take a look-see around."

Seconds later, Smoke melted into the darkness and slipped away.

A few minutes later, a tall, dark figure walked into the camp, a rifle cradled in his arms. "Yo, the camp," he called softly, and Tom Wilson moved into the light cast by the campfire.

"Hey, Mr. Wilson," Pearlie called. "Where'd you come from?"

Wilson put his rifle down and squatted next to the fire, warming his hands. "I made my camp just about a half mile up ahead. I smelled your fire and then I saw the glow."

He glanced at Louis. "You boys should post a guard when you camp. If I'd been an Indian, you'd all be dead."

Smoke moved out of the darkness behind Wilson and walked into the light, his rifle cocked and ready. "Oh, I don't know about that, Tom. I heard you coming ten minutes ago."

Wilson, startled by Smoke's sudden appearance behind him, grinned. "But I didn't make no noise."

"You made enough for these old mountain-man ears to hear you."

"Would you like some lake trout?" Louis said to forestall any further arguments.

"Why, yes, thank you kindly. I'm kind'a tired of beans and fatback."

After Louis prepared a plate of fish for Wilson, Smoke asked, "Where are the rest of your crew?"

"Oh, they're camped about a mile ahead," Wilson said, hungrily devouring the fish on his plate.

"But you said your camp was only a half mile away," Smoke said. "Don't you camp with your men?"

Wilson shook his head, his mouth too full to answer for a moment. "No, not usually," he said. "It's my habit to camp by myself, especially out in the wild."

"Why is that, Tom?" Louis asked.

Wilson shrugged. "I don't know. I guess it's just my contrary nature. I cannot stand to spend too much time around other people, and working with them all day is just about all I can stand." He drained his coffee cup and stood up. "So at night, after we eat, I usually make my camp a little ways off from the others."

He touched his fur cap with his right hand. "Thanks for the grub, gentlemen. I'll see you in the morning and we can all have breakfast together."

After he'd left, Louis shook his head. "What a strange man."

Smoke smiled. "Oh, he's not so strange, Louis. He is a mountain man, after all. The main reason men come up to the mountains is they value their solitude."

"But Bear Tooth and Red Bingham are partners and spend time together, just like Bobcat Bill and Rattlesnake Bob," Pearlie said.

"Yes," Smoke said, "but those men are the exceptions, and they didn't team up until they were quite old. For many years, all of them rode and camped alone. It's the mountain-man way to distrust others, even other mountain men."

He looked over and saw that Cal was slumped in front of the fire, his plate on his lap, fast asleep. He chuckled and shook the boy awake.

"Now, let's hit the blankets, boys."

"I can't believe you woke me up just to tell me to go back to sleep," Cal said grumpily.

"If I had let you sleep sitting up like that, Cal," Smoke explained, "you would be so stove up in the morning you couldn't sit a saddle."

"Oh," Cal mumbled as he crawled beneath his blankets. "Thanks."

"Don't mention it," Smoke said, pulling the edge of the blanket up a little to cover the boy's ears.

# Chapter 25

There was only one doctor in the town of Winnipeg. After Hammer told his men to split up and go to several different saloons to eat their lunch, or in most cases to drink it, so that so many men traveling together wouldn't arouse suspicion, he went to the doctor's office and entered.

Doctor Mack Freeman had his office in an old Victorian-style mansion on the outskirts of town, and he used several of the extra bedrooms as patient rooms for men recovering from injuries or sicknesses.

A lady wearing the white dress and dark blue apron of a nurse met Hammer in the foyer.

"I'm sorry, sir," she said. "The doctor has been called away on an emergency. If you're ill, you may have a long wait to be seen."

"Oh, I'm not sick," Hammer said, holding his hat in his hands. He rarely dealt with women other than of the dance-hall variety, and he didn't quite know how to act when speaking to a lady.

He kept his head down and mumbled, "I'm here to

visit a friend I heard had suffered an injury working on the railroad a while back. A Mr. Albert Knowles."

The woman pursed her lips and frowned. "I'm afraid I don't recognize that name, but most of the railroad employees stay out at the clinic at the rail yard if they need to be kept under observation."

"So, Mr. Knowles isn't here then?" Hammer said, disappointed. He'd gotten himself all fired up to kill the man on sight, and now he was going to have to wait.

"I'm afraid not, but if you want, you're more than welcome to call back later and ask the doctor."

Hammer put his hat on and tipped it to the nurse, trying to control his impatience. "I'm sure that won't be necessary, ma'am. I'll just ride on over to the rail yard and check there."

Hammer left the doctor's house and went to the saloon where he'd left Bull and a few of his other men. He entered and walked directly to their table.

"You done him already?" Bull asked, looking over Hammer's shoulder to see if there were any lawmen on his trail in case they had to leave in a hurry.

"No, damn it!" Hammer exclaimed. "The son of a bitch is evidently in a tent for injured workers over at the rail yard," he added, signaling the waiter to bring him a glass of whiskey and some food.

Bull pursed his lips, thinking. "That ain't gonna be easy, Boss. Going out there, you're liable to run into some of the men on that train that might recognize you."

Hammer sighed. He was getting tired of having to do all the thinking for his men, but the alternative was to have men smart enough to perhaps challenge his leadership. "I know that, Bull," he said, trying to hide his disgust at having to discuss the obvious. "So what I'm gonna do is wait until nightfall, and then I'm gonna sneak into the tent and put a bullet through Knowles's head."

"But Boss, don't you think a knife might be better, seeing as how a gun might wake up the whole place and bring the guards running?" Bull asked innocently.

Hammer started to utter a sharp reply, and then he realized Bull was right. Damn, he thought, even a blind hog will find an acorn once in a while. He smiled and patted Bull on the shoulder. "You know, Bull, you're right. A knife will do just fine."

Just before midnight, after having his men set up camp north of the rail yard so they could get an early start going after Smoke Jensen, Hammer pulled the collar of his coat up around his neck, pulled the brim of his hat down low over his eyes, and walked through the darkness toward the rail yard at the end of town.

Once there, he stopped a man walking back from town who was carrying an almost empty bottle of whiskey and who looked drunk enough not to remember his face. "Say, friend," Hammer said. "Can you tell me which tent is the one where they keep the injured workers?"

The man grunted and swayed on his feet as he looked around. After a moment, he pointed to a tent off to one side that had a single lamp burning just inside the doorway.

"Thanks," Hammer said, and immediately walked toward the clinic tent.

When he got to the doorway, he slipped a large-bladed skinning knife from his right boot and held it under the lapel of his coat.

Pushing the canvas flap of the doorway open, he eased inside and looked around. At a small desk just in-

ide the doorway, a young man sat with his head down
esting on his crossed arms. He was evidently asleep
on the job. Hammer grinned, but just to make sure
ne wouldn't be interrupted in case the man woke up, he
stepped behind the man and brought the steel hilt of
he knife down hard on the back of the man's head,
knocking him off his chair to lie stunned and groaning
on the floor.

Hammer took the lamp from its hook near the door,
urned the wick down low to lower the flame, and carried it in front of him as he walked among the beds in
he clinic.

A couple of men moaned as he passed and laid their
arms over their eyes against the light, but no one chal-
enged him on his journey to the end bed.

He recognized Knowles's face and moved toward the
bed. The light woke Knowles up, and he shaded his eyes
against the light, smacked his lips a couple of times as
ne came awake, and asked in a low voice, "Yes, Doctor?"

Hammer set the light down on the small table next
to Knowles's bed, keeping it between them so Knowles
couldn't see his face. He leaned over the bed, putting
nis left palm over Knowles's mouth, and put his face
close to the injured man's. "I ain't no doctor, Knowles.
Remember me?" he asked.

Knowles's eyes widened and he reached up to try
and grab Hammer's hand over his mouth, but Hammer
slammed the point of the knife into Knowles's throat,
pushing it in all the way to the hilt.

Knowles strangled and gurgled once or twice, and
then blood spurted out over Hammer's hand and the
ight went out of Knowles's eyes and he died, drowning
n his own blood with his good leg doing a little dance
under the covers.

Hammer wiped the blood on his knife and hand off

on Knowles's sheet, and then he slipped the knife back down into his boot and strolled calmly out of the tent, whistling softly to himself.

That's one less problem to worry about, he thought as he made his way to where he'd left his horse. Now, all we have to do is kill Jensen and his men and we don't have a thing to worry about.

As he rode north along the blazed trail by the side of the tracks that had already been laid, he considered how best to accomplish his goal of killing Jensen and the men who rode with him.

First, he reasoned to himself, we have to find them, but that won't be hard if we just follow this here trail. Then all we have to do is keep out of sight until Jensen and his men are off all alone. Then we ride down in force and pump them full of lead.

"Hah," he said aloud to the back of his horse's head. "I'll show that chicken-shit judge who's the baddest hombre around, and it sure as hell ain't Smoke Jensen."

# Chapter 26

Over breakfast the next morning in Wilson's camp, Smoke and his men had a reunion with the four mountain men he'd convinced to come to Canada for a new adventure.

As Bear Tooth put away an impressive number of eggs and flapjacks, he said to Smoke, "Damn but I'm glad you're back, young'un."

Smoke smiled. Only a mountain man who was old enough to be his father would call him a "young'un." "Why's that, Bear?" Smoke asked, doing a fair job on the flapjacks himself.

Bear Tooth inclined his head toward Wilson, who was sitting nearby staring at them over the rim of his coffee mug. As usual, especially early in the morning, Wilson's face was serious, without a trace of a smile or good humor anywhere on it.

"That damned Wilson is plumb near workin' us to death out here."

Almost as if it pained him, Wilson cracked a small smile as Bear Tooth continued. "He looks like a mountain man an' he dresses like a mountain man, but he sure as hell don't work like no mountain man," Bear Tooth groused, scowling at the weakness of the coffee as he took a drink of the brew that for almost anyone else would be considered too strong by half.

"What do you mean?" Smoke asked, winking at Wilson where Bear couldn't see.

"Hell, a real mountain man knows he has to git up with the birds 'fore dawn and git his traps run an' such. But we also know that come noon, a body's natural tendency is to take a after-noonin' nap. After all, ain't nothin' happenin' during the middle of the day. Even critters as dumb as beavers an' foxes know the middle of the day is for sleepin', or at least lyin' around takin' it easy."

He looked around and grinned when Red Bingham, Bobcat Bill, and Rattlesnake Bob all nodded their heads in agreement. "You know we ain't lazy, Smoke, but ol' Tom over there he don't allow hardly no time fer a noon nap at all. He's got us up an' pushin' through the bush from dawn to dusk," he said grumpily.

"An' then some," agreed Red, snorting at the idea of a civilized man not taking a break in the middle of the day like most folks with any sense knew was only right. "A man can't hardly digest his food traipsin' around the wilderness with a full stomach like that."

Smoke looked at Bear's ample gut, hanging over his buckskin trousers. "Yeah, Bear, I can see ol' Tom's damn near working all the fat off you." He grinned. "It's a good thing I got back here to slow him down 'fore you wasted away to a mere two hundred pounds or so."

Bear glanced down and grinned, showing dark yellow stubs of teeth worn down by years of no dental care. "Well, now, Smoke boy, I got to admit I ain't got no grouse comin' 'bout the quality nor the quantity of the food he serves," Bear said.

"'Ceptin' the coffee, dagnabbit," Red added. "He just

won't hardly make it strong enough to be fit for a man to drink. He uses way too much water."

"Yeah!" Bobcat added with emphasis. "We been tellin' the man if'n you don't need a knife to cut it, it ain't near strong enough."

Tom laughed and shook his head as he got to his feet. "Speaking of work, gentlemen," he said. "If you're through stuffing your faces full of my terrible coffee, how about we get the dishes washed and put away and see if we can't blaze a couple of miles today, or do you want to petition Smoke for an after-breakfast nap too?"

Bear stroked his beard, smiling as his eyes twinkled. "Now, I ain't never considered no after-breakfast nap, but if you insist, Tom . . ."

"Off your asses and on your feet!" Tom yelled, pretending to be angry. "Before I take my boot to your hides!"

Bear shook his head and struggled to his feet, groaning and giving Smoke an injured look. "See . . . see how the man abuses us, Smoke?"

While the other men were breaking camp, Tom gestured Smoke over to show him his map. "See here, Smoke," he said, pointing to the map. "Fleming went on across Lake Manitoba, using handmade rafts according to his journal. But since we had to blaze an alternate trail for Van Horne in case he didn't want to bother with a bridge, we've come on south and then back north around the lower edge of the lake. Now we're gonna head for the lower end of Lake Winnipegosis, where we'll turn west again and head for Fort Edmonton."

"What are these lines here?" Smoke asked, pointing to two divergent lines running approximately east and west, one up near Fort Edmonton and the other lower and running more north and south.

"That lower line there is the South Saskatchewan River

and the upper one is the North Saskatchewan River. We'll have to find a good fording place to cross the south branch, but we'll stay south of the north branch and with any luck won't have to cross it," Wilson explained. "In any event, neither of them is much of a river till the spring thaws bring all that glacier water rushing down 'em. Then they can get a bit hairy."

"I see by the map that once we've reached Fort Edmonton, we'll start running into the Rocky Mountains again," Smoke observed.

Wilson nodded, his face grim. "Yes, and that's gonna be really tough going. It may be spring everywhere else, but up this far north, it'll still be winter for another couple of months." Wilson stroked his short beard with his hand as he peered at the map over Smoke's shoulders. "We're gonna be up to our asses in snow, and the horses are going to need more feed and rest after struggling through the snowpack."

"I meant to ask you about that," Smoke said. "Why are we cutting so far north? Wouldn't it be easier going if we kept as far south as possible?"

"It'd be easier going until we reached the Rockies," Wilson explained. "See this little X up here on the map?"

Smoke nodded.

"That's a place Fleming named Yellow Head Pass. His journal isn't too specific about the slopes on the way up to the pass, so it'll be up to us to find out if they're too steep for a locomotive to make the grade."

"And if they are?" Smoke asked.

"Then we either go north to Smoky River Pass, or south and try Athabasca Pass, or Howse Pass, or even farther south to Kicking Horse Pass if we have to," Wilson said.

"Why not try the southern ones first?" Smoke asked.

"Because all the southern ones have large mountains

we'd have to go around to get to them. As you can see by this line here," he said, moving his finger along the map, "the Athabasca River runs almost straight through to the Yellow Head Pass, and over the years it's created a river valley that I hope will be easier going for a train than winding back and forth around five or six big mountains."

Smoke shrugged and grinned. "Well, I can see you've thought all this out pretty well, Tom."

Wilson shook his head. "I don't know, Smoke. The whole idea of trying to build a railroad through this country is crazy, if you ask me." He looked around at the wilderness surrounding them and the massive snow-covered peaks of the northern Rockies in the distance. "After all, who the hell is going to ride on it anyway?"

"You mean Van Horne hasn't given you his dream speech yet?" Smoke asked.

"No, why?"

"It seems Van Horne and his partner and boss, James Hill, have this dream of bringing in thousands of Eastern tourists and visitors to see the wilderness without having to endure any hardships."

"You're not serious?" Wilson asked, his face a mask of disbelief.

"Well, *they* certainly are," Smoke said. "They intend to build big hotels all along the railway routes to house these pilgrims, and make millions of dollars off the fools who decide to take these trips."

"But what about the Stony Indians, and the high-waymen and robbers who infest these regions?" Wilson asked. "Do you think they'll refund the pilgrims' money if they end up getting scalped on their trips?"

Smoke laughed. "Who knows, Tom? Like I said, this is Bill Van Horne and James Hill's dream, not mine. I'm like you, just the hired help who's supposed to make it happen."

Wilson shook his head and folded up his map. He got to his feet and moved toward his horse. "I guess you're right, Smoke. They hired us to do a job for them, not to second-guess their plans."

He climbed into the saddle. "Head 'em up, boys, and move 'em out," he called, and jerked the head of his horse around and pointed it north toward Lake Winnipegosis.

# Chapter 27

Smoke soon discovered the way Wilson liked to work his crew, and he approved of its stark simplicity. While Wilson and the three men from the railroad he had with him, the two McCardell brothers and Frank McCabe, traveled right down the path outlined by Fleming in 1877, he would send out the other members of the team in oblique directions on either side of his middle path.

That way, if Wilson ran into an obstruction that he thought would be too big or severe for the railroad men laying the track to overcome, he would call the other teams back to join him, and would discuss with them what the terrain they'd been over was like. This saved him time, as he rarely had to backtrack if his way was blocked.

The only problem that Smoke could see was that the team's members were separated for much of the day, each smaller team traveling on its own through admittedly hostile territory.

When they broke for lunch the first day, Smoke decided to bring his concerns up to Wilson. As they sat leaning back against pine trees with their plates of food on their laps, Smoke looked over at Tom, who was sitting next to him. "Tom, I've been meaning to ask you about the way we're splitting up the crew during the day."

Wilson returned his gaze and smiled. "You think it'd be safer if we all rode together, huh?" he asked, showing Smoke he'd thought about the dangers as well.

Smoke shrugged. "Tom, this is your country, so I'm not about to tell you how to run a crew, but the thought had crossed my mind that if we were to come under attack by hostiles, either Indians or highwaymen, it might be better to be traveling as a group."

Wilson nodded as he chewed on some deer meat they'd killed the day before. "You're right, of course," Wilson said. "But with Van Horne pushing us so hard, staying just a handful of miles behind us, I'm under some pressure to move as fast as possible."

He paused to drink some coffee and stare at the peaks of the mountains off to their left. "Now, I'm not going to let that make me put my men at risk, no, sir. But right now, we're at least a few days away from Indian territory, at least according to everything I've read in the journals of the men who've traveled across this land before."

Smoke grinned. "Well, I hope the Stony Indians have read those journals, Tom, so they'll know where they're supposed to be."

Wilson laughed in return. "I know, Smoke, I'm taking a slight chance, but I promise you when we get past the Winnipegosis, I'll bring the crew back together and make sure we all travel with our guns loose."

Louis, who was sitting nearby and had listened in on the conversation, spoke up. "Of course, there's one other way to look at it, Tom."

Wilson turned to look at Louis. "Yes?"

"If we're traveling all together and we run into an Indian ambush, we are in real trouble. But if we're divided into three different teams and one of the teams stumbles across the Indians, the other two teams have the option of either running like hell or coming to the first team's aid."

Wilson laughed. "You're right, Louis. In some aspects it would be better that way."

Smoke grinned. "Course, it'd be a mite tough on the team that got jumped," he said.

Louis put on his poker face, hiding his smile. "Well, the odds of being on that team are one in three. In poker, that'd be a good bet."

"If you're betting chips, that's a good bet," Wilson said. "If you're betting your life, the odds are still too high."

He got to his feet with a wry grin on his face. "Well, gentlemen, I'm glad we had this little chat," he said sarcastically. "You've convinced me that no matter how I lead this expedition, I'm damned if I do and damned if I don't."

"Hey," Smoke said, smiling and shrugging, "no one ever said being in charge was easy."

"You got that right, Smoke," Wilson said, and chuckled as he went to wash his plate.

When they'd finished with their nooning, Wilson sent the four mountain men off to the right toward the edge of Lake Winnipegosis, ignoring Bear Tooth's wide yawns hinting at the need of a nap, and he sent Smoke and his three men off to the left, while he and his men took the middle course.

"Remember," he cautioned the men before they took off, "don't get more'n a couple of miles off the course so we don't get too far separated. Keep checking your compasses so you'll stay on line with the other teams."

The mountain men smirked at this advice, thinking anyone who needed to use a compass to find their way in the wilderness had no business being there in the first place.

About two hours later, while riding through some very heavy undergrowth near the edge of the lake, Bobcat told the others to hold on a minute while he took a squat and relieved himself of the lunch they'd eaten.

He pulled his horse over to the side out of sight of the others and got down off his mount, ignoring their taunts about being an old man who couldn't control his bowels until dinnertime.

Bobcat threw his horse's reins over a tree limb and moved off into some bushes. He'd just lowered his trousers and was squatting down when he realized he'd moved into the middle of a wild berry bush.

While he squatted, he reached over and began to pick a few of the wild strawberries, popping them into his mouth and enjoying the bittersweet taste of the berries.

Just as he finished his business and wiped himself with a couple of leaves, he heard a thrashing off behind him in the brush.

"Uh-oh," he muttered, knowing he was in trouble as soon as he heard the high-pitched grunting from a few feet to the side and a much lower-pitched growl from a bit farther off.

"Damn-nation," he muttered, "it's a baby grizzly or my name's not Bobcat Bill."

He knew he had to get out of there fast, for there's

nothing worse than getting mixed up with a grizzly momma when she's got a cub nearby to guard.

As he began to run toward his horse, the cub scampered out of the bushes right in front of Bobcat, and he stumbled over the small animal, making it squeal in terror as they both rolled on the ground.

"Shit!" he exclaimed, knowing he was in for it now, his rifle still in its rifle boot on his horse twenty yards away.

Bobcat jumped to his feet and drew the wide-bladed skinning knife from his boot just as two thousand pounds of furious momma grizzly charged him from the side.

Bobcat crouched and whistled shrilly as loud as he could, both to try and scare the grizzly off and to call to his friends for help.

Seconds later, the grizzly was on him, swatting and batting at him with claws as long as his fingers. The first swipe sliced four furrows across his chest three inches deep and knocked him flat on his back, blood pouring from his wounds.

Bobcat held the knife out in front of him in his left hand while he clawed for his pistol with his right.

The grizzly roared and stood on her hind legs, shaking her muzzle and flinging saliva in all directions as she bellowed her anger.

Just as she pounced on him, Bobcat got his Walker Colt out and got off two shots into her chest, which had no more effect than a bee sting on the massive beast.

When she landed on top of him, wrapping her long arms around his chest and trying to get his head into her wide open mouth, Bobcat grunted in terror and pain and stuck his knife into her throat as hard as he could while ducking his chin into his chest and trying to protect his head from being crushed like a pecan.

Ignoring the knife wound, she chomped furiously at his head, her fangs slipping over the surface and taking half his scalp off with the first bite.

Bobcat fainted just before three shots rang out, blowing the back of the grizzly's head off and dropping her on top of him.

Minutes later, his friends rolled the bear off Bobcat and knelt next to him, trying to stop the bleeding from his head and chest.

Bear Tooth applied pressure with his hands and yelled, "Red, cut some chunks of fat off that bitch and hand 'em to me, quick."

While Red Bingham sliced open the skin of the bear and cut off thick chunks of fat to make a compress, Rattlesnake held his Henry up in the air and fired off several shots in quick succession.

Once that was done, he squatted next to Bear and helped him hold the pieces of fat tight against Bobcat's wounds, slowing the flow of blood down to a trickle.

Red moved over, grabbed the large flap of scalp hanging loose, and pushed it back against Bobcat's head, as if hoping it would stick there.

"Goddamn, Red," Bear growled as the bleeding slowed, "What the hell are you doin'?"

Rattlesnake grinned sourly. "Maybe he thinks that scalp'll take root there and begin to grow again."

"Won't hurt to try," Red said gamely, still holding the scalp pressed down tight. "At least, it'll slow the bleedin' a mite."

By the time the other teams had come to help, Bobcat was conscious again. He lay propped up against a fallen log, his teeth clamped shut tight against the pain. Mountain men, like Indians, put great store in not showing pain at any time, but it was all Bobcat could do not to scream from the agony in his chest and head.

Wilson and his men arrived just minutes before Smoke and his friends galloped up to the attack site.

"Holy Jesus," Thomas McCardell whispered, crossing himself in the Catholic manner.

Frank McCabe turned from the gruesome sight and bent over, his hands on his knees, doing his best not to vomit into the snow on the ground.

Smoke squatted down next to the mountain men, taking stock of what they'd done. By necessity, all mountain men became fairly good at emergency treatment of wounds, or they didn't survive long in the outback.

"How's the bleeding?" Smoke asked.

"Pretty nigh stopped now," Bear said, though he kept a tight grip on the fat he had plastered to Bobcat's chest.

"And his head?" Smoke asked.

"He's lost some hair, but it don't feel like the bones are crushed," Red answered from where he was holding Bobcat's scalp tight against his skull.

"Good," Smoke said, smiling grimly, "then he won't have no brains leaking out all over the ground."

Bobcat's pale lips turned up in a half grin. "Thank God fer that, otherwise I'd be as dumb as Bear here," he said, his voice tight against the pain.

Louis leaned down and held out his brandy bottle. "How about some of this, Bobcat?" he asked. "It'll help with the pain."

Bobcat grinned weakly. "What pain?" he croaked, and passed out again.

"Try to get some of that down him," Smoke told Louis, and he stood up and moved over next to Tom Wilson.

Wilson was digging in one of the boxes on the back of a packhorse as Smoke walked up. "He gonna make it?" Wilson asked as he pulled a long stick out with a funny-looking round tube on the end of it.

"Well, he's lost a lot of blood, but the bleeding's stopped right now. If we can get him to a doctor soon, he should pull through," Smoke said. "The trouble is, I don't think he can stand to be moved by horseback."

"Don't worry about that," Wilson said. "I'm fixing to call for help."

"How—" Smoke started to ask, until Wilson stepped off to the side, struck a lucifer on his pants leg, and held it to the two-inch fuse on the bottom of the tube. Then he quickly bent over, stuck the stick in the ground, and stepped back.

Seconds later, the fuse ignited the gunpowder in the tube and it flew into the air, bursting overhead into a bright red explosion of color high in the sky.

"The Chinese make these for us," Wilson said. "Red is a signal for Van Horne to send help as fast as he can."

"How will we know he saw the signal?" Smoke asked, just as a green explosion in the distance occurred high in the air.

Wilson smiled. "That means he got the message and help is on the way. He should be here in a couple of hours with a doctor and a wagon and some men with guns in case they're needed."

Smoke smiled. "I'm glad to see you and Van Horne thought of everything."

Wilson pulled a heavy blanket out of another box on the packhorse. "Now, let's see if we can keep Bobcat warm until the cavalry arrives," he said.

As he moved to cover Bobcat with the blanket, he glanced over his shoulder at McCabe. "Frank, get us a fire going and heat some water for coffee. I think we could all use some."

"Yes, sir, Tom," Frank said. "I'll cook up some beans and bacon too, just in case anyone's hungry."

# Chapter 28

Hammer Hammerick and his men were following Wilson's blazed trail, going slow and being careful so they wouldn't come upon the surveying party unawares, when suddenly, from not more than a couple of miles ahead, they heard a volley of shots ring out, shattering the stillness of the wilderness.

Hammer's hand went to the butt of his pistol as his horse shied and crow-hopped at the sudden barking explosions up ahead.

"Damn," Bull said, holding his horse's reins tight as it shied also. "You think they seen us, Boss?" he asked, looking around quickly to see where the shots were coming from.

After he'd gotten his horse under control, Hammer shook his head, his expression thoughtful. "No, Bull. Them shots are too far away to be aimed at us."

Little Joe Calhoun rode up next to Hammer, his face pale in the frigid air, his Colt in his hand and his eyes wide. "You think maybe they ran into Injuns?"

Hammer held up his hand and waited a moment, listening for more shots. When there were no more guns being fired, he shook his head. "Not unless there were just a couple of 'em," he answered. "If they was under Injun attack, there'd be a lot more firin' than that."

Suddenly, in the air above their heads, a bright red explosion occurred, sending flaming red shards arching across the sky to slowly fall to earth.

"Holy shit!" Bull exclaimed. "Would you look at that?" he asked, pointing at the bright display above their heads as it spread across the sky.

"What the hell's that, Boss?" Juan Sanchez asked as he stared skyward.

"How the hell should I know?" Hammer answered, as bewildered as his men by the explosion.

"Hey, Boss, looky there!" Jimmy Breslin hollered from the rear of the column of men.

Hammer looked behind him and saw another explosion of green colors spread across the sky behind them.

"That looks like it's comin' from back where the tracks are bein' laid," Shorty Wallace said as he stared at the sky behind them.

Hammer thought for a moment, and then he snapped his fingers. "Hell, boys, it must be some kind'a signal from the surveying crew to Van Horne's men behind us."

"What kind'a signal?" Bull asked, as if Hammer would know what was going on.

Hammer shook his head. "Don't know, but my guess is the boys up front run into some kind'a trouble and they're asking for help from the men back behind us."

"Oh," Bull said, as if that explained everything. "What are we gonna do?"

Hammer sighed. The burden of leading this group of idiots was becoming almost more than he could stand. "I guess the smart thing to do would be to mosey on off this trail and get ourselves hid until we see the lay of the land. If Van Horne is gonna be sendin' some men up here to help the others out, we sure as hell don't want 'em to see us."

Hammer jerked his horse's head to the side, and led his men off the blazed trail and deeper into the woods off to the side. "We'll move on off a couple of miles and set ourselves down and wait and see what happens," he said to Bull. "Leave Spotted Dog close enough to the trail to watch it, but tell him to stay outta sight and not let himself be seen," he ordered.

Bull pulled his horse back to talk to Spotted Dog, while the rest of the men followed Hammer away from the trail.


While Wilson and the others waited for Van Horne and the doctor to arrive, keeping Bobcat warm under blankets and giving him coffee laced with Louis's brandy to give him energy to fight the shock of his injuries, Bear Tooth and Red and Rattlesnake walked over to the dead grizzly bear.

Two of them grabbed it by its fur and turned the body over onto its back. "Well, would you look at that?" Bear said, pointing to the carcass.

Embedded in the bear's throat all the way up to the hilt was Bobcat's skinning knife.

"Why," Rattlesnake said, squatting down next to the body, "that beast was more dead than alive when we shot her." He glanced over at Bobcat. "That hairy old beaver done kilt the bear with his knife whilst she was in the middle of trying to eat his head off."

Red Bingham shook his head. "I ain't never heard of such an act, a man killin' a crazed momma grizzly with only his knife before."

"Come on, boys," Bear said, pulling out his own knife. "Let's skin this critter and cure it up for Bobcat to wear. After all, the crazy ol' coot deserves it after what he managed to do."

They'd just finished skinning the bear when Van Horne arrived in a wagon with a doctor and ten additional men on horseback, all carrying rifles and shotguns.

He jumped out of the wagon, followed closely by the doctor, who immediately knelt and began to take care of Bobcat's wounds, pouring carbolic acid over them to prevent infection and beginning to suture them up, with Bobcat, who was well on his way to being drunker than a skunk, laughing and calling for more brandy.

After Van Horne made sure Bobcat was being well taken care of, he motioned for Smoke and Tom Wilson to join him off to the side, with Louis and Cal and Pearlie standing nearby.

"I've got some bad news, men," he said.

"What's that, Bill?" Tom Wilson asked, wondering what could be worse than one of his men being chewed up by a grizzly.

"Albert Knowles was killed last night while he slept in the medical tent in Winnipeg."

"What?" Smoke asked, remembering how well the man looked when he talked to him.

"Yes. Someone snuck into the tent in the middle of the night, slugged the male attendant on duty, and cut Albert's throat," Van Horne said, his eyes sad and angry at the same time.

Smoke slammed his fist into his palm. "It could only be one man who'd do that," he said. "Hammerick is the only one who had anything to fear from Knowles."

Van Horne nodded. "I agree," he said. "As soon as I found out about his death this morning, I wired the sheriff over at Noyes to see if they were still in jail."

"A dollar will get you five they're not," Louis said, disgust in his voice.

"You're right, Louis," Van Horne said. "The sheriff

said the judge released them on bail a week ago, and they haven't been seen since."

"The son of a bitch barely waited for us to leave town before he set them free," Smoke said, his voice hard and tight. "And now a good man's dead because of it."

"That's not all of the bad news, Smoke," Van Horne said, a troubled expression on his face.

"What else?" Smoke asked.

"On our way out here, while we were following Tom's blazed trail, we found evidence of a lot of horses following the same trail. The prints were fresh and didn't have any snow buildup in them, and since it snowed last night, they must've been made sometime today."

Tom glanced around at the heavy woods surrounding them. "But we haven't seen anyone, Bill."

Smoke smiled grimly. "And you won't, Tom, not until they decide to attack us," he said. "It's got to be Hammerick and his gang. They managed to kill one witness to their crimes, and now they've come to get rid of me and my men to put them out of danger of being hung."

"Well, I won't have that," Van Horne said angrily. "I'll leave these men here with you for protection," he said, but Smoke shook his head.

"No, Bill, that's not the way to handle this."

"Why not, Smoke?" he asked, puzzled at Smoke's refusal of help.

"Because if there are too many men around, Hammerick will just sit back and bide his time until he can catch us alone, and then he'll strike." Smoke shook his head again. "And I'm not going to live looking back over my shoulder and waiting for the son of a bitch to come after me."

"What are you gonna do, Smoke?" Tom asked.

Smoke bared his teeth in a savage grin. "Why, I'm going after him, of course."

"But according to your report, he has over twenty men riding with him," Van Horne said. "It'll be suicide for you to try and go up against that many by yourself."

"No, it's the right thing to do. Hammer won't be expecting me to come after him alone, so when I make my move, he won't be ready for it."

"You mean when *we* go after him, don't you, Smoke?" Louis asked, his eyes flashing.

Again Smoke shook his head. "Not this time, Louis, old friend. I'll stand a better chance and be able to move quicker and faster if I'm alone." He cut his eyes at Cal and Pearlie, who had angry expressions on their faces. "And besides, Sally would cut my throat if I let anything happen to Cal or Pearlie while she wasn't here."

"But Smoke," Pearlie began, until Smoke cut him off.

"This is the way it's got to be, son," he said, not unkindly. "It'll be safer for me this way, and Tom still needs your help in the surveying in case of Indian attack."

Tom nodded, his face sober. "I agree with Smoke," he said. "One man has a better chance out in the wild against a larger force 'cause he can maneuver faster and hit and run better than a group of men, no matter how good."

"If that's the way you want it," Van Horne said, though it was clear he didn't like the idea.

Louis spoke up. "Bill, when you get back to Winnipeg, could you do me a favor?"

"Sure, Louis. What is it?"

"Would you wire the sheriff and Judge Harlan Fitzpatrick in Noyes that no matter what happens to Smoke, I will be paying them a personal visit when this is over to discuss their actions in this matter."

Van Horne felt the hair stir on the back of his neck at

the anger and hatred in Louis's face, and he was glad he would never have cause for it to be directed at him.

"Certainly, Louis," he said. "Anything else?"

"You can tell them Pearlie and me'll be there too," Cal said, "and you can add that they shouldn't make any long-range plans!"

"At least, not any plans that require them to be breathin' to carry 'em out!" Pearlie added.

# Chapter 29

When Van Horne readied the wagon to take Bobcat back to Winnipeg, Rattlesnake offered to stay with Tom and the others, but they all knew his heart was with his partner, so they made him ride back in the wagon with Bobcat.

After Van Horne and his men had left, Tom said, "Until you tell us it's safe and the threat of the outlaws is past, we'll all ride together while doing our surveying. Louis, you and the boys will ride out front, and Bear, you and Red will bring up the rear. The McCardells and Frank McCabe and I will do the actual surveying, with the rest of you acting as guards so we can't be snuck up on."

"That's a good plan," Smoke said. He moved over to his horse, took an extra rifle boot off the packhorse, and added it to the one already on his mount. He put his Henry in one boot, and a short-barreled ten-gauge express shotgun in the other.

While Smoke checked his pistol loads, Louis glanced over at Tom Wilson. "Tom, you got any more of those signal rockets left?" he asked.

"Sure, Louis," Tom said, grabbing a couple off his packhorse and handing them to Louis.

"If somehow you get your back up against a wall, old friend," Louis said as he passed the rockets over to Smoke, "fire one of these off and we'll come running."

"I don't expect that to happen, pal," Smoke said, smiling at he took the rockets. He stuck them in his saddlebags next to a handful of dynamite sticks he'd taken off the packhorse earlier.

"It's what we don't expect that can get us killed, partner," Louis said.

Smoke swung up into the saddle and smiled. "Don't be concerned if you hear some explosions and gunfire tonight, men," he said. "I plan to have a busy night."

It was almost dusk by the time Spotted Dog rode up into the outlaws' camp. Hammer had a small fire going between a couple of large rocks so it couldn't be seen from a distance, and the men were drinking coffee and whiskey and standing as close to the meager flames as they could to try and keep warm.

Spotted Dog hailed the camp so he wouldn't be shot coming in, and jumped down off his horse and hurried over to the fire. "Give me some coffee, quick," he said, his teeth chattering. "I'm 'bout froze clear through."

Hammer handed him a steaming mug, and while Dog warmed his hands on the cup and inhaled the steam, Hammer asked, "Well? What did you find out?"

"The surveying crew had a man injured somehow," Dog said. "I watched when the men who'd come from back down the trail returned with a couple of men in a wagon. One was covered with blankets that had blood on 'em, an' the other was sitting next to him, like he was a friend or something."

"So, Van Horne and his men have all gone back down the trail?" Hammer asked.

"It seemed so. At least they had the same number of riders they had when they went up the trial."

"So, Smoke Jensen and his men didn't get any reinforcements, huh?" Hammer asked, a thoughtful expression on his face.

"I guess not, Boss, an' now they got two less men than they had before up there," Spotted Dog said.

Hammer looked up as snow began to fall and the wind picked up. "Looks like we got us another spring storm brewin'," he said, smiling.

"How come that makes you so happy, Boss?" Bull asked, wrapping his coat tight around him.

"The storm will give us good cover to attack the surveying camp," Hammer said. "While they're sitting around a fire trying to keep warm, we'll ride in and blow them all to hell."

Smoke, who was lying on his belly twenty yards away behind a fallen log, smiled when he heard this. He'd cut Spotted Dog's tracks earlier and followed the half-breed all the way to the outlaws' camp without being seen.

Now, as he lay there and the snow began to fall, he considered his options and how he was going to play things. . . .

As the gang broke camp and mounted up, Smoke ran silently to his horse and jumped up into the saddle. He knew his greatest ally in the upcoming battle would be fear, and he planned to create as much fear and confusion as he could in the men up ahead.

Hammer moved his men slowly through the forest toward where he figured the surveyors' camp would be.

The men walked their horses in single file so as to make as little noise going through the brush as they could.

Smoke rode parallel to the outlaws until he was a little ahead of them, and then he got down off his horse and squatted behind some bushes near where they would pass.

As the outlaws filed by, Smoke pulled out his bowie knife and held it ready at his side.

When the last man in line approached, Smoke leapt out of hiding and jumped up on the man's horse behind him, wrapping his left arm around his mouth and jerking his head back, exposing his throat. Smoke's blade sliced through veins and arteries and tissue like a hot knife through butter, and then he let the man fall to the side. He hadn't made a sound, so far.

Sam Johnson was riding next to last in the line. When he felt and then saw a horse's head moving up next to his leg, he half-turned to tell Jack McGraw to slow down and stop crowding him.

"Hey, Jack," he began, and then he saw fierce eyes staring out at him from under an unfamiliar hat. "What the . . ." he said as the man swung his right arm at him. A burning pain speared his chest, and he looked down and saw a stream of black blood spurting from a hole in the front of his coat. "Oh, shit," he moaned, and then he toppled off his horse and onto the snow.

Smoke reached down and grabbed Johnson's horse's tail, and tied the reins of the horse he was riding to the other's tail. As the two horses followed those in front, Smoke jumped down and jogged along the trail toward the next man in line.

He did this four times until the last four horses in the line were empty and walking with tails tied to reins of the horses behind them.

Smoke finally stopped and waited for the horses to

get almost out of sight, and then he whistled sharply and turned around and ran back to where he'd left his horse tied to a tree.

Jerry Barnes heard the whistle behind him and turned in his saddle, expecting to see one of the gang behind him. Instead, he saw the dim outlines of four horses with empty saddles following him down the trail.

"Jesus!" he whispered, and he drew his pistol and yelled, "Hey, Boss, you'd better come look at this!"

Minutes later, the men were gathered around the horses, all talking excitedly among themselves. "Keep it down," Hammer cautioned, not wanting the sound of their voices to warn Jensen and his men up ahead.

He walked his horse next to one of the empty saddles and reached out and touched a black stain on the side. When he put his hand in front of his face and smelled it, he frowned. It was blood.

He looked angrily at Barnes. "How could somebody kill four men right behind you and you not hear it?" he growled.

Barnes, who now had a sheen of sweat on his forehead, just shrugged. "I don't know, Boss. There weren't no sound to hear is all I can say."

Hammer drew his gun and eared back the hammer. "Spread out, men. It's got to be Jensen and he's right in the area. Find him and kill him," he ordered.

The men all pulled out rifles and shotguns and pistols and moved off in different directions, just as Smoke had wanted them to do. With any luck, he'd have them shooting each other in the dark before it was all over.

As two men approached the tree Smoke had his horse behind, he leaned out and aimed the express gun at them. He let go with both barrels from a distance of less than twenty feet. The shotgun exploded with a roar, blowing flame and molten slugs from the twin barrels that shredded the men in front of him and tore them from their saddles. They never even heard the shot that killed them.

As soon as he pulled the triggers, Smoke leaned low over his saddle horn and spurred his horse away from the area, knowing what was going to happen.

Within seconds, eight guns opened fire from the darkness around him, aiming at the muzzle flash of his shotgun and the sounds of the shots.

Luckily, by this time, Smoke was already gone from the place, and the shots hit the tree he had been behind but missed him by dozens of yards.

Two other outlaws weren't so lucky. Directly in the line of fire, they screamed as their friends' bullets tore into their chests and killed them instantly.

As Smoke rode off, the snow stopped as quickly as it had begun and a full moon peeked through scattering clouds, bathing the forest in a ghostly light.

"There he goes!" Juan Sanchez shouted when the moonlight revealed a fleeing figure among the trees.

Juan and three other men who were nearby began to fire as they spurred their horses after the dark man up ahead.

Smoke jerked his Palouse around a clump of trees, and reached up as he passed beneath a large oak tree. He grabbed a low-lying limb and let his horse's momentum swing him up onto the branch. He leaned back against the trunk of the tree and drew his pistols, earing back the hammers.

His horse, when Smoke's weight lifted out of the saddle, slowed and came to a stop thirty yards from the tree.

As Sanchez and his three companions rode toward the horse, they slowed when they saw the saddle was empty.

"Where the hell is he?" Sanchez hollered, sweeping the area with the barrel of his gun.

"Right behind you, boys," Smoke said softly.

As the men jerked around in their saddles, Smoke let loose with both handguns, firing so fast it almost seemed like one long continuous burst of gunfire.

The four men were slammed out of their saddles and were dead before they hit the ground.

Smoke's pistols were empty, and he needed his rifle in the rifle boot on his horse. He gave a low whistle, and the horse picked up its head and moved slowly back until it was under the tree. Smoke lowered himself into the saddle just as several gunshots rang out and bullets tore bark off the oak behind him.

Smoke jerked his Henry from its boot and spurred his horse into a dead run, whirling around the tree and heading straight for the outlaws who'd fired on him.

Surprised that their quarry was attacking them instead of running away, three men hurried their shots, and Smoke could hear the buzzing of slugs as they passed over his head and to the side.

Shooting from the waist without taking the time to aim, Smoke fired and jacked the loading lever and fired, again and again, until the three men flopped off their mounts and fell dead in the snow.

As he passed them, Smoke threw his empty Colts into his saddlebags, grabbed two more he had there still fully loaded, and stuffed one into his right-hand holster and the other under his belt in front.

When he got to the dead men's horses, Smoke reined his own mount in, fished a cigar from his breast pocket, and lit it with a lucifer.

As he puffed it into life, a shotgun roared from off to his left and he felt the tug in his coat as buckshot shredded the back of it, burning furrows of white-hot pain across his shoulder blades.

The force of the blow almost unseated him, but Smoke fell forward over his saddle horn and kicked his horse forward just as more shots rang out, barely missing him as he fled.

Three more men pulled onto the trail behind him, firing as they rode, some of the bullets coming uncomfortably close to Smoke's head.

As he rode, he reached down into his saddlebag and pulled out a stick of dynamite. Holding the fuse to the tip of his cigar until it caught, he twisted in the saddle and flipped it at the men behind him.

The dynamite went off just as their horses straddled it. The explosion blew men and horses into thousands of pieces, which rained down together in a bloody mix of horseflesh and human tissue for several seconds.

Hammer and Bull and Spotted Dog were the only members of the gang left alive. They'd survived this long because after Hammer sent his men searching for Jensen, he'd signaled the two to follow him while he rode in the opposite direction. He'd remembered the story the judge had told about Jensen and how tough he was, and he wanted to see if his men could take care of Jensen before he tried it himself.

Now, as he peered into the forest in front of him, the filtered moonlight revealed a solitary figure moving slowly toward him, the glowing tip of a cigar between his teeth.

"Bull," Hammer whispered, "you move on off to the right. Dog, you take off to the left. When he gets between you, we'll have him cornered and we can all let go at the same time. He won't stand a chance."

Smoke, whose eyes were as sharp as an eagle's, saw the shadows up ahead as they parted and spread out to his right and his left. He grinned as he moved his horse into the shadows cast by a large ponderosa pine tree, and he slipped out of his saddle.

He pulled the Henry out and steadied the barrel against the trunk of the tree while he took careful aim at the figure to his right. He aimed low, intending to wound rather than kill. Slowly, breathing out and holding it, he caressed the trigger. The Henry exploded and bucked and a second later, a horrible scream rang throughout the forest.

"Oh, Jesus!" Spotted Dog yelled as he toppled from his saddle, "I'm gutshot! Help me, Boss, please, I don't want to die . . . help me!"

Smoke was glad to hear the man call for his boss. That meant Hammerick was still alive and wasn't one of the men he'd already killed.

"You hear that, Hammerick?" Smoke yelled from behind the tree. "Your man is calling for you. Are you going to help him or just let him die?"

"Shut up, Jensen, you bastard!" Hammerick yelled from up ahead.

While Hammer was talking, Smoke took off his hat and hung it from a short branch on the pine tree. Then he took his cigar and wedged it just under the hat behind a piece of bark. Once that was done, he got down on his hands and knees, crawled ten yards away from the tree, and lay on his belly, his Henry aimed out to his left, waiting.

"Did you hear me, Jensen?" Hammer yelled again. "I'm coming to kill you!"

Smoke didn't answer Hammer's taunt; he just waited.

Two minutes later, a shot rang out from Smoke's left and the slug tore his hat off the tree.

Aiming just above the muzzle flash, Smoke squeezed the trigger of the Henry. Like an echo to the gunshot, a scream rang out and a huge figure stumbled out from next to a tree, fired his gun two more times, hitting nothing but air, and then fell onto his face. Bull was dead.

Smoke stood up and retrieved his cigar, and was bending over to pick up his hat when Hammer fired from twenty feet away. His bullets took Smoke in the left shoulder and tore a chunk of flesh from his chest, spinning him around and up against his horse, the Henry flying from his grasp.

As he sank to his knees, Smoke grabbed his saddlebags and pulled them down with him onto the ground.

"How'd you like that, Jensen, you asshole?" Hammer yelled gleefully. "I thought you were tough, mountain man!" he said scornfully as he walked toward where Smoke lay on the ground.

Unable to get to his pistols, Smoke eased the rocket from the saddlebags and positioned it pointing toward the dark shape approaching him. He would only get one chance, so he had to make it right.

Smoke let his head flop down next to the fuse, his eyes squinting along the length of the rocket, taking aim.

"Don't try and play possum on me, Jensen," Hammer growled, raising his pistol and pointing it at Smoke. "I know you ain't dead yet."

"You got that right, killer," Smoke muttered, and he moved his head to touch the fuse with the end of his cigar.

As Hammer grinned, his teeth glowing in the moonlight, he eased back the hammer on his pistol.

With a sudden *whoosh*, the rocket ignited and streaked toward Hammer like lightning.

Hammer's eyes opened wide and he grunted as the rocket struck him in the middle of his gut, doubling him over and knocking him two steps backward.

He straightened up and stared down at his stomach, where the rocket was buried halfway into his abdomen.

He had time to say, "Oh, shit!" before the rocket exploded, sending Hammer to hell in a heartbeat.

# Chapter 30
## Epilogue

Three months later, his arm and chest healed and their work for the Canadian Pacific Railroad completed, Smoke, Louis, Cal, and Pearlie rode into the town of Noyes, Minnesota.

Accompanying them were two U.S. marshals and four deputy marshals.

As they came abreast of the sheriff's office, Luke McCain stepped out, a cup of coffee in his hand. His face paled when he saw the marshal badges on the chests of the men with Smoke, and his hand dropped near the butt of his pistol.

"Please, Luke," Smoke said, his teeth bared in a grin of anticipation, "go for your gun and give me the satisfaction of putting a bullet through that badge that you've dishonored that you wear on your chest."

McCain thought about it for a moment, then smiled ruefully and held his hands up. "Sorry, Jensen, I won't give you that pleasure."

Smoke shrugged. "Then I guess I'll just have to be content to watch you hang."

"Hang?" McCain asked as one of the deputy marshals took his guns. "But all I did was let some men outta jail. I didn't kill nobody."

"No, Mr. McCain, you didn't," the U.S. marshal said, "but the men you let out of jail did, and that makes you what the law calls an accessory."

"And the punishment for an accessory is the same as for the man who pulled the trigger," Louis said with satisfaction. "Hanging from a rope until you are dead."

As they turned their horses toward the courthouse, Smoke could see a wide figure outlined in the window of the judge's chambers.

When they got in front of the building, they heard a shot ring out from behind the window. Smoke looked at the others and turned his horse's head south toward Colorado and Sally. "I guess our job here is done, men," he said, and they all rode south toward home.

# Author's Note

William Cornelius Van Horne was born on February 3, 1843. In 1881 he was asked to be general manager of the Canadian Pacific Railway. His contract was to connect British Columbia to the rest of Canada by building the Trans Canada Railway, at the time the most ambitious project in the world. Van Horne started the railroad in 1882, and completed the project three years later when Donald Smith drove the last spike at Craigellachie, B.C. on November 7, 1885.

He started work in Winnipeg and worked west from there, making about three miles every day, crossing over six hundred miles of mountains in the process.

In the first year alone, over 1500 miles of track was laid. In 1888, Van Horne was named president of the CPR, and was also appointed chairman of the board.

He was awarded a knighthood for his achievements, and spent the last twenty-five years of his life on Ministers Island, which he had purchased. He died on September 11, 1915, in Montreal, and was buried in his hometown of Joliet, Illinois.

In 1882, guided by a Stony Indian, Canadian Pacific Railroad packer (i.e. trailsman) Tom Wilson was the first white man to see Lake Louise. He named it Emerald Lake (later to be named Lake Louise after the daughter of Queen Victoria).

In 1883, railway workers William McCardell, Thomas McCardell, and Frank McCabe discovered hot springs (known today as the Cave and Basin) at the foot of Sulphur Mountain, near Banff.

In 1888, the original log-framed Banff Springs Hotel was opened for business by the CPR.

In 1889, Van Horne and the CPR brought in Swiss guides to the Rockies to lead tourists to the summits of the mountains.

Look for the next novel
in William W. Johnstone's
Mountain Man series—
*Ambush of the Mountain Man*—
coming from Pinnacle Books
in December 2003.

## THE ASHES SERIES BY
## WILLIAM W. JOHNSTONE

# THE CODE NAME SERIES BY
# WILLIAM W. JOHNSTONE

__Code Name: Payback
0-7860-1085-1                                  $5.99US/$7.99CAN

__Code Name: Survival
0-7860-1151-3                                  $5.99US/$7.99CAN

__Code Name: Death
0-7860-1327-3                                  $5.99US/$7.99CAN

__Code Name: Coldfire
0-7860-1328-1                                  $5.99US/$7.99CAN

__Code Name: Quickstrike
0-7860-1151-3                                  $5.99US/$7.99CAN

## *Available Wherever Books Are Sold!*

Visit our website at **www.kensingtonbooks.com**